DAYS

OF

MASHIACH

Collected Stories

DAYS

OF

MASHIACH

Tzvi Fishman

Shorashim • Jerusalem

טוב להודות לה׳

Computer typesetting and layout: MK

Shorashim - Fishman
19 Shoshana St. Apt. 8
Jerusalem, Israel 96149

Contents

This book is dedicated to the brave, holy Jews of Judea, Samaria and Aza whose day-to-day valor infuses the nation of Israel with endless Divine favor and strength.

Eliahu teaches:
"There are six thousand years to this world:
2000 years of Chaos;
2000 years of Torah;
and 2000 years of
Days of Mashiach."
Sanhedrin 97A

THE TSHUVA
OF
DAVID DOR

1

D avid Dor sat in the windowless briefing room of *Shin Bet* headquarters in Gilo, one of the neighborhoods which were growing like vineyards on the hillsides surrounding Jerusalem. *Shin Bet* was the familiar name for the *Sherut HaBitachon HaClalli*, the Israeli Secret Service. For the past two years, the young agent had served in New York, in the narcotics-control division, quietly dealing with Israelis involved in the drug trade. The top-secret assignment he was to receive that morning was the reason the "*Shabak*" had transferred him back to Jerusalem.

At precisely ten o'clock, David's liaison officer, Behar, entered the room, followed by Amos Tamir, the Head of all *Shin Bet* forces. Surprised, David stood at attention.

"Relax," the former *Tat Aluf* said.

Seemingly bored, the aging war hero sat down with his famous nonchalance. But when his sky blue eyes peered at David, the young man felt his heart pound in his chest.

"Sit down, David," Behar, code-named *Bet*, said. "I think we can do without introductions. The *Rosh HaShabak* has studied your file, and everyone is satisfied that you can handle the job."

"I want to nail these fanatics," Tamir stated, laying a fist on the long conference table. The masquerade of indifference, which for twenty years had helped him survive a Ferris wheel of prime ministers and governments suddenly vanished. "These radicals are a threat to this country, and I want their whole movement crushed."

On the outside, David made sure he looked calm, but an involuntary shudder ran through his body.

"I don't like them. I don't like their beliefs. I don't like their holier-than-thou attitude."

The blue eyes widened like Siberian lakes.

"I don't care if we have to throw all of their rabbis in prison. Is that clear?" the country's security chief asked.

Amos Tamir glared at the young agent. His blue and white eyes, like tiny Israeli flags, shone with a towering patriotism. For all of David's confidence, he was finding it hard to breathe.

"I am putting all of our resources behind this," Tamir continued. "As of today, this is our number one project, and you are the key."

The people who Tamir wanted to stop were the settlers, religious Jews who insisted on Israel's biblical right to settle all of *Eretz Yisrael* , including the infamous "West Bank" which Israel had recaptured from attacking Arab forces during the miraculous Six-Day War. Though their numbers were relatively small, like all idealistic groups, their influence was a powerful force in the country. Their tenacity had pushed governments into sanctioning tiny caravan villages which had grown into the *Gush Emunim* strongholds of Ofra, Shilo, Hevron, Bet-El, Kedumim, and Gush Katif, to cite but a few.

For the past two months, the young agent Dor had undergone a rigorous training program, studying the rudiments of religious practice and prayer. He, his wife and two children would be moving to Pincus, a small religious settlement on the West Bank. Posing as a *baal tshuva*, a Jew recently returned to the faith, David would study in the local yeshiva and infiltrate the community. Pincus, the Security Services suspected, was a hotbed of rightwing extremists who were planning a reprisal against leaders of the Palestinian Authority in Shechem. Such an attack, and Israel's failure to stop it, could cause an international uproar. Intelligence experts were convinced that given the present volatile situation, the year-long Intifada could explode any moment into an all-out Middle East war. "This is a campaign 'Green Dollar,'" Tamir emphasized, meaning that no measure was too extreme to achieve the

objective. "You are to look on these people as your enemy.
I want no compassion. Forget that they're Jews. You are to
look upon them as drug pushers or terrorists. Is that
understood?"

"Yes, sir," the young agent answered.

The Head of the Service stood up. He shook David's
hand. Then, without further ado, he turned and strode out
of the room.

"I gave a good report about you," *Bet* said. "Don't let
me down."

"I won't, sir," David replied.

Horowitz, the *Shin Bet's* chief equipment specialist,
hurried into the room, carrying a stack of books up to his
chin. With a grunt, he set the giant-sized volumes down
on the table. Rabbi Schwartz wheeled in a cart laden with
religious paraphernalia. Schwartz, a former Conservative
rabbi from America, had his own personal score to settle
with the Orthodox settlers. He had been David's instructor
for the last two months. Finding a real Orthodox rabbi who
was willing to work against the religious had always proved
problematic for the Security Services. *Satmar* Hasidim
might be vocally opposed to *Chabad*, and *Breslov* to *Neturei
Karta*, and *Neturei Karta* to *Gush Emunim*, but man for man,
the religious were as loyal as brothers.

"I'm sorry we're late," Horowitz said. "But we had
some mechanical difficulties in the lab."

Proudly, like a father showing off a precocious child,
Horowitz proceeded to demonstrate the gadgets he had
fashioned to aid the young agent on his mission.

"First, your *tefillin*," he said.

Gingerly, he extracted them from a small cloth sack.
David had learned how to wear them during his classes
with Rabbi Schwartz. One of the tiny black boxes was
strapped around the left arm, opposite the heart, during
the morning prayer service. The other was placed above
the forehead. It was one of the 613 commandments of the

Torah, reminding the Jew to keep G-d always in his mind and always in his heart.

"Of course," Horowitz added, "these *tefillin* are special."

Carefully, he stripped off the false bottom of one of the boxes. With a tiny screwdriver, he opened the leather encasing and pulled out a small microphone.

"There's a wire in the strap which serves as a ground," he said. "Any conversation you have will be picked up by one of our satellites. Finger pressure on top of the box turns the mike on and off."

"Remember that after you touch the *tefillin*, the custom is to kiss your fingers," Schwartz said.

"Kiss your fingers?" the liason officer asked.

"To show how much you love the commandment," Schwartz explained.

Next, Horowitz displayed the *mezuzot* David was to affix to the doorposts of his house. Each wooden case housed a miniature bugging device whose signal would be received at the Army Base #3 below the Pincus settlement.

"Remember to hang one in every room in your house, excluding the bathroom," Schwartz said. "The book I gave you has illustrations showing how. But don't worry if you forget something or make a mistake. A *baal tshuva* isn't expected to know eveything."

Schwartz explained that the giant tomes were part of the standard religious-home library, a twenty volume set of *Gemara* and the *Shulchan Aruch* of Jewish Law. Volume Two of *Hoshen Mishpat* was hollowed out to house a sophisticated Sony recorder.

"What if someone wants to read it?" David asked.

"Don't worry," Schwartz said. "No one will."

Finally, Horowitz held up a framed photograph of Jerusalem, an aerial view with a majestic building superimposed in the area of the Temple Mount, in place of the Dome of the Rock.

"The Temple," Schwartz said.

David had learned lots about the *Beit HaMikdash* in his two-month, cram course. The First Temple of Solomon had been destroyed by Nebuchadnezzar. The Second Temple had been razed by the Romans. For two thousand years, Jews had been praying three times a day that the Temple be rebuilt. The site of the Temple was the holiest place in Judaism. Israel had recaptured the Mount from Jordan in the '67 War. To appease the Arabs, Moslems were given permission to keep worshipping in the mosque they had built on the site. Jewish prayer was forbidden, restricted to the area of the Western Wall, outside the Temple Mount proper.

"Hang this picture up in a conspicuous place in your house," Schwartz advised, "and you'll instantly be a part of the club."

Horowitz concluded the presentation. The liaison officer, *Bet*, handed David a file that included the biographies and photographs of the bearded faces he was to befriend. Finally, he was supplied with a list of contacts and communication channels.

"Until the end of the operation, you are not to be seen around headquarters," *Bet* insisted. "Is that understood?"

"Of course," David answered.

The team shook his hand, and David was left alone in the room with his new *tefillin* and library of Jewish books.

2

David's wife, Rita, sat in stony silence on the long drive from Ramat Aviv to Pincus. She stared out at the moving van on the road in front of them and felt like she wanted to cry. Her whole life, like her furniture, was being uprooted. She loved her country with all of her heart and had always stood by David in his work, often through long, lonely nights when he was away on dangerous assignments. Always, she had hid her fears from the children. She had been a good, faithful wife. But this was too much, dragging the children off to live in the middle of nowhere, in a settlement of religious fanatics, surrounded by hundreds of thousands of Arabs.

"Not this time," she had threatened. "I won't go with you. I won't let you do this to the children."

But her protests hadn't helped. Her husband would not be dissuaded. His job, he insisted, came first.

Just before the Hyatt Hotel in Jerusalem, the moving van turned north. David had chosen to take the long way through Jerusalem because he was unfamiliar with the shorter route through the Shomron. Before long, elaborate three and four story villas surrounded the highway. Tall TV antennas, like miniature Eiffel Towers, sprouted from the rooftops. The architecture was gaudy and grand, on the style of a potentate's brothel, each mansion many times the size of the Dor family apartment in the suburbs of Tel Aviv.

"Who lives in these houses?" she asked.

"Arabs," David answered.

"I thought they all lived in refugee camps."

"Only on CNN News. Money from Saudi Arabia and Jordan is smuggled in by the Palestinian Authority to finance the building," David explained. "Every day another villa goes up, even houses that no one will live in, just to build up a presence here. From here up to Pincus, it's all the West Bank."

Rita didn't answer, as if it didn't interest her. But it did. Never in her life had she been in this part of Israel, and she was startled to see that the oppressed Palestinians lived like sultans and sheiks. Mercedez after Mercedez whizzing by with colored Arab plates were a lot roomier than their cramped Subaru sedan.

"Are we going to live in houses like these?" Orit, the nine-year-old girl asked.

"Not quite," David said.

"Does our house have a tower?" Danny, the six-year old, wanted to know.

"No," David said. "But we can build one."

An army jeep was stationed by the roadside on the turn to Bet-El, but otherwise, there was no *Tzahal* presence at all. At this very spot, a school bus on the way to pick up Jewish children had gone up in flames, and a little up the road, a settler had been gunned down at the wheel of his car. But David said nothing to Rita. He drove along, whistling a carefree tune, as if they were journeying through one of America's national parks.

"Are we in Pincus yet?" the little boy wanted to know.

"Not yet," David said. "We're passing the settlement of Ofra. Up on that mountain is an army intelligence base that keeps a close watch on Jordan."

"Where?" the boy asked, pressing his small face to the car window.

"Don't you see the radar balls on the hill?" his sister answered, as if it were common knowledge.

"Wow," Danny said.

David didn't mention that dozens of settlers had had their cars stoned along this same strip. He didn't want to worry his wife.

"Can we go there one day to see the soldiers?" the boy asked.

"Sure," David answered. "I promise."

For a while they drove in silence, awed by the winding mountain road and the stark beauty of the Shomron. Olive trees dotted the landscape. The hillsides were terraced with grapevines, just as they had been in biblical days.

"That's Shilo." David said. High on a hillside was a cluster of houses, almost as big as the Arab homes they had seen. David handed a travel guide to his wife. "Why don't you read to them what it says about Shilo," he suggested. "Why don't you?" she replied, refusing to look at him. The beard he had started to grow and the knitted *kippah* on his head made her furious.

David sighed. He opened the book with one hand, and with one eye on the road, he flipped to Shilo and started to read as they drove past the renewed Jewish settlement.

Orit reached forward. "That's dangerous, *Abba*. I'll read from the book."

The girl took the travelogue from her father and read.

"Shilo was the religious center of Israel prior to the conquest of Jerusalem, and the nation's first capital. Here, the *Mishkan* and the Holy Ark rested for 369 years. Here, Hannah composed her stirring prayer to *Hashem*."

"Who's *Hashem*" Danny asked.

The car swerved in response to his words. With both hands, David brought it back on the road. Husband and wife glanced at each other sharply. Rita's eyes flashed, as if challenging him. It was one of the reasons she was so against the move to Pincus – the education of the kids. She was terrified that her children would be inculcated with primitive religious beliefs.

David himself didn't know how to answer the boy. He, like his wife, wasn't the least bit religious. But how could he tell his children that he didn't believe in the Bible, now that he had to pretend that he did?

"It's another word for *Elokim*," he said.

"Do we believe in *Hashem*?" the girl asked.

"Of course," he replied. "That's one of the reasons we're moving. So that we can all learn more about Him."

"In a moment, I'll wake up and this nightmare will be over," Rita muttered.

Both Rita's and David's parents had come from Europe to build a new home in Israel, wanting only to be people like everyone else, with a land and national flag of their own. They strove to escape the dark past, but the past reappeared in religious political parties, in laws banning El Al flights on *Shabbat*, in settlers with biblical claims, and with the ludicrous *kippah* which David now had to wear on his head.

"What's the Ark?" Danny asked.

"A box the Ten Commandments were kept in," Orit told him.

"Commandments? Like what?" the boy asked.

"Honor thy father and thy mother," David said. "That's the most important one of all."

"What are the other nine?" the curious lad inquired.

David didn't know. Between he and his wife, they managed to come up with six. Orit counted on her fingers. She wanted to know the last four.

"You'll learn them in Pincus," the father said.

The road wound back through centuries to a world of shepherds and Arabs riding on donkeys. Ascending a long, steep incline, the moving van slowed to a crawl. When they finally reached the summit, a magnificent valley stretched out in a panoramic vista before them. Two mountains towered like bodyguards over the ancient city of Shechem. David stopped the car by the roadside. The moving van rolled off down the hill.

"He's getting away from us," Danny said nervously, worried about his *doobey*, his favorite teddy bear which had been packed into a crate with the rest of his toys.

"Well?" David asked his wife.

"Well what?"

"Aren't you going to read?"

Rita threw him the guidebook. The young, *Shin Bet* agent laughed, determined to be in good spirits. He knew that his success in the field depended upon a happy family at home.

"Shechem sits between the mountains of Gerizim and Eval," he read. "The spacious valley was the first place

Avraham came to when he entered the land of Canaan.
Yaacov purchased the field on the site of the ancient *tel*.
Here Yosef is buried. Yehoshua gathered the Children of
Israel between the mountains of Gerizim and Eval when
he brought them into the Promised Land. Here the
Covenant was confirmed – a blessing for those who follow
the Torah, a curse for all those who turn away."

"If you ask me, this is the curse they were talking
about – that we have to live here," Rita said glumly.

"Give it a chance," David answered. "It won't be so
bad."

Rita wasn't appeased by his big show of confidence.
She was mad.

"According to that book of yours, we certainly have a
strong connection to all of these places," Rita said to annoy
him.

"So?"

"So maybe the settlers are right."

"Nonsense," David answered. "The United Nations,
not the Bible, gave us the right to live in Israel."

"Who is Yosef?" It was Danny again. He was a lover of
stories.

"You know – Yosef," Orit answered, as if it were
something that everyone knew. "He's the one who was
buried in Yosef's Tomb. The place where the Arabs threw
out the Jews. We saw it on TV, remember?"

"Maybe," the boy said, not really sure.

"Pincus is on top of that mountain," David announced.

Rita had to squint through the strong sunlight to see
the red rooftops at the peak of the mountain. Other small
Jewish settlements, Elon Moreh, Itamar, Bracha, and
Yitzhar were scattered far apart on the surrounding hills.

"Who lives in Shechem?" Danny asked.

"Arabs," her father replied.

"There aren't any Jews?" Orit wondered.

"No. Only an army base close by. There used to be a

yeshiva in Yosef's Tomb, but the Arabs forced the Jews out. The students now learn in Pincus. I'll be studying with them."

"You're going to be studying with the fanatics from Yosef's Tomb?" Rita exclaimed in surprise.

"That's right."

Rita was furious. Her mouth hung open. Her face was red.

"I want to turn back," she said.

"Sweetheart, please."

"Why didn't you tell me?"

"I thought that you knew."

"You told me it was a school for *baale tshuva*."

"It is. That is, they have a program for *baale tshuva* too."

But Rita was right. He had been purposely vague. He didn't want to upset her. The settlers who had studied in Yosef's Tomb were the most radical of the lot. They lived in the settlements surrounding Shechem, dreaming of the day when they would return to the holy compound that *Tzahal* had abandoned.

"Aren't you too old for school, Dad?" Orit asked.

"Your father still thinks he's a boy," the mother sarcastically answered.

"I want to go to yeshiva too!" Danny decided.

Rita was furious. She felt trapped.

"If you don't turn the car around this minute, I'll get out and walk," she threatened.

The children sat wide-eyed, wondering what would happen. David stared at his wife. When he didn't answer, she opened the front door and climbed out. "Rita," he called. Angrily, she opened the back door to take out the kids. "I'm not going to let you destroy the minds of our children," she exclaimed.

"I want to go with *Abba*," Danny shouted. "I want to live in Pincus too." The children edged to the other side

of the car, out of their mother's reach. Frustrated, she
strode down the road, heading back toward Jerusalem.
David jumped out of the car and ran after her.

"Stop it!" he said, grabbing her arm.

She was frightened, he knew. Scenes like this had
happened in the past. It was common in marriages like
theirs. The man was trained to overcome danger and fear.
The wife was far more unprepared.

Up ahead, a car heading toward Pincus had stopped.
The driver, a tall man with a gray beard walked toward the
arguing couple. David let go of his wife.

"Any trouble?" the man asked. His voice was hoarse,
his face sun-scorched, like a prophet come up from the
wilderness. The man's searing gaze silenced Rita
immediately.

"No, no, everything is fine," David said, recognizing
him instantly. "We were just stopping to admire the view."

"It isn't the best place to stop," the man said, facing
David as if his wife weren't there.

The children leaned out of the car window to watch.

"We're on our way now," David said.

"Where to?" the man asked.

"Pincus," David answered. "We're moving there."

The man's gazed focused on the secret-service agent.
His penetrating stare made all of David's private concerns
seem trivial in the great flow of history and time. A small
smile formed on his lips. "You'll be learning in the new
program for *baale tshuva*?"

"Yes," David answered. "That's right."

"Very good," he said. "I wish you success. May your
coming be for a blessing. Follow me. I'll show you the
way."

The man turned and walked back to his car. His
presence seemed to have soothed Rita's anger and fear.

"Who is he?" she asked on the way back to the
children.

"Yehoshua Gal," David answered.

"The rabbi?" Rita asked.

David said yes. His photograph was in the young agent's file. The children also wanted to know who he was. David told them he was the rabbi of the *yishuv* they were going to live in.

"He looks like Moses to me," Orit said.

"Who's Moses?" the little boy asked.

3

The road climbed and climbed until they were literally in the clouds. Gal's car vanished in the heavy fog which swirled over the mountain. At the summit, a soldier stepped out of a guard booth. He walked over and lowered the chain that stretched across the entrance to Pincus.

"Why is there a chain?" Danny asked.

David could feel his wife's silence. "To keep the wind from blowing people off the mountain," he answered.

"That's silly," the girl said.

The moving van was parked beside one of the small asbestos houses. The settlement's forty families lived either in caravans, or in the box-like asbestos supplied by the Jewish Agency. Obviously, the people who lived here did so for ideological reasons and not for material pleasure.

David's *kippah* flew off his head the moment he stepped from the car. The children had to fortify themselves to stand up straight in the strong gusts of wind. David knew what his wife must be thinking. The mountaintop in the middle of nowhere, the howling gusts, the bearded men and kerchiefed women who began to appear from their houses – they were images from the worst of her dreams.

A settler as big as the mountain lumbered over and greeted them with a hearty *shalom*. His hand enveloped David's, his arm clamped around the newcomer's back, and his great round face beamed in a joyous smile.

"I'm Shimshon," he said. "We live next door. Whatever you need, let us know. I've got a cord on my telephone that can reach your house. You're welcome to use it until you get your own line. Tonight, you'll eat dinner with us. And you're invited for *Shabbat*, all three meals."

"Thanks," David said.

Shimshon headed for the moving van to help with the unloading.

"My wife's name is Esther," he yelled. "Whatever your kids need, just ask."

Another three guys appeared, with giant *kippot* on their heads, Uzis slung over their shoulders, and *tzitzit* dancing in the wind. After greeting the settlement's new family, they began to grab the tables, beds, and chairs that were coming off the truck. Rita was quickly surrounded by women. She alone didn't cover her hair. As for the kids, they had run off with a group of miniature settlers toward the playground. More people gathered. Rita felt embarrassed as all her possessions paraded by for everyone to see. But only she paid attention. Everyone else was too busy, carrying things into the house until the truck stood empty.

Crates and cartons jammed the modest abode. There was hardly room for Rita to enter. The front door opened onto a small area that tripled as kitchen, dining room, and salon. Down the hall were two small bedrooms, and a bathroom that had a niche for the washer and dryer, a shower stall, and toilet with just enough room for one's knees.

Before Rita could sink into a monumental depression, a procession of women arrived, all carrying trays and plastic containers of food – six cakes, three roasted chickens, four *pashtidot*, and enough salads to cater a wedding.

"Just to help you get started," they said.

In America, David and Rita had hardly made a friend. In Ramat Aviv, they had gotten used to a secluded lifestyle. Instead of neighbors, they had TV. Life in Pincus was obviously different, Rita observed right away.

In all the coming and going, she remembered the kids. "Where are Orit and Danny?" she asked.

"In the playground," David answered.

"Don't worry," a friendly face said. "Kids love it here. There's plenty of space to play, everyone knows everyone and looks out for each other's children, and you don't have to worry about cars."

In New York, when they had moved into their Queens neighborhood, they had received a letter from the school asking permission to fingerprint their children – so the police could identify their bodies in the event of a kidnapping or murder. If you wanted your child to play with someone else, you had to arrange for an appointment and a ride. It was forbidden to let a child go out on the New York streets alone. In Ramat Aviv, the situation was better, but you still had to keep a sharp lookout.

"You've got to go say hello to the *Rav*," Shimshon said, wrapping a large persuasive arm around David.

"We met him out on the road," the young secret-service agent replied.

"That's not official. You've got to go to his house. *Kevod HaRav*."

"After I help my wife unpack," David told him.

"The women will help her," the huge settler said. He practically carried David out of the door. The newcomer managed to make eye contact with his wife before his over-friendly neighbor whisked him away. Rita looked totally lost.

Shimshon led him across the mountaintop *yishuv*. He slapped him on the back, raised his free hand to the sky and started to sing, "*Am Yisrael Chai.*" David was forced to join in. When in Rome, do as the Romans do. In his role of a *baal tshuva*, he was supposed to act happy, as if he had just won the Lotto's first prize.

The rabbi lived in an asbestos like the Dor family, only theirs had an extra bedroom for their eight kids.

"The *Rav* is a serious man," Shimshon said on the way. "You probably heard a lot about him from his activist days. Now he's gone back to learning. He hardly ever comes out of the house."

"Maybe we shouldn't disturb him."

"That's what he's here for. What's a rabbi without someone to ask him a question? You can ask him anything you want. It's the best way to learn. Understand?"

"I really should be helping my wife," David said.

Ignoring his protest, Shimshon rapped on the door.

"Come in," a woman's voice called out.

Shimshon pushed David inside. The rabbi's wife stood cooking in the kitchen. She was the picture of a rabbi's wife – pregnant, busy with housework, and pale in the face, as if she had never been outside in the sun.

"The new *tzaddik*," Shimshon said.

The woman smiled quietly. "Welcome," she said.

The walls of the room were covered with bookcases. Unlike David's collection, these books had been used. Bindings were worn and peeling. Here and there were photos of other settlements where the Gal family had lived – Hevron, Keshet in the Golan Heights, Atzmona in Gush Katif. David recognized the picture of Rabbi Kook on the wall, and the photograph of his son, HaRav Tzvi Yehuda. A montage of the Third Temple enjoyed the most honored place in the house. Horowitz had given the same picture to David with the order to hang it where everyone could see it.

Without waiting for an invitation, Shimshon led the way down the hall and knocked on the door of extra bedroom which the rabbi now used as his office. Most of the children, David later discovered, were either married, in the army, or boarding at school.

Yehoshua Gal sat at the end of a table. His head was bent over a volume. After a few seconds, he glanced up. Seeing David, he smiled broadly, stood up and stretched out a hand. David stared into the rabbi's clear blue eyes and involuntarily trembled, as if he were standing in front of Amos Tamir.

"I hope you will be happy here," Gal said. "Materially, the conditions are not the most luxurious, but the people are very friendly and outgoing. My family are newcomers too. They asked me to come after the yeshiva was closed down in Shechem."

For a few seconds he paused, as if remembering the sorrowful day. In his eyes, David could see the TV news footage of Joseph's Tomb burning. Then the gaze of the rabbi turned back to the room, as if returning from a distant journey.

"I agreed to move here on the condition that I only teach two classes a day. But don't be afraid to come and ask questions. It doesn't disturb me. A rabbi learns the most from his students. You have a job?" he asked.

The question startled David.

"I have some savings."

"Then you can study full time?"

"I hope so."

"G-d willing," the rabbi said.

He motioned for David to sit. The yeshiva's new student hadn't noticed that Shimshon had left. Gal's wife brought in a pitcher of juice and two glasses, which she placed by the dish of cookies on the table. David thought about his own wife, all alone with the cadre of settlers' wives. She had been in tough situations before and she had managed. She would have to manage now.

Gal told him to take some refreshment. David poured

some juice, carefully said the blessing he had learned, and drank. He noticed his hand was shaking. In all his time on the force, that had never happened to him before.

"I was once in America," Yehoshua Gal said. "They told me you lived there. To come back to Israel, and to Torah, are very great things. Very difficult things. They asked me to go there to speak to *yordim*. You have to be very strong to have an effect on Israelis who have abandoned the land. The impurity of America is very deep. The Jewish Agency tries to entice them with houses and jobs, but the material life is far better there. And most of them have lost contact with the spiritual life. So how can you influence them? I warned them that their children will marry gentiles, but most of them don't care. They think only of the moment. When they look to Israel, they see only darkness. Darkness because of the light. There is a light of holiness so bright here that it must be hidden by darkness. This is the way it must be until we can build the vessels to contain the great light. These vessels are *Eretz Yisrael* and the Temple. Today, those without Torah don't see the great light. They see only the darkness in Israel, the problems with the economy, with the Arabs, with our political system. It's our job to teach them. But first we must learn to see the great light for ourselves. We must learn to see the sparks of redemption in our return to Hevron and Pincus. We must learn to appreciate the miracle that after two-thousand years of persecution, we have a Jewish government and Jewish army to defend us against the enemies who rise up to kill us."

The wise eyes gazed down at a cookie. In his hand, it seemed like a trivial thing. He told David to take one, but in the heat of the moment, the young *Shin Bet* agent wasn't sure of the words of the blessing. He felt a drop of perspiration form under his arm.

"Do you understand what I said?" Gal asked.

"Yes," David said.

"Good," the rabbi said with a smile. "It took me twelve years of study to understand, and you understand in a minute. You have a very bright future in Torah."

David felt like a fool. Like a little boy. As if Gal's laser eyes saw right through him.

"What made you come back to Israel?" the older man asked.

"For our children," David answered. "I realized that I wanted them to grow up in Israel."

The rabbi nodded. "And what brought you back to the Torah?"

"I really don't know."

"A good answer," Gal said. "Sometimes it happens to very big souls – a sudden yearning for G-d. The person may not even know why. This powerful yearning emanates from the foundations of the nation, from the inner soul of our people to return to our pure life of holiness."

David thought about the guys in the army base down the mountain who were listening in on the conversation via the microphone in the *mezuza* that David was wearing around his neck. As for David himself, he wasn't impressed with the lecture. Every psychiatrist, guru, and preacher had his version of the very same speech. To David's way of thinking, rabbis were outdated. Policemen, judges, and secret-service agents were society's true healers, the defenders of the real foundations of the nation, democracy and law and order.

"Maybe your wife needs your help," Gal said. "I'm sorry I detained you."

"No, no, I enjoyed it. I hope we can talk often. That's why I came here – to learn."

"Very good," the rabbi said.

After mouthing a blessing, he stood up, surrounded by four walls of books and escorted his new student back to the front door.

"Where did you serve in the army?" he asked, catching

David off guard.

The *shabaknik* stiffened. "Battle corps engineer," he replied. "Explosives."

Gal didn't comment. He simply nodded his head. His wife handed David a tray of cookies to take home for the children. On his way out, the frazzled agent remembered to touch the *mezuza* on the doorpost and then give his finger a kiss.

Outside, the wind was still howling.

"Pawn to king four," David said.

The match had begun.

4

T he house looked in much better shape when David returned. Empty cartons were stacked in the yard. Rita was sitting in one of the bedrooms, putting clothes into a dresser. A white kerchief was wrapped on her head. She gazed up at her husband and blushed.

"Do I look ugly?" she asked.

A surging of love rose up inside of her husband. Rita was trying. Once again, she had taken her place at his side. He sat down beside her and held her hand in his.

"I'm sorry that I blew-up today on the road," she said. "I guess I was scared."

"I should have filled you in sooner," he said.

"You did what you had to," she responded, tugging at the kerchief, which had slipped to one side of her head. "I'm sure I must look like my grandmother."

"You look pretty," he told her.

"You really like it?"

In a strange way he did. It made her look pure. "It fits you," he said.

"Are you sure you're not acting a part?" she asked.

"I'm off duty," he quipped.

Playfully, she moved him in front of the mirror that she had leaned against a wall. There they were – she in her kerchief, and he in his *kippah* and beard. They both had to laugh.

"Where are the kids?" he asked.

"At our neighbor's. Esther said the work of unpacking would go faster without them at my feet."

"There's enough food here for an army," he noted.

"Isn't it amazing? Who are those cookies from?"

"The Gal family."

"You met his wife? What is she like? They all say she's special."

"Her cookies aren't bad."

Rita tasted one, as if that would give her a better insight into the woman. "You spoke with the rabbi?" she asked.

David nodded and bit into another cookie.

"What did he say?"

"He told me I had a very big soul."

"What else?"

"The usual speech about the Temple. Which reminds me, when you come across the picture they gave me, we've got to hang it up."

"What else did you talk about?"

"He asked where I served in the army."

"What did you tell him?"

"Explosives."

"You're not wasting any time, are you?"

"I wonder why he asked me," David reflected, sharing his puzzlement with his wife.

"It's a common question, that's all."

"He's not a common man."

"Well maybe he tries to be, to put people at ease."

"Maybe," David said. "Anyway, I'll go get the kids."

"I think they'll like it here," Rita said. "There are plenty of children their age."

"What about you? Will you like it?" he asked.

"Well, the house isn't very big. And the wind outside drives me crazy. But for your sake, I'll try."

"My woman of valor," he said. "Many woman do valiantly, but Rita outdoes them all."

As it turned out, that was the first thing he hung up – a framed calligraphy of the "Woman of Valor" proverb. Schwartz said it was standard issue in every Orthodox home. David hung it above the shelf holding their Sabbath candlesticks. Beside it, he hung up the photomontage of the Temple. After checking his notebook for the list of things he was supposed to do, he nailed *mezuzot* onto the doorposts and filled up some bookshelves with books. It wasn't long before Shimshon knocked on the door to drag him off to his first congregational prayer.

The cloud over the mountain had cleared. The afternoon sun was a giant red orb over the Mediterranean Sea. The coastline stretched along the horizon, with Tel Aviv's skyline visible in the haze. To the north, Shimshon told him, you could sometimes see the peak of Mount Hermon. To the east, on a hillside across the valley, was the settlement of Elon Moreh, where Avraham had been promised the Land. On neighboring Mount Gerizim, a small band of Samaritans continued to practice their break-off religion, including the roasting of a Passover lamb, something forbidden outside of the Temple. Below, set between the mountains, was the city of Shechem.

The synagogue was housed in two empty caravans that had been connected together like two pieces of Lego. Shimshon introduced David to the other Pincus settlers, as if he were part of his family.

"Maybe you know some rich people in America who can donate some money so that we can build a real synagogue?" the *gabai* asked.

"I'll think about it," David answered.

"It's a big *mitzvah*," Shimshon assured him, "to build a synagogue in *Eretz Yisrael*."

David surveyed his new neighbors, as if he were photographing them in his mind. Many were young, in their twenties, with long, unkempt hair, large *kippot*, and dangling *peyot*. One wore a Clint Eastwood poncho. Another walked in carrying a guitar. There were some older settlers too, with graying beards and sweaters. Everyone waited until the rabbi arrived. Gal sat in a chair near the *Aron HaKodesh*, and the prayer "*Ashre*" began. David went through the motions, swaying his body and mouthing the words. Some of the faces he recognized from his album. Yaacov Perl had been one of the teachers at the *Od Yosef Chai* Yeshiva in Shechem. Moshe Goldman was an activist with *Kach*. And the beardless Shlomo Shapiro was the *mazkir* of the Itamar settlement with a long list of arrests for attempting to pray on the Temple Mount. Shimshon, for all of his spirited friendliness, had a police file that filled up five pages, including arrests for demonstrating without a permit, property damage (smashing Arab car windows) and aggressive bodily assault. To his credit, he had never been convicted on any account. And, of course, there was Yehoshua Gal. Pincus was his fifth home since the Six-Day War. When a settlement reached the stage of asphalt roads and two-story villas, the Gal family invariably moved on.

"I'm Yosef," an American said to David right after prayers. "But most people end up calling me Joey."

It was strange to hear English again. Especially up here in the clouds. But, after all, the Americans had made it to the moon. Why not to Pincus, David thought?

Yosef was perhaps twenty-five. A few months before, he had married a Yemenite girl. He too was a *baal tshuva*, a Carlebach freak and a self-styled expert on Israeli-Arab affairs.

"For a year, I spoke only Hebrew – out of principle," he said, escorting David out of the *Beit Knesset.* "But I blew out my brain cells. Now I speak English with my wife. She realized a few months after our marriage that I hardly understood a word she was saying."

"That can happen to a husband and wife even when you speak the same language," David answered in his well-practiced English.

"I understand you lived in New York. What a sewer. A graveyard for Jews. Only they think it's good for them there. All of my friends married *goyim.* You know what America is in Hebrew? *Amareka.* The empty nation."

David nodded. It always made his work easier if suspects liked to talk.

"Don't get me wrong," the hyped-up *baal tshuva* continued. "I'm not blind to the problems in Israel. But there's a big difference. Here in Israel, the Jewish people are sick, but we are on the way to getting better. In America, the Jewish people are dying."

The evening sky seemed impossibly clear. Lights glittered all along the seacoast, from Tel Aviv to Haifa.

"Just look at it," Yosef said. "Every time I see the view from this mountain I get goose bumps. Moshe *Rabbeinu* didn't make it here, and here we stand. And they talk about giving up *Yesha.* From here, an Arab with a sophisticated katyusha rocket could hit any target in Tel Aviv. It's suicide for us not to be here."

"Unfortunately, a lot of Jews think the opposite," David said.

"And look who agrees with them. The Arabs and the gentiles. That should tell you something right there."

An interesting point, David thought. He tried to keep his own personal politics out of his job. He wasn't a diehard leftist, like some of his friends in the Service, but he certainly wasn't a rightwinger either. But standing on the mountaintop, gazing down on the twinkling population centers of Israel, it was hard to see the logic of surrendering settlements like Pincus to the Arabs. Just from a strategic, military point-of-view, the spot where he was standing was vital.

They walked on, circling the hilltop. A small building with a Coca-Cola sign turned out to be the local grocery. Another simple structure was the yeshiva. There was a kindergarten, playground, basketball court, and a *mikveh*. A few large army antennas towered over their heads. That was the sum total of Pincus. There wasn't even a school. Older children were bused every day to Elon Moreh.

Their stroll led them back to the synagogue trailer for evening prayers. G-d had brought on the darkness of evening, and, like for everything else, He had to be thanked. When David got home, the kids were already in bed. They had come home from Esther's exhausted. Rita couldn't figure out how to bathe them in the tubless shower, so she had sent them straight off to sleep.

David sat down at the dining-room table and wolfed at a leg of chicken and one of the *pashtidot*. Rita kept unpacking boxes and stacking dishes and glasses into the cupboard above the kitchen sink. *Rav* Yehoshua was giving a class for women that evening, and Rita wanted to attend.

"*Rav* Yehoshua?" David asked.

"That's what everyone calls him."

"I thought I was the one who had come here to learn," David said.

"You want me to win the confidence of the women, don't you?"

"Of course," he said. "I'm glad."

He asked for another piece of chicken, but had to take it himself. Esther came by and Rita rushed off with a smile and a wave. David felt relieved. The busier she kept, the less time she had to feel blue. He was halfway through the chicken when someone knocked on the door. Joey bounced in clinking four bottles of Maccabee beer.

"Monday is bachelor night," he said. "Your wife leave you too?"

David nodded. Joey sat down. Like a native Israeli, he pried off a bottle cap with the dull edge of a fork. From his windbreaker pocket, he pulled out a pack of sunflower seeds and spilled them out onto he table. "*L'chaim*," he said, then made a blessing and drank. He slid a bottle over to David.

"Excuse me," David said.

He had taken off his *mezuza* in the bathroom. Quickly, he walked down the corridor to the small cubicle. After waiting a minute, he flushed the toilet, as if he had used it. Then he stepped into the bedroom and slipped the wired *mezuza* back over his neck. When he returned to the dining room area, Joey was opening another beer.

"Maybe we can study together," Joey said. "I can learn a little *Gemara* in Hebrew, but after a while, my brain fizzles out and I have to switch into English."

"Fine," David said. "But I haven't learned much *Gemara* before."

"You'll catch up to me fast. I'm not the sharpest student you'll find. I want to learn for a while so I'll be able to learn with my kids, then I want to go out and help build the land."

"Doing what?" David asked.

"Whatever is needed."

"How will you know?"

"There are big people who know. Like *Rav* Yehoshua. He can just look at you and tell what's inside."

David sipped on his beer and let Joey talk. In any interrogation, winning the confidence of the suspect was the key, and just listening with a smile was still the best technique.

"The Torah is compared to an ocean," the energetic American said. "Guys like me and you are just getting our feet wet. Other guys are out there swimming. The best of them have snorkels and masks to glimpse what's below. Then come the scuba divers, the Torah scholars, who are doing their thing underwater. And down at the bottom are the deep-sea divers like *Rav* Yehoshua, digging around in the sunken treasures of Kaballah."

"He studies Kaballah?" David asked.

"He lives Kaballah," Joey said. "Like *Rav* Kook and the Maharal, may the memory of *tzaddikim* be for a blessing. Those guys were in another league altogether."

"Submarines?" David suggested, extending the metaphor.

"More than that. They were so merged with Torah, they were like fish."

David laughed. His new friend had the imagination of a different kind of swimmer. The name of that ocean was drugs. In a sea where most swimmers drown, the young American had latched onto the lifeline of religion. David had seen it happen to some Israelis in New York.

This time the knock was unmistakably Shimshon's. His hand hit the door like a sledge. As usual, he had someone in tow under one of his arms, a bushy-bearded settler who carried a guitar.

"Where's all the cake?" Shimshon asked.

He sat at the table, grinned, and waited to be served. Joey introduced Tzvi. "He's an American too. But don't let him know that I told you. He tries to pretend he's Israeli."

Tzvi didn't smile. He didn't bother to shake David's hand. "What did he say?" he asked in a very Israeli voice. Obviously, he had worked on his accent.

Shimshon pounded the table. "What's going on here? I come over to give a Jew a chance to do a *mitzvah*, and I'm ignored."

After a moment, David caught on. The *mitzvah* was *hachnasat orchim*. He hustled out of his chair and prowled around the kitchen until he found the cakes. Shimshon wanted the cookies which the rabbi's wife had baked.

Finding out that they had all been eaten, the big settler moaned, stood up from the table, and said, "Let's go." Joey pulled him back down to his chair.

The moment Tzvi played his first notes, a different dimension took over. Call it time, or space, or spirit. His fingers flicked over the strings with a life of their own, producing a sound almost sweet. Slowly, his body rocked back and forth as is he was praying. His eyes closed, and at first, he just whistled. A whistle with wings, transporting his listeners back thousands of years. Shimshon started humming deep down in his chest. The strumming grew stronger and soon the caravan echoed with a Carlebach tune.

The song ended two hours later. Thirty settlers squeezed their way into the room at one time. Everyone found something to eat and somewhere to perch. Tzvi gave them a concert, leading them through song after Carlebach song. Shimshon called it a *Hanukat Habayit*, a celebration over the Dor family's new home.

"When the children return to their borders," they sang. "*Veshavu banim, veshavu banim, veshavu banim, l'gvulam.*" When Rita returned, she could hardly find a place in the kitchen. Then Shimshon stood up and dragged David and Joey to their feet. Soon, everyone was dancing, arms locked together, dancing in a circle around the table.

Down the mountain, in the Army Base #3, a *Shin Bet* agent was tapping his feet and singing along with the settlers, "*Veshavu banim l'gvulam.*"

5

David and Rita sat on the sofa, relaxing after such an exhausting day. They were both overwhelmed by the singing and gladness which had filled their new home. Even now, the music reverberated in their ears.

"Tzvi used to play rock," David said. "In America, he had his own band. Joey has two of his tapes."

"You know, it's funny," Rita said quietly. "I don't think we've had so many people in our house since we were married."

David didn't answer. He knew what she meant. Plus, there was a real depth to the people on the mountain. Like Shimshon, their friendliness, simcha, idealism and spirit were all bigger than life.

"How was your class?" he asked.

"Incredible," she answered. "Before I went, I made up my mind not to like it. But he's really something. He didn't look at me once, but the whole evening, the way he was speaking, I felt I was the only one in the room."

David wanted to know what he said.

"Well," she began, "The class was on a book called *Mesillat Yesharim*. He said that man's task in life was to get close to G-d. The way a Jew does this is through the commandments. Everything else is a test to see if we follow after G-d, or after our own desires. The biggest test for most people is their ego. That's the true battle, he said. To turn off the ME, ME, ME voice and listen to the Torah. That's when I knew he was talking to me. As if he had some kind of radar machine. I mean there must be something to it. Think how Jews have clung to the Torah for so many thousands of years. David, are you listening to me?"

Her husband answered with a snore. He sat with his head dangling to the side, mouth open, totally exhausted. With a smile, Rita covered him with a blanket. Locking the front door, she looked at her little house and felt strangely satisfied.

"Please, G-d," she said in the dark. "If I haven't lived right, please forgive me. Please show us the way to be better Jews."

Then she turned off the light and tiptoed down the hallway to peek in on her peacefully sleeping children.

6

A t first, David thought he was dreaming. When he opened his eyes, it was dark. Again, he heard someone knocking. His watch read five-thirty.

Barefooted, he hurried to the door. "Who is it?" he asked.

"Me. Joey," came the English reply. David opened the door. "Come on," the youth said.

"Where to?"

"You'll see."

"I'm still sleeping. It's nighttime," David protested.

"Trust me," the American said in a hush.

David told him to wait. Who could tell? Maybe the kid wanted to show him a cache of explosives. He dressed quickly and quietly. The night air was cold, but at least the raging wind had calmed. Galaxies stretched out above them. The eerie wail of Moslem prayers sounded from loudspeakers in the valley below.

Joey led the way toward a small building at the edge of the *yishuv*. "Rabbi Nachman says it's the best thing there is for the soul."

"What is?" David asked.

"A *mikveh*."

Joey opened the door with a key. David had never been inside a *mikveh* before. In fact, he thought it was something for women. It resembled a small locker room with a sunken jacuzzi.

"The gas heater's been busted for almost two weeks,

but the water's not really that cold."

"Forget it," David said. "I'm not going in."

"Don't worry," Joey assured. "Rabbi Nachman used to immerse himself in ponds frozen over with ice."

The enthusiastic *baal tshuva* began to undress. David wanted to run, but just then a dark figure entered the building. Like a shadow, Yehoshua Gal whisked past into the lone changing room.

"He comes every morning," Joey whispered.

He stripped and climbed down the steps to the pool. Once, twice, three times, he ducked down under the water. Four times, five times, six. David counted the splashes till nine. Reluctantly, he undressed. He had impersonated drug pushers and addicts, and one time a queer, but immersing in a *mikveh* was the craziest thing of all. When Joey emerged from the pool, the private door opened, and Gal hurried down the steps. David counted another nine splashes. Stripping down to his boxer shorts, he trembled. Not from the cold. For the first time in his career, the young agent felt truly frightened. Not by the water. By the *mikveh* itself. What if the ritual bath really worked? After nine dips, who would he be when he came out of the water?

Gal finished and disappeared back into the changing booth.

"Go for it!" Joey said.

David's foot protested when it landed on the first step of the pool. The water was freezing. With a gasp, he plunged in. He thought he would go into shock. Up and down, he splashed, trembling from the cold. When he reached seven, he stood up, out of breath, eyes and mouth opened wide. So what if he only made seven? Did that make him any less of a man? Gasping, he splashed his way out of the pool.

"Great way to wake up, isn't it?" his study partner said, handing him a towel.

"You said it wasn't cold."

"This is nothing. You should try the *mikveh* of the *Ari* up in Tzfat."

Outside, the sky along the eastern horizon was filling with light.

"Quiet," Joey said, holding an arm out to stop David from walking. "Just watch."

"When in Pincus, do as the settlers do," David thought.

Not since his training days in the army had David taken the time to observe the sun come up over the mountains. He had to admit it. There was nothing like the timelessness of a sunrise in Israel. Floating on the gentle morning wind was the whisper of something eternal, of a glory long past that echoed over these very same hillsides today.

"To me, it's the most beautiful sight in the world," Joey said.

It truly was something, but standing exposed on the mountaintop, David was certain he would come down with pneumonia. His hair was still wet, and ever since his childhood, he had been prone to quick colds.

"I'll meet you at the synagogue," he said and ran back to his house to get his *tefillin*.

"What are you looking for?" his sleepy wife asked.

"My *tefillin* bag."

"It's in the suitcase on the floor."

He grabbed the blue sack and headed back off for the six-thirty *minyan*. The trailer was already full. Shirtsleeves were rolled up and worshippers were strapping on the little black boxes. David removed the prayer shawl from his bag and swung it over his head like he had practiced. But he blew it when he tried to strap on his *tefillin*. The box kept falling off of his left bicep. He tried to remake the loops, but couldn't get the strap to come out in the right direction and continue down his arm. The praying had already started. Finally, Shimshon came over and gave the black

strap a twist. David managed on his own after that.
Reading along with the prayers, the *shabaknik* kept an
eye on the settlers he was to place under surveillance.
Every few minutes, it seemed like someone would catch
on fire and shout out verses of prayer. *Shema Yisrael* was
intoned in a unified roar. Then David bobbed up and
down like the others for the long *Amidah* prayer.
Everything went smoothly until the *gabai* called David up
to the Torah.

"David ben..." he asked, waiting for David to fill in his
father's name.

"Ben Yehuda," David answered.

But he didn't know the blessings for the Torah.
Schwartz, the Conservative rabbi, had neglected to teach
him. He stood by the scroll of the Torah, waiting for
something to happen. "*Baruch...*" Gal called out. The
gabai's finger pointed to a line in the prayer book.
Embarrassed, David read it aloud. The congregation
responded. The finger moved down the page.

After the Torah reading and the final blessing, the
congregation broke out in song, celebrating the Dor
family's arrival.

"*V'shavu banim, v'shavu banim, v'shavu banim l'gvulam.*"

By the end of the prayer service, David was drained.
One by one, the settlers came over and shook his hand.
Except for Yehoshua Gal. He sat in his corner, praying.

"You're going to be a big rabbi some day," Shimshon
said with a "*yasher koach*" slap on the back.

The rock musician, Tzvi, told him not to worry about
flubbing up the blessing. "In the eyes of Hashem, we're
all just beginners," he said.

David wound up his *tefillin* straps like Schwartz had
instructed. Then he folded his *tallit*, as if he had been
folding *tallitot* all of his life. When he left the caravan,
Yehoshua Gal was still praying.

7

D avid spent his first day in Pincus helping Rita fix up the house. The children played outside. Furniture that they couldn't find room for was stored in an empty caravan down a dirt path. Unlike their Ramat Aviv apartment, which had American-style closets built into the wall, their new accommodations were far less luxurious. The rooms didn't have closets. If you wanted to store something, you had to buy an additional house, or put up a do-it-yourself closet that ate up a third of the room. Once again, Shimshon came to the rescue. He was driving into Jerusalem in the *yishuv's* all-purpose van. He offered to buy them a closet like he had in his house and to bring it back to Pincus. Rita gave her O.K. after a quick visit to Esther. It wasn't the most attractive closet in the world, but it seemed sturdy enough. When David said he would come with him to help, Shimshon refused.

"It's a bigger *mitzvah* to help your wife," he said, driving off with one of the Dor family's checks. A few hours later, he was hauling the long planks through the front door.

He worked for two hours non-stop. A plank here, a piece here, a screw there, a bang, "*kacha*," with his foot, and a whack with his hand. David practically stood by the sidelines and watched. Each time he tried to help him, the big settler would growl and wave him away. Sweat was pouring down his face when he stepped back to have a look at his finished creation. David had to laugh.

"What's so funny?" Shimshon asked.

The closet stood slanting over, a good fifteen degrees off center, as if it were about to fall over.

"It looks like the Leaning Tower of Pisa," David said.

"The what?" Shimshon asked.

"There's a famous tower in Italy that looks like its going to fall over," David explained.

"So what if it's crooked? It works," Shimshon said, opening and closing the doors.

Rita wasn't amused. "If that's how it is going to look, I don't want it in my house," she declared.

This time, David insisted on helping. The work took them another hour, but at least the closet stood straight.

"Sometimes," Shimshon confided to David, "women can drive you nuts."

When her clothes were hanging in the closet, Rita was much more at ease. With their familiar belongings in place, the mountaintop abode seemed far less threatening and foreign. And Rita's worries about the children proved groundless. They ran around all day outside like gazelles born and raised in the wilderness. Come bedtime, they snuggled into their blankets like little earthbound angels.

David told Joey that he'd take a rain check on the next morning's *mikveh*. Following breakfast, the security agent drove off in the Ford van with Shimshon and the American *baal tshuva* to pick up some new *stenderim* for the yeshiva. A Hasidic song boomed over the *Arutz*-7 radio station, transforming the van into an amplifier on wheels. Shimshon sang along while he drove. When the "beep beep beep beep beep" of the eight-o'clock news sounded, Shimshon let out a "Shhhhh!"

"Maybe the *Mashiach* has come!" he said in a voice filled with suspense.

Apparently, he hadn't. A terrorist bomb had exploded on the roadside in Gush Katif. There had been sporadic firing throughout the night in Hevron and Psagot. Rock throwers had been apprehended near Kedumim. In all of the incidents, no Jews had been wounded.

"*Baruch Hashem*," Shimshon said.

The curves in the mountain road jolted David back and forth. Before long, the van left the paved road completely and bounded down a rocky incline. In the middle of nowhere, Shimshon braked. Grabbing a pair of binoculars, he climbed out of the vehicle.

"Come on," Joey said.

Curious, David followed after them along a path leading through the boulders on the side of the hill. Joey carried his own pair of binoculars, along with an M-16. Ironically, David, the government agent, was the only one unarmed.

Shimshon sat down on a rocky perch that looked out over Shechem. Holding the binoculars to his eyes, he focused and started to sob.

"Why, why, why?" he moaned. "Yosef, Yosef, forgive us."

David thought he was nuts.

"What is it?" he asked.

"*Kever Yosef*," Joey answered. "Take a look."

Teary eyed, he handed the binoculars to David. He scanned the streets of the city below until the familiar round dome of the tomb came into sight. David recognized it from pictures. Only now the dome had been painted green to look like a mosque. A Palestinian flag waved on the roof. A Palestinian policeman stood in the shade of a fig tree, guarding the holy tomb, where the bones of Joseph had been buried by the Children of Israel more than three-thousand years before. Nearby was the ancient *tel*, which the patriarch Jacob had bought for his family. Schwartz had taught David about Dina's rape and how the brothers, Shimon and Levy, had revenged their sister's honor by killing every male in the town. At the beginning of the *al-Aksa Intifada*, Arabs had overrun the yeshiva on the site, killing one of the Israeli soldiers on guard.

"Oh, Yosef, oh, Yosef," Shimshon sighed. "Yosef the *Tzaddik*, forgive us."

"We'll return there; don't worry," Joey assured.

"By force?" David asked.

"Of course by force," Shimshon exclaimed. "That's the only thing the Arabs respect."

"Supposing a group of settlers reconquered it. They'd never be able to hold on to it," David said.

"The army will reconquer it," Joey corrected.

"What army?" Shimshon laughed. "The government is afraid of its shadow. We have to save Yosef. Then the army will have to come in to defend us."

"Yosef wasn't the only one with dreams," Joey said. "Shimshon comes up with a new scheme every day. Don't take him seriously."

David peered through the binoculars.

"You ever see Shechem before?" Shimshon asked.

"Can't say that I have," David answered.

"Looks nice and peaceful, huh?"

"It seems to be," David agreed.

"You see those uniformed schoolchildren walking to school?"

David panned with the binoculars, and the orderly line of schoolchildren came into focus.

"They learn rock throwing, Jew hating, and media relations. Physical education consists of live firearm training."

David laughed.

"You think I'm kidding," Shimshon asked.

"Exaggerating a little, that's all."

"Remind me to show you a video of the rallies they hold for the kids. Achmed Kabril is fond of telling them that they won't be servants of Allah until they dance on Jewish graves. There are so many stone throwings and shootings around here, the army doesn't bother to report them. If you want to smoke a cigarette, all you have to do is hold it outside your car window and a molotov cocktail will whiz by and light it. Our soldiers can't go into their

shetach, so the terrorists aren't afraid they'll be caught."
"They're all afraid of Shimshon," Joey said. "They call
him 'The Ugly Israeli.'"
"*L'hitraot, Yosef HaTzaddik*," Shimshon said, standing
up. "Don't despair. We saved you from *galut* in Egypt, and
we'll rescue you from this *galut* too."

After picking up the *stenderim* in Elon Moreh, the van
returned to the *yishuv*. David let Rita know he was back,
then walked over to the two caravans which housed the
yeshiva. Pictures of *Rav* Kook, the Lubavitch *Rebbi*, the
Temple and Joseph's Tomb hung on the walls. In the *baal
tshuva* division of the yeshiva were Joey; a former
kibbutznik; an Ethiopian boy; a new Russian immigrant still
in the process of thawing; two Sephardis fresh from the
army; an Israeli youth with hair down his back; two
brothers from France, and David. Tzvi was already learning
in the *kollel* with the serious guys.

It was the month of *Elul*, a few weeks before the New
Year, so they were learning the *Gemara* of *Rosh Hashana*
with *Rav* Shmuel, a young Torah scholar from Yitzhar
whose tremendous white kippah covered his head. Then
came a class in *halacha*, and a lecture on the writings of
Rav Kook. After the afternoon prayer, David went home
to eat lunch. Refreshed from a half-hour nap, he returned
to the study hall to learn *Mishna*, the Book of *Yehoshua*, and
something called the *Kuzari*. David enjoyed the last two
classes the most. The rest to him was a bore.

As the week passed, *Gemara* seemed an insurmountable
challenge. The Aramaic was strange to his ears, and the
flickering *Rashi* script made the young agent's eyes hurt.
Joey moaned and grumbled and banged his fist on the
table when he struggled with a difficult point.

"Why bother if it's so painful?" David asked.

"Not according to the knowledge, but according to the
toil is the reward," he answered. "I grew up with baseball
and movies. I want to give my kids something more."

In *halacha* class, the laws seemed so picayune and irrelevant that David couldn't understand how any intelligent person could believe that a G-d so great could concern himself with particulars so small.

"That's one of the things which makes Torah so great," Joey said. "It brings G-d into everything on earth. I love it, I love it, I love it!"

Yehoshua Gal taught the class in the *Kuzari*, a discourse on Jewish fundamentals. It was strange, David had to admit, that he knew nothing about the roots of his own Jewish culture. He had studied world history, psychology, philosophy, anthropology, sociology, politics, literature, economics, and art, but he had never studied anything about Judaism. Sure, he had learned some Bible stories in school, but they were taught as if they were Greek myths.

When David returned home that Thursday evening, he stumbled through the salon to the bedroom, and collapsed face down on the bed.

"What happened to you?" Rita asked from the doorway.

He lay without answering, spread out on the bed like a blanket.

"David, is something the matter?" she asked in alarm.

"I won't make it if I have to do this every week. There's no way. I can't."

Rita sat down beside him. Through all of the years she had been with him, he had never spoken about a job so despairingly.

"There's a boy from Ethiopia," David continued. "Two years ago he didn't know Hebrew, or how to eat with a spoon. He understands *Gemara* better than I do."

"I get it," she said. "Your ego's been hurt."

When her husband didn't answer, she knew her hunch was right. David was a perfectionist. In everything he did, he wanted to be the best.

"It's hard at the beginning, that's all," she said.

"Where are the kids?" he asked, suddenly aware of the

silence.

"Shimshon took them to Elon Moreh with his kids."

"What for?"

"I don't know." David sat up. "Why'd you let him?"

"You know Shimshon. He lifted them up and threw them in his van."

"The guy's irresponsible," David declared.

"Oh, I think he's harmless," Rita said.

"Yeah, for someone who wants to recapture Joseph's Tomb. In addition to having been arrested fifteen times, dislocated a soldier's shoulder, pulverized a half dozen Arab automobiles with a hammer, and killed eight Syrian soldiers in Lebanon, he's an ideal babysitter for our kids."

"If he killed Syrians in a war, so what?"

"And the cars of the Arabs?"

"Maybe it was coming to them," she said.

David grumbled. He didn't mention that the Israeli soldier had dislocated his own arm trying to drag the giant settler out of the road during a sit-down demonstration protesting the deteriorating security situation in *Yesha*.

"How was your day?" he asked, sitting up.

"OK. I organized the house some more and took the kids for a walk."

"Where to?"

"To the grocery."

"Yeah? You know I haven't yet been there. What do they sell?"

"Milk, bread, Sabbath candles."

"Everything a Jew needs," David kidded.

"We circled around the *yishuv* a few times until I got dizzy. Orit said that tomorrow we can walk in the opposite direction, and then it will seem like we're doing something new."

"In other words, you're going stir-crazy."

"Well, to tell you the truth, it isn't Tel Aviv, is it?" she said. "I guess you could say that I'm suffering from some form of culture shock, that's all."

David walked into the kitchen and opened the refrigerator door, hoping to find a beer.

"Incidentally, I spoke to *Rav* Yehoshua for an hour," she confessed.

David felt his heart skip a beat.

"Close the fridge door," she told him.

He pulled out a plate of cold chicken and sat down at the table to eat. "Is that so?" he said, feeling that his life was beginning to slip out of his hands.

"I made a decision," she said.

She said it with a tone of finality. When she told him, a piece of chicken lodged in his throat. Gagging, he spit it back to the plate.

"I want to keep kosher," she said. "Otherwise, it isn't fair to these people. They'll be coming here and eating. It wouldn't be right to betray their trust. They have certain beliefs, and we should respect them while we are here."

"What if I don't want to keep kosher?" he asked.

"I'm in charge of the kitchen," she said.

"True, but I'm in charge of the house."

"In that case, I'll take the children and go back to Ramat Aviv," she threatened.

"It's so important to you?" he asked her.

"To be a good person, yes."

"Did you ever think that our being here may be betraying their trust in a bigger way?"

"That's different. Your work is something that affects the whole country. I'm talking about a personal interrelationship between people."

"What's that got to do with Gal?" David asked.

"I went to ask questions about *kashrut*."

"Stay away from him. I'll buy you a how-to-keep kosher book. The less he knows about us the better."

"Sometimes you're paranoid, you know that?"

"I get paid to be paranoid. Heat up this chicken, will you?"

"I can't," Rita replied.

"Why can't you?

"The stove isn't kosher. We'll have to buy a new one. Gal says there are ways to kosher a stove with a blow torch, but it isn't always effective, and I want a new model anyway."

"And who's going to pay for it?" he asked.

"The company."

"Whose company?"

"Your company. It's the same as a business expense."

"The chief will get a kick out of that."

"We can do the microwave ourselves, but we'll need another set of silverware and dishes, a new toaster oven, a whole new set of pots and pans."

"Your very generous with the company's money."

"Everyone else takes advantage. Why shouldn't we?"

"I'm glad to hear you haven't become religious completely."

"Don't be foolish," she said.

David lost his appetite for the chicken. When he couldn't hear anything over the noise on his cell phone, he walked over to Shimshon's house to borrow the phone. Esther handed it out through the bedroom window. Shimshon had rigged up a cord that reached into the Dor family's salon. No doubt, David thought, it was bugged.

"Hello, Uncle," he said to the agent who answered. "This is David, calling from Pincus. We ran into a little money problem, and we need to buy a new stove..."

"An Electra Deluxe," Rita whispered.

"An Electra Deluxe, my wife says. And a toaster oven."

"Silverware," Rita whispered.

"And two sets of new silverware. Otherwise, I'll be up here in Pincus without a wife and kids. And if you could get us a telephone line, it would be great."

"I'll see what I can do," the voice said.

"Thanks, Uncle. Goodbye."

"Satisfied?" he asked when he hung up the phone. Rita nodded. That was Rule Number One for success on the job. Make the wife happy.

A blast of Hasidic music sounded outside. Shimshon drove up to the house in his van. Danny and Orit ran in the door.

"*Abba*, we saw Joseph's Tomb with binoculars," the girl excitedly said.

"And Arabs threw stones at us," Danny reported.

"Pebbles," Shimshon said from the doorway. "Nothing serious."

David was angry. "Are you crazy? Taking kids to a place like that? They could have shot at you."

"Wooo. A little nervous today," Shimshon said.

"Goodnight," David said, closing the door.

Shimshon reached out a paw before it could shut. "You've got my telephone," he said.

David handed him the phone and closed the door on the big, smiling face.

"You shouldn't behave like that," Rita said.

"Why not? Isn't it kosher enough for you?"

"You lost your cool."

"I didn't lose my cool," David argued. "He took the kids to a very dangerous place."

"So did you," she said. "When you agreed to take this assignment."

David fumed.

"Where's our TV?" Danny asked.

"We left it in Tel Aviv," Rita said.

"I want to watch it," he insisted.

"Religious people don't watch television, dummy," his sister said.

"We're not religious," the boy answered.

"We're pretending to be," the girl said.

Husband and wife exchanged worried looks. If the kids spoke that way with their friends, that would be the end of the mission.

"We're not pretending to be," Rita said. "We're learning how."

"I used to think religious people were scary," Orit said. "But the people in Pincus are nice."

"Go to bed," David told them.

"If I can't have a television, then I want a gun like Shimshon's," Danny said.

"When you grow up, I'll get you a gun," David promised.

"I need it now. What if Arabs come and you're not around. Who'll protect *Eema*?"

"Go to bed," David warned in his assertive voice.

"Dad?" the boy asked.

"What?"

"Why do we have idols in our house?"

"Idols?" Rita exclaimed in surprise.

The small boy pointed to the two oriental statues that stood on a shelf in the kitchen. One was a delicate Geisha girl made of porcelain, and the other a green dragon. Rita had purchased them in Chinatown in New York.

"Those aren't idols," the mother said. "They're for decoration."

"Jews aren't supposed to have statues," the boy answered.

"Where did you learn that?" David asked.

"From Shimshon's kids," Danny said.

David frowned.

"We don't worship them," Rita explained.

"Well somebody does," Orit said. "In China or somewhere."

"That's it for me," David exclaimed. "I'm beat. You put them to bed. I get enough of this brainwashing at the yeshiva. It's too much for my head to absorb. Maybe when

I wake up, I'll be back in the army, a bachelor, before we got married, when I had a chance to sign a contract to play soccer with Maccabee Tel Aviv."

He was on his way to the bedroom when Orit asked the evening's last question. "If we're going to be religious, are you and *Eema* going to have any more children?"

"Not for a while," David said. "You and your brother are enough."

Two hours later, when her family was peacefully sleeping, Rita carried the trash bag out of the house. Alone, in the moonlight, she felt a little like Abraham. Inside the trash bag, the two oriental statues clanked together and smashed into pieces when they landed in the bin.

Overhead, the heavens sparkled with stars.

8

The very next morning, as David was winding up his *tefillin*, Yehoshua Gal appeared at his side.

"Where did you get your *tefillin*?" he asked.

"My *tefillin*?" the *shabaknik* responded in surprise.

"Are you sure that they're kosher?"

"Kosher? Sure they are kosher."

"Where did you buy them?" the rabbi asked.

"From a store in the city."

"Which city?"

"Jerusalem," David replied, feeling his palms sweat.

"Which store?"

The guy probably knows every *tefillin* store in the city, David thought in panic.

"I don't remember the name of the place. A friend took me there."

"Not every store selling *tefillin* checks the merchandise

that they sell. Very often, the parchments inside aren't written according to the *halacha*. *Tefillin* are like a cellphone to G-d. If they are not written correctly, the channel of communication remains closed."

Gal looked deeply into David's eyes. The large drop of sweat that had formed under the agent's armpit dripped down his arm like a tomato falling off of a vine.

"If you want, I can examine the parchments for you," Yehoshua Gal volunteered.

"He knows they're not real," David thought. "He knows that they're wired!"

Gal's eyes peered right through him, as if reading all of his secrets.

"It's a simple procedure to open the *batim*," Gal said. "I'll have them back to you by tonight."

"I'm certain they're kosher," David mumbled nervously. "My friend's a *Chabadnik*. He wouldn't steer me astray."

"Very well," Gal said. "If there is anything else I can do for you, don't hesitate to drop by for a visit."

"Thank you, sir, I mean *Rav*," Dor answered.

He took a deep breath when his inquisitor walked out of the caravan. With trembling hands, he placed his *tefillin* back in their sack. All the way home, he wondered if Gal really knew about the hidden microphone. How could he? It was a case of paranoia, that's all, David thought. It was known to happen to agents. But maybe Gal had learned Kaballah and could tell what David was thinking.

Just to be sure, the moment David returned home, he dialed his special emergency number.

"This is David. I'd like to speak to my Uncle," he said.

"Your Uncle is not available," a voice answered.

"Tell him that I need a new set of kosher *tefillin* by tomorrow."

"One second, please," the voice said.

"What's the matter with the *tefillin* you have?" Rita

asked as she swept up the room.

David didn't answer. He waited until the voice returned to the line.

"Your Uncle will be in the store today at five o'clock."

"I'll be there," David said.

He breathed easier the minute he hung up the phone.

"What was that all about?" Rita asked.

"Gal offered to check my *tefillin* to make sure that they're kosher. I think that he knows."

"Nonsense," David's wife answered. "How could he know? I'm sure he was just trying to be helpful, that's all."

"I have the feeling that the guy sees right through me."

"You mean he makes you feel guilty. I have the same feeling too."

"Guilty for what?" David asked.

"Well, we aren't exactly being honest in our being here."

"Either is he," David answered. "This is occupied territory, remember?"

"He thinks it's his land."

"So do the Arabs."

"I know that they do. But you have to understand Gal's point-of-view too."

"I don't have to understand anything," David said. "I just have to do my job."

"So do I," Rita answered. "So hurry up and eat breakfast, and let me clean the house."

After scrambling a few eggs, the new student gathered his books and headed off for the yeshiva. Seeing Shimshon's van by his house, he decided to stop by and borrow a book of the Chofetz Chaim that he needed for class.

Esther directed him toward the back of the house. Shimshon sat at a computer in the combination children's room and makeshift study. Surprisingly, the equipment, including the professional scanner, was expensive and new.

"Take a look at this," the big settler said, moving back from the screen.

Shimshon was watching a video of the attack on *Kever Yosef* taken on the day that *Tzahal* had abandoned the site. Hundreds of Arabs surrounded the Tomb, firing rifles and throwing rocks and molotov cocktails.

"You see him?" Shimshon asked, freezing the image. With a deft move of the mouse, he switched to a close-up of a high-ranking Palestinian officer. "That's Kibril," he said, "the henchman of Schechem."

With another flick of his wrist, he switched the digital disc to another selection. This time, Kibril could be seen firing shots out of a window with a Russian *Kalatchnikov*.

"What's he shooting at?" David asked.

"*Kever Yosef*. But this is from the riots of '96, after Netanyahu opened the tunnels of the *Kotel*. Shooting down from the building next to the Tomb, Kibril killed two of our soldiers."

"How'd you get this footage?" David asked.

"We have our channels," was all Shimshon said.

"Foreign newsmen?" David queried.

Shimshon shook his head no.

"*Mashtappim?*"

Again, the big head shook back and forth.

"From the *Shabak?*"

"Let's just say we have friends," Shimshon answered.

He clicked the mouse and opened another folder. This time, Kibril was standing in a school playground, lecturing students.

"What is he saying?" David asked.

"He's telling them that the Arabs of Shechem will not give up armed struggle until they dance on the graves of all the Jews in Samaria. The very next day there was a drive-by shooting by Ariel, and two Jews were killed."

"If the *Shin Bet* knows this, why don't they take the guy out?" David asked.

"Politics," Shimshon answered. "It's all rotten politics." Once again, he opened another file. This time, Kibril and two other Arabs were seen dancing on the dome over Joseph's Tomb.

"Here he is with Omir Faraki, head of Palestinian Authority Propaganda, and Ibraham Mouward, Arafat's head commander in Ramallah."

"What are you doing this for?" David asked.

"I'm making an album," his new neighbor replied.

Shimshon reached up to a shelf and pulled down an album of photos. On page after page, there were pictures of gun-toting Arabs taken from an assortment of riots.

"Look at this," Shimshon said, drawing David's attention back to the screen.

The zoom lens of a video camera was focused on a house. Two Palestinian policemen stood outside. The front door opened and Kibril emerged carrying a briefcase. He walked to the driveway and swung open the driveway door. A minute later, his Mercedez backed out onto the street. The two policemen hurried into a waiting car and followed Kibril down the block.

"He leaves home at six o'clock every morning."

"So what?" David said.

"So if some brave Jew wanted to get him, that's the best time."

"They say that walls have ears," David warned him.

"They've arrested me so many times, I don't let it worry me anymore."

"Yeah, well, be careful. In the meantime, let the army do their job."

"I wish that they would," Shimshon said. "But the truth is that the lefties control the army, and they don't want us here either."

The undercover agent left Shimshon's house with a copy of the Chofetz Chaim's book, *Shmirat HaLashon*. The rest of the day, he spent learning, but the video kept replaying in his mind. He left the yeshiva early to drive into the city. "Uncle" was to be waiting for him at the fish counter of the Co-op in Pisgat Zev. But instead of finding his liaison officer, the young agent discovered the *Shabak* chief, Amos Tamir, disguised with a walking cane, false moustache, and cap.

"This is the fish that you wanted," the retired *Tat Aluf* said, handing David a package that was wrapped like a fish. "Any problems?" he asked.

"No, sir. Well, I don't know, sir. You see, I don't want to take any chances. Sometimes, they check *tefillin*, and I don't want my microphone found."

"Understandable," Tamir replied. "Any progress?"

The icy blue eyes peered down at David, making him feel like one of the frozen fish in the counter.

"I'm working on winning their confidence."

"What about Sylvester Stallone?"

That was the code name for Shimshon.

"He dreams about recapturing *Kever Yosef* and forcing the army to come back into Shechem, but I think it's just talk. And he has a fetish for watching videos of Achmed Kabril, as if he's planning some sort of action."

"You fellas want anything?" the fish salesman asked on the other side of the counter.

"Fish *shnitzel*," Tamir said.

"Aisle three," the worker replied.

David followed his boss down the aisle.

"Videos?" Tamir asked.

"He says he got them from us."

"That's interesting."

"You're not trying to encourage him, are you?" agent David Dor asked.

The Secret Service chief didn't answer. Instead he reached down and picked up a box of frozen fish *shnitzels*.

"My wife likes the Nile perch," he said, nonchalantly. "Plus, if you amass enough labels, you can win a roundtrip flight to Kenya for two."

With a tip of his cap, the dapper-looking man walked away toward the check-out.

"Keep in touch with your Uncle," was all that he said.

9

D avid had a lot to think about by the time he got home. Could it be that Tamir was setting Shimshon up? Or maybe an agent had given Shimshon the tape on his own. After all, it was possible that an agent could sympathize with the settlers. Not every agent in the service was a card-carrying leftist like Amos Tamir.

Rita was heating up soya *shnitzels* in the toaster oven. Danny was playing on the floor with Shimshon's son, Ariel.

"I need a beer," David said, unnerved by his meeting with Tamir, and by the long, winding drive home to Pincus.

"We don't have any," Rita answered.

"No beer?"

"I forgot to buy in the *makolet*. Why didn't you buy some when you were in Jerusalem?"

"I guess I forgot too."

He glanced down at the children. They were playing a game of toy soldiers. Danny's forces were defending a shoebox. On top of the shoebox was a cereal bowl, turned upside down to look like a dome. Ariel's troops marched on the enclave, led by a formation of tanks. Danny's snipers on the roof of a box of corn flakes kept the tank force at bay.

David sat up on the couch, realizing he was watching a dress-rehearsal for the conquest of *Kever Yosef*.

"Now!" Ariel called into a toy cell-phone.

Lifting a helicopter into the air, he stood up and circled around behind the corn-flake building. The gunship opened fire, blasting Danny's snipers off the roof.

"That's great," David said, sarcastically. He stood up and walked over to his wife in the kitchen. "Do you know what our son is playing?" he asked.

"Soldiers," Rita replied calmly.

"Israeli soldiers recapturing Shechem is more like it."

Rita glanced over. "What did you expect? They are growing up in Pincus, not in Ramat Aviv."

David let out a sigh. "Where is Orit?" he asked.

"I don't know."

"You don't know?"

"Outside playing somewhere."

"Outside playing somewhere on the top of a mountain overlooking a city of one-hundred thousand Arabs?"

"Maybe she's at the house of a friend."

"Shouldn't we find out?"

"Oh, David, try to relax. Do you want me to worry every minute? I'd go crazy up here if I did."

A "humff" passed through David's lips, but he realized that Rita was right. For some reason, he was awfully uptight.

"I forgot to tell you," Rita said. "Shlomo Shapiro came by to see you."

"Shlomo Shapiro?' What did he want?"

"He didn't say."

"That's interesting," David reflected.

Shlomo Shapiro was the administrator of the neighboring settlement of Itamar. In addition to being a round-the-clock workhorse for settler causes, he had written several pamphlets about the Temple Mount. Since the Dor family's arrival in Pincus, the busy Shapiro had hardly found time to say hello to the yeshiva's latest *baal tshuva*. Why had he suddenly come for a visit, the young *Shin-Bet* agent wondered?

Even though the summer had barely ended, David slipped on a jacket.

"Where are you going?" Rita asked.

"To see Shapiro."

"What about your *shnitzel*?"

"I'll eat it when I get back."

Sure enough, a cold wind blew over the mountainside. The lights of Netanya sparkled in the distance. Stars filled the sky. The Shapiro house was situated at the end of the *yishuv*, facing the cluster of caravans that had been recently set up on the adjacent hillside. With an uncharacteristic smile, Shlomo Shapiro welcomed David inside.

"Sorry, we haven't gotten around to inviting your family for a *Shabbat*, but the truth is we've been away a lot the last month working on a *kiruv* project getting communities around the country to support the settlements in our *gush*."

David nodded, noticing the paintings of the Temple on the walls. After a few minutes of small talk, the serious-minded Shapiro got down to the point.

"I thought that maybe you could help us in Itamar," he said. "We've got a lot of problems with the *mikveh* that was built in the early days of the *yishuv*. I wasn't working there then. The construction was unprofessional, irresponsible, if you ask me. Anyway, pipes are leaking, and the foundation is falling apart. In short, we have to build a new *mikveh*. And, of course, we don't have the money, so we are looking to cut costs. The site that we have is almost all rock, so we have to blast before we can build. Regular contractors want a fortune. I heard you know something about explosives. We can get a hold of the material. We need someone who can rig us some charges."

The earnest settler stared at David like it was the most normal request in the world.

"I worked with some explosives in the army," the

secret agent said, "but I wouldn't say I'm an expert."

"We don't need an expert. We just need somebody who isn't going to blow himself up in the process."

"What about the *Misrad HaDatot*? Can't they help?" David asked.

"Yeah, they help a little, and other people have promised me funds here and there, but it doesn't even cover half of the costs."

"I've got a guy who works at blowing up construction sites. He's willing to volunteer his engineering know-how, but he doesn't work with the explosives themselves. He'll show us where to put them.. According to his figures, we need eight TNT charges at 30 kilos each."

David whistled. "It must be a pretty big *mikveh*," he said.

"The *mikveh* isn't so big, but the rock it's sitting on is," Shapiro replied.

"Look, if I can help, I'll be happy to. Maybe I can even get you a better price on the charges. I can look into it if you like."

"*Tizke l'mitzvot*," Shapiro said with a grin. He shook David's hand like a vice, as if he had been doing construction work all his life.

"Knight to queen bishop three," David said to himself as he walked toward his home.

He was feeling his usual confident self by the time he stepped in the door. Things were picking up. He was winning people's confidence faster than he thought. Either his new settler friends were naïve or desperate for all the help they could get. But his good mood was short-lived as his wife dropped a bomb of her own. The kids had gone to bed, and Rita was finishing the dishes when she told him.

"You'll have to sleep on the couch tonight," she said with a blush.

"Huh?" he muttered, not understanding.

"You'll have to sleep on the couch until we get separate beds," she said, nervously pulling at the kerchief she wore on her head.

"What are you talking about?" he asked.

"I want to start keeping the laws of family purity," she answered.

"The laws of family purity? What's that?"

"You know what it is."

David was stunned. He shook his head as if to wake up from an unpleasant dream.

"You mean....?" he stuttered, unable to get out the words.

Rita nodded yes.

"Are you crazy?" he asked.

"I suppose so," she said. "I must have been to come here with you. But we're here, aren't we?"

Her husband didn't know what to answer.

"Esther came over this morning after you left. I was changing our sheets. We got to talking and she asked me about our bed. Religious people don't sleep in double beds. I guess your conservative rabbi forgot to tell you that. Did I ever turn red in the face! We spent the rest of the morning learning the laws from a book she brought over."

"You're really serious," he said.

Rita didn't answer.

"Please, Rita, tell me you're kidding," he begged.

Remembering the *mezuza* he was wearing, he stripped it off his neck and stuffed it into his pocket. The guys down at the base didn't have to know everything about his personal life too.

"I want to try it," she answered. "In a way, I think it's beautiful. It shows real respect toward the woman."

"But why separate beds?"

"For one thing, you know why as well as I do, and for another, we'll never convince anyone that we're religious if we sleep in one bed."

"So we'll buy separate beds and still sleep in one."
Rita rose from the table. "I'll set up the couch," she
said with firm determination.
David grumbled. "Please, sweetheart,'" he appealed.
"This is going too far."
When he reached out his hand, she pulled away with
a sudden gesture, as if he had some kind of plague. He
gazed at her with a mixture of hurt and disbelief.
"You can't," she told him. "Not for another two
weeks."
"Two weeks?!"
"Twelve days to be exact."
"*Eizeh basa*," he groaned.
David couldn't believe it. What was happening? What
had he gotten himself into? What was going on with his
wife? Was she being hypnotized by the place, by the
classes, by the women of Pincus, and by Yehoshua Gal?
She came back into the room and dumped his blanket
and pillow on the sofa.
"If this is what makes her happy," David thought with
a sigh.
That was the first rule of the job. And to David Dor,
success on the job came before everything.

10

They arrived at David's parent's house at noon,
dropped off the kids, grabbed their bathing suits, and
headed off for the beach. David took off his *kippah*. Rita
felt a little twinge when she pulled off her kerchief and
loosened her hair, but within minutes it felt perfectly
natural. After a month in Pincus, it felt like a honeymoon
to both of them – as if they had been let out of prison.

They strolled along Dizengof like tourists, looking at the people and the stores, laughing together like teenagers and remembering the days of their courtship and youth.

They sat down in a restaurant and David ordered the most unkosher shishkabob he could find. Rita chose fish. When their salads arrived, David held his lettuce leaves jokingly up to the light.

"Oh, stop it," Rita said.

"Is something the matter?" the waitress asked.

"I want to make sure that the lettuce is loaded with insects," he answered.

"Insects?" the girl asked.

"He's joking," Rita told her with a disapproving look at her husband.

After the meal, they walked to the beach. Rita put on her bikini in the dressing room, but she couldn't bring herself to walk out. She felt naked. She felt embarrassed, as if all of her skin was exposed. Blushing, she stepped back outside, still wearing her dress.

"Where's your bathing suit?" David asked.

"It's too small on me," she said.

"So let's buy a new one."

"That's all right. I'll just sit here and relax."

"OK. Have it your way," he said. "I'm off for a jog."

He handed her his clothes and ran off. In the army, he had been one of his platoon's fastest runners. Even though his joints were stiff from sitting in yeshiva all day, the running came easy. It was a hot afternoon in the middle of September and the beach was packed. Suddenly, another runner appeared, keeping pace at his side.

"You should have left word you were leaving Pincus for *Shabbat*," the fellow jogger said.

An agent, David realized. They were as tenacious as flies in the Negev.

"Can't a guy have a vacation?" David asked.

"Not when he's on an assignment," the other runner

replied.

"Well this is part of my role. Everyone goes away for *Shabbat* now and then."

"To the beach in Tel Aviv? You're supposed to be religious, remember."

With that word of caution, the runner veered off toward the water and splashed into the ocean. He dove into the waves underwater where a submarine was probably waiting to pick him up. Disheartened, David circled back to his wife.

"That was quick," she said.

She stood up and shook the sand off her skirt.

"I'm a bit out of shape," he replied, grabbing his clothes and heading back to the dressing room.

The sound of the surf and balls plonking against paddles followed them back to their car. When they arrived back at his parents' apartment, the dining room table was laid out with a white tablecloth, *challah*, and wine.

"What's going on?" David asked.

"Your kids insisted I go out and buy things for *Shabbat*," his father replied.

His parents weren't the least bit religious. Outside of lighting Hanukah candles and eating some *matzah* on *Pesach*, David couldn't remember celebrating any of the holidays in the house.

"They learned that in Pincus," David told him.

"Where is Pincus anyway?" his father asked. "I looked at a map and couldn't find it."

David told him. Vaguely, he described his assignment.

"I just hope it isn't dangerous," his mother said, carrying plates to the table.

"Don't worry, Mom, I'm stuck in an office most of the time," he relied to make her feel more at ease.

Danny ran into the room and jumped into his father's arms. "Dad studies in a yeshiva," he announced.

David winked at his parents, as if to say, "That's what

we tell the kids."

"Where's your *kippah*?" the little guy asked.

David took the crumpled *kippah* out from his pocket and set it on his head.

"Please let it be just a part of your job," his mother said nervously.

David laughed. He told Danny to bring him a Coke and waited until he disappeared into the kitchen. "Remember when I had to dress up like an Arab?" he said to his parents. "Now I have to dress up like a Jew."

Smiling, he pulled the strings of his *tzitzit* out from his pants. His mother let out a whelp.

"Oh no! *Ribbono shel olam*! Anything but that!"

"I'll say one thing," Yehuda Dor said. "You've got to give credit to the settlers. They are the pioneers of today, there's no question about that. Politics aside, they're strong people. They still have a dream. The rest of us lost it when Ben Gurion died."

Ben Gurion was his father's hero. He had grown up in one of his youth movements. The biography he wrote about him won him several prizes and secured him a place on the history faculty of Tel Aviv University. He still voted for Labor, but he remained on the hawkish side of the party.

"You think Ben Gurion would have been in favor of the settlers?" David asked.

"No question about it. He was a settler. The whole nation in his days was made up of settlers. He wasn't soft with the Arabs. To his way of thinking, this was our country and that was that. It was his followers that raised the white flag. They made Zionism into a dirty word. Today it's capitalism, westernism, and egoism. We've made bigger Zionists out of the Palestinians than out of our own children."

"Where are the candles?" Orit asked, walking into the room.

"I don't think I have any," her grandmother answered.
"Don't worry, I brought some," Rita said, appearing in
a pretty Sabbath dress.
"But you're still going to vote Labor, right, *Abba*?"
"Probably," the older Dor admitted.
"This time I'm voting Likud," *Eema* Dor said.
David was surprised. In his family, a vote for Likud
could be grounds for divorce.
"I'm voting for Gandi," Danny announced.
When evening came, the boy asked his father why he
wasn't going to the synagogue. David said he wasn't
feeling well. Rita explained that they had come to *Saba*
and *Safta* to "*L'hitavrer.*" Since there wasn't a prayer book
in the house, Orit helped her father remember the words
of the *Kiddush*. Not wanting to insult her mother-in-law,
Rita ate the food that was served, but she felt bad about
not keeping kosher. After the kids went to bed, husband
and wife drove back to the city. Rita was silent,
uncharacteristically depressed. Lately, she didn't know
what was happening, but she felt she was changing inside.
Her thoughts, her feelings, her outlook on life were all
undergoing a revolution. Even her body felt different. Like
a butterfly emerging from a smothering cocoon, a
metamorphosis was occurring. Yehoshua Gal said it was the
magic of *tshuva* – the process of cleansing and discovery
that caused a person to be created anew in the healing
light of G-d's love. In a way, Rita had to laugh at herself.
Here she was, Friday night in Tel Aviv, feeling guilty
about driving in a car. But it was a joke that she had to
keep to herself. That's what caused her depression – her
loneliness in not being able to share this incredible new
journey with her husband, who was only acting a part.
     Their friends were waiting for them in their old
hangout, a dimly lit bar at the north end of Ben Yehuda,
not far from the Yarkon. Arik and Bonnie were like family,
the only couple they had stayed close to over the years.

The tall, handsome Arik had the face you expected to find in an Israeli high-tech brochure. He had come up in the company with David. Their loyalty to each other was as binding as love. Rita had felt jealous of their relationship until she had become like a sister to Bonnie, an English girl who had met the charismatic Arik when he was still a soldier.

Everything in the bohemian bar had stayed exactly the same during the twelve years they had been meeting for hamburgers, conversations, and beers. The lampshades, the Greenwich Village decor, the Billie Holiday music, even the customers all seemed the same.

"Should I wish you a *gut shabbos?*" Arik teasingly asked.

Bonnie laughed. "Really, Rita. How can you do it? Do you cover your hair? Tell me. I'm dying to hear."

She laughed with the cultured disdain that the Tel Aviv crowd harbored toward the religious. Yet Rita saw in her friend's gaze a true desire to hear. She recalled her own antipathy, once upon a time, toward the religious, as if they were the real Jews and she was *treif*.

"I like your beard," Arik said. "It fits you."

"I think it's cute," Bonnie added. "Are you going to grow *peyes* too?"

David asked about their children. They were almost the same age as Orit and Danny. Drinks were ordered and the conversation split into pairs. The women spoke about their families, and the men talked about guys they both knew, about basketball, videos, and America. Rita never understood their fascination with jump shots, sprained ankles, and last-minute baskets. Their talk about giant Black athletes and movie stars sounded strange to her ears, which had grown accustomed to discussions about *Moshe Rabeinu* and the redemption of *Am Yisrael*. To her new, refined senses, against the background of beer bottles, John Denver songs, and teenager chatter, the man that she loved seemed rather immature and boring. To her surprise, she found herself talking about the *Kuzari* and *Rav* Kook.

"You mean you really keep kosher and go to a *mikveh?*" Bonnie asked her as they were walking alone around the block.

It happened each time that they met. The men would hang out in the bar for another few beers while the women stepped outside for a little fresh air.

"I know you'll think I'm crazy," Rita confessed, "but in a way I think that it's good."

"Living on a mountaintop surrounded by thousands of Arabs is good?"

"That part isn't so easy, but the lifestyle is really wholesome. I may sound square, but I think it is a good experience for the children."

"If they're not brainwashed completely by the time the assignment is up."

"I suppose that's one of the risks of the job."

For a moment, both women fell silent, as if they were in separate worlds. Suddenly, Bonnie stopped, hid her face, and started to cry. Rita was startled.

"What is it?" she asked.

Bonnie shook her head. Tears streamed down her face. She tried to smile, but she couldn't stop crying.

"What Bonnie?" Rita asked.

"Arik," she said. "He is having an affair."

Rita was stunned. For a moment, she didn't know what to say.

"Oh, Rita, that's not all. I am too," her best friend admitted. "Both of us are. For over a year. Oh, Rita, I feel so awful."

Sobbing, she cried in Rita's arms. Her whole body shook, as if shedding layers and layers of anguish. Cars and taxis sped by on the street. Slowly, Bonnie's outburst subsided.

"It's all right," Rita said, not knowing what else to tell her.

"No it isn't," Bonnie responded. "I try to pretend that it is. I play a great game. After all, when in Tel Aviv, do as the Romans do."

She sniffled into a Kleenex.

"You're the first person I've told. Help me, Rita. You're my best friend. I don't want to continue. What should I do?"

Rita didn't know what to say. "Does Arik know?" she asked.

"Of course. We talk about it. That's the worst part. He acts like it's the epitome of modern living, what every cultured couple should do."

Bonnie took a deep breath to bring herself under control. "I'm sorry," she said. "I didn't plan on spilling my heart. Forget about it, all right? I suppose everyone has his own little soap opera. I guess I just had to tell someone, that's all."

When they got back to the bar, the fellows were feeling no pain. Their table looked like a bowling alley with all the bottles of Carlsberg grouped together like pins.

"Are you guys collecting beer bottles or are you planning to go bowling tonight?" Bonnie asked, assuming her usual cool.

"Hey, that's a great idea!" David said. "Why don't we open a bowling alley in Pincus? It would give people something to do at night."

"You know that might be a great therapy for the settlers," Arik joked. "You could stick little *kefiahs* on the pins. By knocking them down, they could work out all of their anger."

"How about the two of you wise guys coming to Pincus for a *Shabbat*?" Rita suggested.

"Hey, what a super idea," Bonnie said. "Me with a kerchief and Arik with a *yarmulke*. Like extras on the set of a movie."

"I wouldn't drive there if you sent me a tank," Arik

quipped.

"We'll parachute you in," David kidded.

"Let's do it," Bonnie said. "We can leave the kids with your mother."

"We'll see," Arik answered.

"Say yes," Rita urged. "It will be fun."

It was past one o'clock in the morning when they said goodbye on the street. Rita was happy. She was glad they had come. She felt as if she had been sent from Above to help Bonnie.

11

O n *Motzei Shabbat*, Yehuda Dor helped David carry their bags down to the car.

"Now I remember about Pincus," he said. "Yehoshua Gal lives there."

"You know him?" David asked.

"I spent the better part of two days with him, doing research on the paper I wrote on the modern Zionist settlement. The paper was published, by the way, in the *Princeton University Journal*."

Surprised, David set down the suitcase he was carrying. "You never told me," he said.

"I guess you were in America at the time. Besides, when did you ever care about *Gush Emunim?*"

"You went to Hevron?" David asked.

"I spent three days there. To tell you the truth, I expected to find a nest of religious fanatics. Instead, I met a lot of nice people. Gal included. He turned out to be an extremely intelligent man. A man with a real vision, I'd say. He even knows a great deal about history and literature. Agriculture too. We had a great many things to talk about."

"Did you speak about me?" David asked.

"About you? I don't know. Maybe. I think we did talk about family and children. I may have mentioned you were working in America."

"Working for who? The Service?"

"I never speak about that."

"Are you certain?" David asked, feeling a groan in his stomach.

"I don't remember everything, but I'm sure I didn't say anything problematic concerning your work."

That destroyed the whole weekend for David. On the long way back to Pincus, he drove in moody silence.

"I know your father," Rita tried to assure him. "He's as tight-lipped as they come. I'm sure he said nothing at all."

"You don't know my father at work. When he likes somebody, he can talk without stopping. I've seen him when he interviews people. He talks a mile a minute to put them at ease."

Pulling the carpet out beneath a guy's feet wasn't the word for it. David's confidence was shattered. If Gal really did know that David was in the *Shin Bet*, the family might as well pack their belongings and head back to Tel Aviv. Why prolong the charade? Distracted by the weight of his thoughts, he didn't notice that the car's gasoline level was low. Turning away from the shore, they headed east, passing the tennis stadium where David had won a competition in high school. In no time, they sped by the Morasha Junction and headed into the hills. In the distance, the mountains of Samaria loomed dark and foreboding. Passing the Oranit army checkpoint, David flicked on his brights.

"Are you sure we don't need gas?" Rita asked as they neared the Elkana gas station. David was surprised to find the needle on empty. Switching on his blinker, he eased the car into the turn leading to the affluent settlement.

"Are we home?" Danny's sleepy voice asked.

"Not yet," Rita said.

To David's dismay, the service station only sold diesel. Banging the wheel, he let out a curse.

"What's the matter?" Orit inquired.

"Nothing. Go back to sleep," David told her.

"Now what?" Rita asked.

"We have enough gas to make it," he said.

"The needle's on empty."

"There's always more than it says."

Slowly, he pulled back onto the road. Almost immediately, it was like they had left the country of Israel behind. Arab factories and stores lined the roadway. Not a pedestrian was to be seen. At that hour of the night, everything was closed.

"Are we lost?" Orit asked, gazing out at the Arab village along the highway.

"No," her father answered crisply. "We're on our way home."

"Are the Arabs going to kill us?" the little boy asked.

"Don't be silly," his mother said, flashing her husband a glance.

David flicked on his blinker, slowed, and pulled to a stop at the side of the road by a yard filled with garden statues and vases.

"What are you doing?" Rita asked.

"Getting my gun."

Quickly, he got out of the car and walked to the trunk. He kept the weapon hidden in the compartment with the tools. It took months for the Ministry of Interior to issue a gun permit to a new settler, so it wouldn't have looked normal for him to be toting a Magnum on his very first day in Pincus. But in a situation like this, he wanted the gun at his side.

"Why don't we go back to Rosh Ayin and fill up with

gas," Rita suggested when he returned to the wheel.

"Why waste an extra hour?" he answered.

"At least that way we'll get home alive," she responded.

Not one car had passed the whole time they were stopped. The Arab village bordering the road was deserted. Apparently, Saturday night wasn't a night on the town for the Moslems. The only sign of life was the carcass of a dog run over on the road. The sky was black. The stretch of highway they were traveling on didn't have street lamps. David could sense his wife's tension.

"I have to pee," Danny said.

"Not now," Rita told him.

"But I have to!" the boy insisted.

"Hurry," David told him. "Get out."

He palmed the gun in his hand and climbed back out of the car. Outside, as he stood in the darkness guarding his son, he slipped in a clip. The sky up above was vast and unknown. There were times in the army when he had experienced a great exhilaration in the isolation and depth of the night. But with a wife and two children to protect it was different. In the Israel he loved, he felt uncomfortably wary.

"Let's turn back," Rita said, when they were back in the car.

"Don't worry," he answered. "There's a gas station in Ariel. It's just another five minutes away."

The car never made it. The engine went dead. David pumped the gas again and again, but the motor wouldn't ignite.

"What's the matter?" Orit asked.

"We're out of gas," Rita told her. "Your genius father forgot to fill up when we left Tel Aviv."

"Blame me. That will help," David said tensely, glancing outside at the dark olive grove bordering the highway.

A truck carrying vegetables rumbled by on the way to some market. Danny climbed over the front seat to sit by his mother.

"Now what?" Rita asked.

David didn't know. He couldn't push the car to Ariel, and he couldn't get out and knock on the nearest door for help. The only thing he could do was flag down a car and pray that the driver was Jewish.

"Don't worry," David told his family. "I'll get us a ride in a minute."

Once again, David got out of the car. Taking out his cell-phone, he put a call in to Uncle. David figured they'd send an army jeep out in no time. A Mercedez swerved around the corner, it's headlights shining in David's eyes. Gripping the gun in his hand, the *shabaknik* caught a glimpse of the Arab plates as the vehicle passed. Inside their car, Orit climbed into the front seat to huddle against Danny and her mother.

"Please G-d," David prayed as he stood alone in the night. "Get us out of here fast."

Another pair of headlights appeared down the road. This time, the license plate was Israeli. The driver saw David wave. The station wagon passed, slowed, then stopped and reversed. It belonged to a family with four kids, heading home to Elon Moreh. When the driver heard that David's car had run out of gas, he insisted there was plenty of room in his station. *Chick-chock*, he herded his drowsy children into the baggage compartment and offered the rear seat to his guests. David locked up his car, and the Peugot wagon sped off.

They made it to Pincus in just half an hour. The settler offered to drop off his family at home, round up some gas, and drive David back to his car, but Shimshon insisted that he have the *mitzvah*. Rita herded the kids into the house without saying a word to her husband. Shimshon said he had a cannister of gas in his van. He told David to wait as he hurried back to his house to fetch a tape player, a big bottle of Coke, and some cake.

"We have to have a *Melava Malka*," he said.

Placing the tape on the dashboard, he turned up the volume of a spirited Carlebach tune, and the old Ford rumbled off down the mountain like a stereo speaker on wheels.

"We'll wake up the Arabs for a change," Shimshon laughed. Making a *bracha*, he wolfed down a handful of cake.

"Do they really get up at four in the morning when that wailing begins?" David asked.

"Just the guy who has to turn on the tape," Shimshon answered.

"It's a tape?"

"Sure. What do you think? Don't make them out to be such *tzaddikim*."

They made it back to the olive grove before the first side of the Carlebach tape had ended. Shimshon slowed the van instinctively when he saw the bright fire. Two army jeeps were parked by the roadside, and soldiers were directing traffic.

"It looks like we got here too late," David said, watching his car go up in flames.

"You have fire insurance?" Shimshon asked.

"I think so."

"Then you should get the full *mechirone* price. Just like if they stole it."

David got out to speak to the soldiers. While they were writing up a report, Shimshon lumbered over.

"If there were a real army in this country, the Arabs would be afraid to come out of their houses at night," David said, playing his part.

"If there were a real army in this country, there wouldn't be Arabs," Shimshon added with a grin.

A fire truck from Ariel arrived on the scene. There was

nothing else to do. When the flames died out, a tow truck would drag the remains away to a scrap metal yard.

"Try to look at the bright side of things," Shimshon said as they were driving away. "At least you weren't inside the car. I know people who had the skin burnt off their faces for life."

A short way down the highway, Shimshon turned onto a side road and headed into an Arab village.

"Where are you going?" David asked.

"To deliver a message."

In the middle of the *kfar*, he stopped and put the van into neutral.

"You drive," he said, hopping out with his Uzi. Opening the rear door, he pulled out a baseball bat.

"Put the music up loud," he commanded.

David obeyed the order. The voice of Shlomo Carlebach echoed through the sleepy Arab village. David drove slowly, following Shimshon up the street in the musical van. The baseball bat swung in the air and smashed out a car windshield. Another mighty swing through the air and it punctured a hood. The Jew continued down the road, clutching the baseball bat in his hand like a jawbone, pulverizing car after car. When shutters began to open, a burst of fire from the Uzi sent curious villagers to the floor of their flats. At the end of the block, Shimshon jumped back into the van.

"Where did you get that?" he asked, nodding at the Magnum in David's hand.

"I used to work nights guarding construction sites," David answered, stepping on the gas.

With a smile, Shimshon finished off the rest of the Coke.

"An eye for an eye, a tooth for a tooth, a car for a car," he said.

With a rag, he wiped off the handle and head of the baseball bat.

"It's Joey's," he said. "I wouldn't want him to get into trouble."

True to his words, the police showed up in Pincus the following morning. They led David to a police van and shut him inside.

"You don't know a thing," Joey whispered in his ear.

Through the wires covering the van window, David waved to Rita and the children. When they arrived at the Ariel police station, Shimshon was already there. Three Arab villagers sat on a bench in the back of the room. When they saw David, they all got excited and pointed their fingers at him. David felt more relaxed when he spotted an agent he knew.

"They're lying," Shimshon said.

The police asked David questions. Was the Subaru his car? They showed him the scorched license plates. How did he get home? Where had he driven after returning to the site? Who was with him?

"They know I was with you," Shimshon cut in.

"Somebody beat up ten Arab cars last night in a nearby village," the investigator said. "I don't suppose it was the two of you?"

"Us? Absolutely not," David answered.

Shimshon smiled. The Arabs protested loudly. One of the cops told them to shut up and led them out of the room.

"You mean to say that you gave your report to the soldiers and drove home to bed?" the investigator asked.

"That's exactly what happened," David agreed.

"And I suppose big hailstones rained down from the sky on the Arab village, damaging their cars."

"Could very well be."

The investigator shook his head. "I'm in no rush," he said.

"Look fellas. Have some compassion," Shimshon said. "I'm starving. Let's make this short. We would have been pretty stupid to do it, having been seen in the area, right?"

"That's right, but what about the Arabs who saw you?"

"Put us in a line-up with ten other settlers. To them, we all look alike."

Since it was lunchtime, the police left Shimshon and David in the interrogation room and went off to the mess hall for something to eat.

"Don't worry," Shimshon assured the initiate. "The food here is pretty decent. One time, I gained a kilo when they detained me here for a week. If we behave nicely, we'll be out by the end of the day."

Shimshon was wrong. They ended up spending three days in jail. Gilo headquarters decided that a little prison time would boost their undercover agent's image with the settlers. Sure enough, upon his return to Pincus, David was welcomed like a hero. Overnight, he became one of the *hevre*.

Except to Yehoshua Gal. His all-knowing eyes seemed to smile with a secret that only he and David shared.

12

The week before *Rosh HaShana*, Joey informed David that Itamar wanted to blow up the bedrock at the new *mikveh* site right after the holiday. David called his Uncle, made a few stops at hardware stores in the city, and took the opportunity to look for a second-hand car. When the day came, Shlomo Shapiro drove David across the valley to the settlement of Itamar.

On a neighboring hillside, an Arab shepherd gazed through a pair of high-powered binoculars to watch the explosion. It was Horowitz, the *Shin Bet's* number-one equipment specialist. He wanted to be on hand for the fireworks. In the Gilo headquarters, Amos Tamir watched on a large TV screen, via Israel's spy-satellite hook-up. The young agent, Dor, was doing so good a job of winning the confidence of the settlers, Tamir didn't know whose side he was on. The explosion seemed to shake the floor of the command room itself. A cloud of dirt rose into the sky. Seconds later, an echo of explosions shook the hillsides surrounding the *yishuv*. David and Shlomo Shapiro stood behind a bunker, a safe distance away. When the dust and smoke cleared, a crater the radius of the golden dome on the Temple Mount, appeared instead of the rock.

"Where's the eighth?" Horowitz asked through the neck mike hidden under his caftan.

"The what?" the Tamir asked.

"The eighth explosion. I rigged him eight charges. Only seven went off."

"I only heard two," the chief said from headquarters.

"There were seven," the equipment specialist answered. "I counted them."

"You're certain?"

"Have Levy check it."

Horowitz's assistant, Levy, already stood in the command room, holding the seismograph report in his hand.

"We recorded seven explosions," he confirmed.

Tamir glared at the screen. The settlers were standing at the lip of the huge crater, congratulating one another on their success.

"They're building a *mikveh*, just like I'm donating my salary to Chabad," the security chief wryly remarked. "That's a test rehearsal for a terrorist bombing if I ever saw one."

David Dor was thinking the very same thing as he stared down into the gaping hole in the hillside. In some other place, an explosion like that could trigger a cataclysmic world war.

13

"**R**elax," Joey said as they drove back to Pincus. David was still fuming over his argument with Shlomo Shapiro concerning the missing charge.

"What kind of *fryer* does he take me for?"

"He explained what happened."

"Sure. His kid threw one of the charges in the bathtub! Does he expect me to believe that?"

"You know what they say – kids will be kids. Anyway, don't worry. Shlomo is a *tzaddik*."

"He better not ask me to do him any more favors. It isn't my idea of professionalism."

"Forget it," Joey said. "You did a big *mitzvah*. Listen, tomorrow, a group of us are *davening* at the *Kotel* for *Selichot*. Why don't you join us?"

"What time are you leaving?" David asked.

"Three in the morning."

"You've got to be kidding?"

"A friend of Shlomo who works for the *Misrad HaDatot* has a key to the underground tunnels. It's really a treat."

"Shapiro is going with you?" David asked.

"Sure – it's his idea."

"I'll think about it," the *Shin Bet* agent said.

In truth, David had been waiting for an invitation. Since the *Selichot* prayers had started, Shlomo Shapiro had been leaving the *yishuv* in the middle of the night to make the long drive to the *Kotel*. His visits were making Gilo headquarters crazy and exhausting the agents who had to be staked out at the Wall. Shlomo and his friends prayed in the Western Wall tunnels that extended deep into the Moslem Quarter. They prayed in the spot exactly opposite the site of the Holy of Holies, where the Ark and the Tablets were housed. Ever since David had supplied Shapiro with the TNT charges, Israel's security forces had been put on maximum alert. A Temple Mount blast meant *jihad*. In response, the usual cursory search at the entrance to the Kotel had been stiffened. Whether they belonged to settlers, *Haredim*, or tourists, *tefillin* sacks were to be passed through the metal detector along with everything else.

Rita mumbled and continued to sleep when Joey knocked on their window. David jumped out of bed as if he were a fresh recruit in the army. Shlomo was waiting outside in his van. Waking up in the middle of the night was habit to him. Even before the month of *Elul*, all through the year, he woke up at one in the morning to pray the midnight prayer, mourning the destruction of the Temple, a practice that only the most pious maintained. Often, Joey said, Shlomo would stay up all night studying the laws of the Temple sacrifices.

"History will judge us," he said weightily, as they sped along the deserted highway toward Jerusalem. "If we pray with all of our heart and soul, tomorrow the *Mashiach* will come, the Temple will descend miraculously from Heaven, and the *Kohen HaGadol* will enter the *Kodesh HaKodashim* on *Yom HaKipporim* and win forgiveness for *Am Yisrael*."

"You really believe that?" David asked.

Everyone in the car was completely silent. By their reaction, David realized he had made a big no no, as if he doubted that the *Mashiach* was really on the way.

"I mean do you really believe the Temple will come down from the sky? I understand there are other opinions," he said.

"Shlomo wrote a whole book on that," Joey said.

"A pamphlet," Shapiro corrected.

"The foundation of the Temple will come down from Heaven and then we'll build the rest," Joey said. "Isn't that right, Shlomo?"

"You have it backwards," he responded. "First we must do our part, and then G-d will complete our work."

"Don't we first have to get rid of the mosques on the Mount?" David asked.

"We're working on that," the Temple scholar replied cryptically. "Each prayer brings us closer."

Then, not wanting to speak anymore, he put on a tape. It was still night when they arrived in Jerusalem. They parked outside the southern wall of the Old City, across from Ir David. Hasidic apparitions darted through the darkness on their way to the pre-dawn prayer. The Wall shone with a mystical light. David trembled when he saw the great ancient stones, as if they were a connection to a past he preferred not to explore. The soldier at the gate stopped them and carefully checked their gun permits. Another soldier went through their *tefillin*.

"What are they looking for?" David asked.

"Your missing explosion," Shapiro replied.

A *minyan* of settler types was waiting by the entrance to the tunnels. With a ring of keys, Shlomo's friend unlocked the steel gate that led into an arched passageway. Opening an electric box, he switched on the lights.

Slowly, they descended through history, traversing epoch after epoch of the razed and rebuilt city. An iron gateway led down a long Hashmonean corridor to the 100-ton stones of the *Kotel*, so heavy that no modern crane could lift them. They stopped in a small, candlelit enclave directly opposite the Holy of Holies. Shlomo claimed that on the other side of the Wall, deep underground, the Tablets of Law had been hidden.

David joined in with the others as they wailed out the prayers for forgiveness. Their shouts were joined by their echoes and by the supplications of two thousand years. Though David wasn't a very spiritual person, he felt deeply moved. On the other side of these boulders, fifty meters away, was the foundation stone of the world. Even the *Shin Bet* agent had to admit, it was eerie.

After the prayers, Shlomo led him to a break in the Wall that had been sealed by thick blocks of cement.

"This was once a gate used by impure *Kohanim* who had to leave the grounds of the Temple," the Temple historian explained. "It's exactly where the Mishna states. Teddy Kollek had the entrance sealed off so that Jews couldn't tunnel their way to the *Kodesh HaKodashim*. The passageway leads up Mount Moriah to the rotunda under the Dome of the Rock."

"How thick is the cement?" David asked.

"About a meter," Shapiro answered.

David nodded and stared at the closure.

"What are you thinking?"

"Well, I was thinking that a simple explosive, about the size of the charge that was lost, could easily reopen the passage."

"Funny, but whenever I stand here, I always have the same thought," Shapiro said.

Nothing more was said. Retracing their steps back through the tunnels, David could feel his microphone *mezuza* bump up and down on his chest. Later that morning, when the tape was played for Tamir, he ordered that Shapiro, Joey, and David be tailed, round the clock, twenty-fours hours a day.

"These people are crazy," he said. "And I don't want to take any chances."

14

*Y*om *Kippur* arrived and Israel's sins were forgiven. Unfortunately, the Arabs in the country didn't seem to have heard. Riots erupted with the vengeance of a late summer *sharav*. Bonnie and Arik canceled their visit to Pincus. Travel on the road leading up to the *yishuv* became increasingly dangerous. Shootings were so common that newscasters failed to report them. Terrorist bombings shocked Haifa and Ashdod. In addition, forest fires set by the Arabs were raging inside the Green Line.

"That shows you that Israel isn't their land," Joey said. "I mean, who burns their own land? It's like a mother burning her child. Can you imagine a Jew purposely setting a forest on fire in Israel?"

It was an interesting observation, David thought.

When a motorist from a neighboring settlement was slain at the wheel of his car, Yehoshua Gal called for an emergency meeting. Every settler in Pincus squeezed into the dining room of the yeshiva. The men sat on the right; the women to the left. Baby carriages and children crowded the aisle in the middle. In a hoarse, rasping voice, Gal called for attention. His speech surprised David. Judging by the reaction of many of the settlers, it obviously disappointed a lot of people in the room. Instead of a call for revenge, the once fiery rabbi spoke in a moderate tone, calling for patience and trust. A lack of faith in our chosenness; a lack of adherence to Torah; and a lack of brotherly love had all brought a black cloud over Israel, he said. The strike of health-care workers and hospitals that the country was suffering was an expression of the spiritual malaise of the nation. The out-of-control forest fires symbolized the rage of the land. Rather than obliterate His nation under a Heavenly boulder, G-d forbid, *Hashem*, in his mercy, was breaking the boulder into small stones and throwing them at us one-by-one, to give us a chance to repent. Only on the foundations of *tshuva* could water put out the fires, and soldiers put down the riots. Without a deep, searching *tshuva*, he said, water and soldiers weren't enough. They could only temporarily bandage the sore.

"*Tachlis!*" a voice yelled out impatiently. "What are we supposed to do?"

"I think we should go to the Prime Minister and tell him the danger we face," a woman asserted. "We should go to the army and demand that they provide security for every car on the road. We should push the leaders of the government to act."

"We've talked already," Shimshon called out. "A hundred times. They couldn't care less."

"We should go back and talk a thousand times if that will help," Gal boomed back.

"What about my children? I'm worried about my children!" another woman cried out.

"All the Arabs understand is a strong hand," ben Moshe, the Yemenite Jew who ran the *makolet*, declared. "If we don't strike back ourselves, we're finished. They'll think we're weak and broken."

"Doesn't the Torah say if someone comes to kill you, stand up and kill him first?"

David almost fainted. It was his wife, Rita. Sitting there with the women, she looked just like the wife of a settler. For a moment, the hall was silent. Not because of what she had said, but because she had said it so challengingly in front of the *Rav*.

"That's correct," Gal replied calmly. "That's the law."

"Do we wait until they start throwing hand grenades?" Tzvi, the American guitar player, asked.

"Of course we have to defend ourselves. That's why we have the Israel Defense Force," Gal answered.

"What if the Israel Defense Force isn't doing its job?" Joey asked.

"Our own Jewish government has turned us into sitting ducks because they're afraid of the *goyim*," a *Kachnik* yelled out. "It's a *Chillul Hashem* that must be erased."

Yehoshua Gal never got a chance to respond. The shouting grew louder. Soon, any form of order was gone.

The meeting broke up without a decision, a position, or a unified plan.

A half-hour later, there was a knock on David's door. Four of David's classmates stood outside: Tzvi; the Kachnik; Daniel from Ethiopia; and Alex, a Russian *baal tshuva*. David invited them in, but Tzvi said that they didn't want to disturb David's kids from sleeping.

The *Shin Bet* agent followed them down the road toward the basketball court.

"We've decided to do something, and we'd like you to join," the musician confided when they were a safe distance away from the houses.

"Like what?" David asked.

"We've thought of some options. What do you say? Are you with us?"

"That depends," David answered.

"If people ever rioted in Moscow," the Russia immigrant said in his heavy accent, "the authorities would impose a solution in a day. It's gotten to the point where I feel as much in *galut* here as in Russia."

"I feel the same way," the soft-spoken Daniel agreed.

His Zionism could hardly be questioned. His family had walked hundreds of miles through sand to get to the airplane that took them to Israel. It all seemed so obvious and natural to them, whereas David, who had been born and bred in the country, felt strangely left out.

"I'll think about it," he said. "I'll let you know."

David could sense their disappointment. In a way, he felt he was letting them down. But he didn't want them to get into trouble. They were like innocent babies. He felt certain there were bigger fish in the sea. Returning to his house, he paused on the doorstep and whispered into the *mezuza*, "Tell my Uncle that we need more security here. The army better do something fast. Otherwise, there's going to be anarchy."

In a way, he was following the rabbi's advice that they

intensify their appeals to the government. These people had a serious problem, and he wanted to help. He had an open line to the authorities that could be used in two ways. In the meantime, he decided to spend more time with Shimshon and Shlomo. They were the ones, he felt, who could blow the Middle East time-bomb sky high.

He didn't have to wait long. In the middle of the night, there was a knock on his bedroom window. It was Shimshon. Dressed in his pajamas, David opened the front door.

"We're moving some caravans down to the site of the shooting," the big settler said.

"Now?" David asked. "It's two o'clock in the morning."

"If we work hard, we can set up a new settlement before the army takes notice."

"Sounds good," David said.

"It's the *Rav's* idea," Shimshon replied. "I think we need a stronger response, but in the meantime, it beats spending the whole night in bed."

"Will the army let us stay?"

"I doubt it, but it will make the Prime Minister look really bad if he has to give an order to drag us away."

"Give me two minutes to dress," David said.

"Take your *tefillin*," Shimshon told him.

Shlomo Shapiro and three guys from the yeshiva were waiting in Shimshon's van. Joey and his wife ran out of their house to join them. Before heading down the mountain, Shimshon stopped at the Gal house. In another minute, the rabbi climbed aboard, wearing an army *doubon*.

The murder of the motorist had occurred between the Tapuach Junction and Ariel. By the time they arrived, the two caravans were in place on the hillside overlooking the road. David joined other young settlers in unloading a truck of furniture. Other workers carried the furniture into the homes. The noise of a generator echoed over the dark landscape. Lights were set up and hot coffee was served. During a break, Shimshon led the workers in a cheerful song. Gal, Shapiro, and other settlement leaders met in a tent. Within an hour, the two caravans were furnished, including flower pots on the front steps. A group of spirited *chevre* who had learned in *Kever Yosef* danced in a circle, their *peyes* and *tzitzit* flying in the wind. What a difference from the teenagers in Tel Aviv, David thought. An Israeli flag was raised over one of the caravans. Groups of young settlers kept arriving in cars for the showdown that was sure to come in the morning. Children flocked up the hill, followed by mothers with carriages. Others carried babies in pouches strung over their necks. David had to give them credit. They were lovers of *Eretz Yisrael*, that was for sure.

By dawn, army jeeps and buses carrying soldiers filled the roadway below. A commander walked up the slope to the *giva* and spoke briefly with Gal. Shaking his head, he walked back down the hill. TV crews started filming while the settlers were praying *vatikin*. As more buses and army trucks arrived on the scene, the settlers sipped coffee. Others spoke furiously on cell-phones, calling reinforcements to the scene. From the number of soldiers down on the road, it looked as if *Tzahal* was preparing to wage a small war.

"*Halevai* they would use the same manpower to go after terrorists that they use to keep Jews from building new communities in *Eretz Yisrael*," Shimshon sarcastically told a reporter.

Once again, the heavy-set army commander climbed up the hillside to speak with Gal and the other settlement leaders. Apparently, the powwow ended in a stalemate. Once again, the commander walked off down the hill. Gal herded his young troops together, warning them not to resist the evacuation with force. No one was to raise a hand against a soldier.

"Remember, they are our brothers," he said, "just

carrying out the orders of a mistaken government policy."

In the sky, an army helicopter circled the hillside. Officers ordered the TV crews away from the scene. The military sealed off the area. David climbed up on a caravan roof with the yeshiva students from Pincus. After a series of ultimatums were shouted out over a megaphone and ignored, the evacuation order was given. Rows of soldiers headed up the hill. Young women soldiers grabbed a hold of the female settlers. Teams of soldiers grabbed the men and dragged them away. David joined in the protests from the rooftops.

"*Bolshevikim*! Police state!" he yelled.

Down below, five soldiers dragged Shimshon out of a caravan. One of the settlers let out a groan and fell to the ground, holding his lower back. Shimshon lay like a beached whale, screaming out bloody murder, as if he were being tortured. The evacuation took nearly two hours. Time and again, David pushed away the ladder that the soldiers tried to lean against the roof.

"Look!" Joey called out from below. "It's a settler on the roof!"

Obviously, the soldier who knocked him down from behind didn't appreciate the joke. But it was true. The nostalgic days of the fiddler were gone. In the eyes of the world, the Jew of today was a settler.

Finally, the roof was stormed on all sides.

"You call yourselves Jewish soldiers?!" David yelled out as they dragged him away.

He resisted passively, like Gal had commanded, but that didn't make the task of the soldiers any easier. When he wouldn't walk down the ladder, they slid him down as if it were an airplane's emergency chute.

His acting stopped when he hit the ground with a bang. His coccyx rang like a bell. A razor-sharp pain ran the length of his body. When a soldier yanked him to his feet, David shoved him back angrily. Another soldier pounced on the undercover agent from behind.

"This is *Eretz Yisrael*, not Germany!" Gal was screaming when they hauled David away.

To David's good luck, he was thrown into a paddy wagon with Shimshon and Shapiro.

"Nice going," Shimshon said with a contented smile. "You really laid that guy out."

"You too," David replied. "One of the soldiers who tried to lift you was carried away on a stretcher."

The neighbors shared a good laugh. David could tell he had been accepted as one of the crowd.

"Don't worry," Shimshon said, "they will release us by the morning."

"It's all a waste of energy," the stern-faced Shapiro exclaimed. "Our fight is with the Arabs, not with *Tzahal*."

The mood in the paddy wagon turned serious.

"He's right," Shimshon said.

David nodded and said, "I agree."

"Playing cat and mouse games with the army doesn't work anymore," Shapiro asserted. "We've got to wake up the nation."

"How?" David asked.

Shlomo Shapiro lapsed into silence, his pensive continence locked in reflection. The wire door of the lock-up swung open and another two settlers were herded inside. Then the stern image of Yehoshua Gal appeared outside the police van.

"*Kimah, Kimah*," he said. "A little at a time. The redemption of the Jewish people comes in small steps – a little at a time."

15

The very next day, two teenage girls from a settlement near Pincus were missing. Over four hundred settlers joined in the search. Hours later, their bodies were found in a cave, their skulls crushed and dozens of stab wounds mutilating their bodies. The nation reacted with shock. Thousands marched in the funeral procession to the windswept cemetery on a hillside overlooking Shechem. David and Rita felt lost in the crowd. On that day, all the Jewish people were settlers.

In the evening, David and Rita went over to Shimshon's to watch the TV news. Seeing the coverage of the funeral, they once again relived all the pain. Afterward, Achmed Kabril was interviewed in Shechem. Joey pulled out his handgun and aimed it at the screen.

"As head of the Palestinian Authority police in this area, do you condemn this horrible murder," the reporter asked him.

"When Israeli soldiers kill our young people, do your people condemn the killing?" he questioned in return. "The Israelis are conquerors and oppressors of the Palestinian people. The settlers are the Nazis of today. There can be no peace as long as the settlers continue to occupy Palestinian land."

"Bang!" Joey said, pulling the trigger with a harmless click.

"Not in the house!" Shimshon yelled.

"It's empty," Joey insisted.

"Not in the house," Shimshon repeated.

"Kibril's got to go," Joey said.

"He's number one on my list," the big settler

answered, getting up to switch off the TV.

That night, David received a phone call from Shapiro. "We want to start construction on a new Talmud Torah building in Itamar," he said. "It's going to be twice as big as the *mikveh*. Do you think you can help us?"

"Maybe," David said. "I'll have to know more of the details."

They arranged to meet the next day in Jerusalem. David had to be there anyway to buy a second-hand car. And Rita had some shopping to do. Shimshon drove the family to Tapuach, and from there, they boarded a bus to Jerusalem. While they were approaching Ofra, a barrage of bullets rained down on them from the hill along the road. Luckily, no one was hurt. Settlers jumped off the bus, inserting clips in their rifles, but soldiers in the jeep escorting the bus kept them from firing.

In the city, Rita took Orit shopping. David took Danny to the lot where he was buying a used car. For the time being, the insurance company had rejected David's claim, maintaining that David's negligence in abandoning the car had led to the mishap. David had hired a lawyer, and the Company was picking up the tab for a used station wagon. Once the auto was theirs, and the papers all stamped, they drove to Meah Shearim to buy the *arba minim* and a portable *sukkah* which David tied down to the roof rack of the car. To pass the half hour before his meeting with Shlomo, David led Danny along the festive, music-filled street to buy some colorful *sukkah* decorations. He lifted the lad on his shoulders to give him a bird's-eye view of the crowd. Jews of all sizes and shapes bent over bright yellow *etrogim*, searching for microscopic flaws. A Hasid held a *lulav* in the air as if he were sighting down the barrel of a rifle. David had no idea what they were looking for. There had been a short class in the yeshiva, but without seeing the four species in front of him, he didn't understand what the teacher was talking about.

Shlomo Shapiro was waiting at Kikar Shabbat. His own seven-year old son sat on his shoulders, waving a *lulav* in the air like a sword.

"I want one too," Danny said.

"I'll get him one," Shlomo promised. "A friend of mine has a booth here. Have you bought your *arba minim* yet?"

"Not yet," David said.

"I'll get you a good price for a really nice set, and a *posul lulav* for your kid so he'll have something to play with."

David followed his neighbor down the noisy street, trying to keep at his side. With all of the holiday music, the *Shin Bet* agent doubted he could get their conversation on tape.

"We want to start work on the foundation next week," Shapiro informed him.

"How big a building?" David asked.

"Two stories on a *shetach* of 600 square meters."

"That's a lot of material. Maybe you should get someone professional to do it."

"We don't have the money."

David stopped at a quieter corner. "You're talking about a lot of fire power. Maybe twenty charges. That's a big job for me," he said.

"Still worried about the last job?" Shapiro asked.

"I think about it," David admitted.

Shapiro reached up and lowered his son to the ground. "Remember when we started to build the new *mikveh* in Itamar?" he asked him, bending down to his height.

"Yeah," the boy answered.

"What did you do with one of the explosives?'

"The big firecracker?"

"That's right."

"I put it in the bathtub with my toys," the seven-year old said.

"Some battleship, wasn't it?" his father asked.

"It was a submarine," the boy corrected. "It sank right down to the bottom."

Shapiro smiled and stood up. "Have you seen the work we've been doing on the new *mikveh*?" he asked David. "The foundation has been poured, and we have the water conduit in place."

David was surprised to hear it. He had come to think that the *mikveh* was all a big story. Either Shlomo was on the level, or he was a very good liar. The *shabaknik* wasn't sure which. They walked a little further down the street. Shlomo's friend wore a big knitted *kippah*. Shlomo picked out a nice-looking *etrog* and *lulav* for David and gave little Danny a quick lesson on *hadasim*.

"I hope you understand my reservation," David said as they walked back toward his car.

"Who's your rabbi?" Shapiro asked.

"*Rav* Gal," David answered.

"Why don't you ask him?"

"Okay," David agreed. "I will."

Rita was waiting with Orit by the *Mashbir* in the center of town. David was worried that she'd be angry because they were late, but she had a smile on her face from ear-to-ear. What was so funny, David wondered? The *sukkah* and long palm branches on the roof of the car? But when she climbed into the front seat, she didn't say anything about them, or about the new car.

"What are you so happy about?" he asked her.

"Guess," she replied, beaming like a bride.

"You bought a new dress for the holiday?"

"Better than that."

"A new microwave."

"Even better than that."

"I give up."

"*Eema's* pregnant!" Orit exclaimed.

David looked over at his beaming wife.

"You were at the doctor?" he asked.

Rita nodded.

"Why didn't you tell me?"

"I wanted to be sure. Are you surprised?"

David was so surprised, he drove straight through a red light. Suddenly, a car appeared in front of him, like a close-up in a movie. The driver honked and stopped short. David had to slam on his brakes to avoid a collision. Instinctively, he shot out an arm to hold Rita back.

"Be careful," she said.

"You kids all right?" he asked.

The other driver was screaming. Cars honked, anxious to get through the intersection.

"Sorry," David called out, swerving around the car in front of him and negotiating his way out of the jam-up.

"Put on your seat belt," he told Rita.

"There isn't one," she said, looking around.

"Oh, how stupid of me. I should have checked it out before we left the lot."

"Are these safety windows," Orit asked.

"Yes," David answered. "For the money, it's not a bad car."

"What's pregnant?" Danny inquired, getting back to the top news of the day.

"It means that there is a baby in Mommy's belly, and she's going to get fat like all the other women in Pincus," Orit observed.

"That's what I call really getting into a role," David joked.

Leaving the city, they had just passed the Adam junction when David heard a THUD on the roof. Suddenly, they were enveloped in the heat of a fiery explosion. Air whooshed out the window, and a flame streaked into the car like an arm. The children screamed. David lunged across Rita and opened her door, shoving her outside on the street. Flames seared his flesh as he jerked back, opened his door and tumbled outside. In a second,

he was up on his feet, pulling at Danny's locked door, but
the fireball blew him aside. He smashed out the back
window with his fist, opened the door from inside, and
pulled out his burning son. He fell to the street,
smothering the boy in his arms, until he put out the fire.
On the other side of the car, a passing motorist had rescued
Orit. Miraculously, she was unhurt. But the boy's clothing
was scorched and his body was covered with blood. Rita
ran over and gasped. The boy was unconscious. Soldiers
arrived at the scene and blocked off the road. For the
second time in two-weeks, David watched his car go up in
flames. The palm branches and *sukkah* had saved them,
keeping the initial burst of fire up toward the roof. The
thrower of the molotov cocktail had fled. As an ambulance
siren sounded in the distance, David held his son in his
arms, rocking him back and forth, praying for the L-rd to
save him.

16

David rode in the ambulance with Danny. Rita and
Orit followed them to the hospital in a police car.
The race to Hadassah Ein Kerem took thirty minutes. A
medic held a portable oxygen mask over Danny's face all
during the drive. His limbs hung loosely at his side, his
face was pale white, and he hardly seemed to be breathing.
The medic said that in addition to the burns, the boy was
in shock. In the emergency room, a special burn-trauma
team took over. They gave him adrenaline and a glucose
infusion, and he was wheeled away for a long operation,
hooked up to a respirator and heart machine. Afterward, he
was brought to a special recovery room, where he lay
attached to pipes and wires under a plastic tent. The

doctor who spoke with the parents couldn't find a smile. In addition to shock and prolonged heart failure, there was no way of knowing the damage caused to the brain. Burns covered most of the boy's body, and excess fluid loss was likely to cause renal failure. Plus, the doctor continued, the immunological system was crippled in cases like this, impairing the burn patient's ability to fight against infection and to heal on his own.

"I'm afraid that only a miracle can save him," the doctor solemnly told them.

Rita trembled and clutched her husband's arm. David refused to believe it. It couldn't be true. Certainly at some other hospital, with some other treatment, the boy could be helped. But he knew that Hadassah's burn unit was one of the best in the world.

As David led his wife away down the corridor, the first person he saw was Yehoshua Gal. The rabbi was sitting in the waiting area, staring down at the book of Psalms in his lap.

"Oh no," David thought. "The stupid assignment."

In the middle of everything, he would have to continue playing his role. It seemed so meaningless now after what had happened to Danny. Gal stood up. The expressions in the eyes of the young couple told him everything. Instead of bothering them, he spoke to the doctor.

Shimshon's wife, Esther, grabbed Rita's hand. The big settler told David that he had given orders not to let reporters enter the ward. David could see them gathered like vultures outside the corridor door.

"What do you want me to tell them?" Shimshon asked.

"Whatever you want," David replied apathetically.

"How's Danny?"

"Not good," David said. "Did they catch the animal who did it?"

"It seems so. Their car flipped over into a ditch on the way toward Atarot."

"Are they alive?"

"Unfortunately."

"How does the police know it was them?"

"They found some more molotov cocktails in the back of their car."

"Animals," David said.

Shimshon walked away to speak with the reporters. Gal was talking on a pay phone. He motioned David over.

"What's the boy's name?" he asked.

"Daniel," the father answered.

"Daniel ben Rita," Gal said into the phone, arranging for prayers to be said at the *Kotel*. Then he sat back down and continued saying Psalms. He started at *alef* and read through to the end of the book. Then he started all over. He prayed from the late afternoon till late in the night. Without eating, without drinking, without speaking another word. His lips moved silently, but occasionally a torrent of verses would burst from his mouth and his fist would wave through the air.

A group of settlers arrived from Pincus to visit the Dor family. Doctors with serious faces looked in on the boy round the clock. In the evening, the President appeared with a squad of security guards and a flash of TV lights. He said a short prayer, promised that the terrorists would be punished, and left. The father declined to be interviewed. Instead, the giant Shimshon stood in his place and let the world know that peace would only come to Israel when all of the Palestinians were transferred to Iraq. Amos Tamir winced when he heard it. For the first time in his career, he was uncertain what to do. He picked up his phone to the Prime Minister and asked him if it was wise to drop the investigation or not.

"Continue the investigation, but protect the *Shin Bet* at all costs," was the answer.

In other words, it was immediately arranged that six months before the Dor family had moved to Pincus, David

Dor had been officially fired from the service. In the event that he did something foolish, or if his cover were exposed, the *Shabak* would deny all involvement. If problems arose, then for the past half a year, Dor had been acting on his own. As proof, Dor's signature was forged on an official release paper. He was a free stringer, just another crazy religious nut.

At ten o'clock, David's parents arrived. They had seen it all on the news. When Gal saw David's father, he nodded. The two men shook hands. Then the rabbi sat back down to pray. By midnight, the crowd had left. The settlers from Pincus had driven off to the *Kotel* to pray. Yeshivas had been alerted, and a prayer vigil began on behalf of the child.

Only Shimshon, Joey, Yehoshua Gal, and Shlomo Shapiro remained in the darkened sitting room of the burn ward. The great hospital was silent. Occasionally, a beep from a monitor sounded from inside the intensive care unit. David donned a germ-free gown and mask and walked inside to stare through the plastic tent at his motionless son.

His friends from Pincus were still gathered around Gal when David came back to the room. David's parents had taken Rita and Orit to their home for the night. The rabbi glanced up at David for news.

"The same," David told him.

"He will be all right," Gal said in an assuring voice.

"The two Arabs they found in the overturned car were Palestinian policemen from Shechem," Shapiro reported. "Two of Kibril's personal bodyguards. There's no doubt that he sent them. If we had any hesitations before, I think this closes the issue."

"I agree," Shimshon said. "How many people have to be killed before we react? The politicians make promises every day on TV, but it always ends there."

No one disagreed. Joey kept respectfully silent. As a

newcomer to Israel, he felt he had nothing to say in matters as weighty as this. All eyes were on the deadly serious Shlomo.

"Along with Kibril, the two biggest inciters are Omir Faraki, the head of Fatach propaganda, and Ibrahim Mouward, Arafat's strongman in Ramallah. If something were to befall them, in one swoop, everyone will get the message loud and clear."

Gal was silent.

"Are you with us?" Shapiro asked David.

"Leave him out of this," Shimshon said. "He has enough on his mind."

Shlomo faced Gal.

"You know what I think," he said. "This is a job for the army and the security services. This isn't a personal thing. The whole country's at war."

Gal turned to David with his penetrating eyes. David was sure that he knew. But why was he letting the masquerade continue? Why didn't he tell the others that David was a *shabaknik*? How could he lead them astray? How could he let them go ahead with a plan that would lead them to jail?

"If I can help you, I will," David told them.

The rabbi stood up and walked over to the door of the intensive-care unit to continue his prayers. The settlers agreed that he would not be involved in the action. David was to supply the explosive charges "to be used in breaking ground for the Itamar school." Shimshon and Joey would do the necessary reconnaissance work. Shlomo would recruit other specialists to round out the team.

After the three settlers left, David drifted off to sleep in a chair. The last image he saw was Yehoshua Gal, pacing back and forth in front of the intensive-care room in prayer. When David awoke, Gal was still praying.

He prayed all through the *Sukkot* holiday. It was a time when Jews left their comfortable homes to dwell in frail wooden huts to show that salvation comes, not from material might, but from G-d. Gal stayed in the hospital ward, eating snacks of fruits and water. Someone who was needed to care for a sick person didn't have to dwell in a *sukkah*, he said. On *Hoshana Rabbah*, Danny moved his hand. On *Simchat Torah*, he opened his eyes. His parents stood by his plastic *sukkah* and cried. The next day, the child started to breathe on his own.

"I itch all over," he said.

David and Rita embraced. The physicians were at a loss to explain the startling recovery.

"It's a miracle," they all said.

Outside the burn unit's intensive-care room, Yehoshua Gal continued to pray. David watched him and trembled. There was no doubt that G-d had answered his prayers. In a way, David had fallen in love with the man. More than the classes in Torah, or the beauty of *Shabbat*, or his wife's inner peace, it was the incredible kindness and faith of the rabbi that convinced him.

"You can go home," David told him. "Danny's out of danger."

"*Baruch Hashem*," Gal answered with a shine in his eyes.

"Thank you," Rita said.

"I didn't do anything," Gal answered.

"For your prayers."

"Prayers don't heal. G-d heals. He grants doctors the power to heal. If you need me, please call."

Gal started to leave. David hurried after him.

"About the other thing...." He began.

Gal waited silently.

"I'm not sure I can do it. I'm not sure it's for me. I mean, I think it is dangerous for the others. The authorities will be on the lookout for something like this."

"I think you are right. In principle, I am against individual acts of revenge. That's the job of the army. But

I understand the frustration that people are feeling. Your son was lucky. Maybe the next victim won't be."

David was tempted to disclose the whole story right then and there. He wanted to tell Gal the truth and lift the heavy load from his heart. But he didn't. Call it training. Call it loyalty to the job. When you worked for the Secret Service, you weren't your own man.

That afternoon, he and Rita went home to Pincus together for the first time in over ten days. After greeting neighbors, they spent a quiet evening at home. But after putting Orit to bed, David got tense. Seeing Danny's empty bed made him angry. There was still some unfinished business he couldn't put out of his mind.

"I'm going for a walk," he told Rita.

"Want me to come?" she asked.

"That's all right. I just want to get some fresh air."

"Do you really want to go on with what we are doing?" she asked.

"I'm not sure," he replied. "I haven't made up my mind."

Rita nodded. David waved goodbye and kissed the *mezuza* as he walked out the door. He spent the rest of the evening with Shimshon, watching his stock of secret tapes. Sure enough, the two Arabs who had thrown the firebomb at the car were Achmed Kibril's bodyguards. There they were on camera, standing outside Kibril's villa in Shechem, waiting to escort him to work.

"The man is evil," Shimshon said as he appeared on the screen, opening the door of his house. "Believe me, the world will be a better place without him."

David made up his mind the next day in Jerusalem. Rather, Amos Tamir made the decision for him. At first, when one of Jerusalem's finer hotels offered David and his wife a room free of charge for the duration of Danny's convalescence, David thought it was a wonderful gesture of kindness, and perhaps some good publicity for the hotel.

Only when the desk clerk handed him a note did David understand who was behind the gesture. It was an invitation to visit the hotel's health spa. The time 20:00 was scribbled in pen and underlined with a double green line, signaling an urgent *Shin Bet* communication.

A few minutes before eight, David showed his room card to the health-spa receptionist, who smiled and handed him a towel. Inside was a large swimming pool with a lifeguard and a half dozen swimmers. A few heads stuck out from the sudsy Jacuzzi. The young agent cruised through the men's locker room and was headed back toward the pool when a swimmer passed by and said, "Try a steam bath. It will do you good."

David stripped to his under shorts and wrapped the towel around his waist. He followed the signs to the steam room and opened the door. A hot wet cloud enveloped him. The door clicked, closing behind him. Groping his way through the thick steam, he made his way to a bench. Hot air filled his lungs. His feet burned, but he couldn't see them through the fog. Then he heard a familiar cough.

"Is that you, Dor?" the gruff voice asked.

Immediately, the young agent jumped to attention.

"Sit down," Tamir commanded.

Like a blind man, David poked around in the fog for the bench. His hand came to rest on the security chief's thigh.

"Hey! Watch it," he said.

"Sorry, sir," David apologized.

He sat down on the bench by the towel-clad commander.

"It's already 8:15," he disapprovingly noted.

"It took me a while to find the place," David answered.

"In the meantime, I'm burning my bottom."

David peered through the steam. The older man lay on his back, his belly bulging out from the towel like a beach ball. David was surprised how skinny his legs were. Pipes rattled and a new burst of steam filled the room.

"Why meet here?" David inquired.

"Would it be more convenient for you if I drove up to Pincus?" the chief answered sarcastically. "Actually, I'm here every Tuesday night."

The young agent always perspired when he spoke to Tamir, but now droplets of sweat poured off his body.

"This time my patience is spent," the angry voice said. "This time, they've crossed the line."

"The people from Pincus?" David asked.

"No. The Arabs. No one makes an attack on an agent of mine and gets away with it. It's a *boosha*."

"I'm sure they didn't know who I was," David said.

"I don't care if they knew. It's gotten out of hand. We're fighting a war. No one is safe anymore. Even inside the Green Line."

David kept silent. He didn't see the difference between an agent, a settler, or any other Jew. But he was there to take orders, not to offer his personal beliefs. Besides, he wanted to get out of the burning steam room as fast as he could.

"I'm glad your son is better," the chief said. "We had the top specialists from all over the country looking in on him."

"Thank you, sir," David said.

"At first I was afraid that you were getting too close to these people, but now it's a good thing. They trust you. You've succeeded in that. We'll let them go ahead with their plans. And you'll continue to help them. The charges, you'll have to rig by yourself. I don't want anything to be traced to the lab. Also, all calls to your Uncle are out. But don't worry. We'll be backing you up. And we'll make sure no one gets caught."

"No one will be arrested?"

"That's right. We are going to let them do the work for us. We want to nail Arafat's key people as much as your friends do, but if we do it, Israel will catch international hell."

"What about the police?" David asked.

"No arrests means no arrests," Tamir insisted.

If the first rule of the job was to make your wife happy, the second was not to trust anybody at all. The world, David had been taught, was built on deceptions and lies. To untangle the web, the security forces had to be the biggest deceiver of all. As the door of the steam room clicked open, and another towel-clad man stepped inside, the young agent wasn't sure if he could trust his own boss.

The man's accent pegged him as a tourist from New York.

"This is the life," he said, sitting down. "Whoever thought you could find a steam bath in Israel? It's getting to be you can find everything here. They even have Nathan's hotdogs, would you believe it? And Ben and Jerry's ice cream! I'd move here in a minute if it weren't for the stinking government. Why don't they throw out the Arabs already? You know what I mean?"

"Sure," David answered, feeling he was going to have a heart attack from the heat.

"They always bow down to American pressure," the tourist continued.

"*Tipesh*," Tamir muttered in Hebrew.

David heard the door open and close. Gasping for breath, he hurried out of the steam room in pursuit of his boss. Cold air rushed into his lungs. Bending over a sink, he splashed cold water on his face until his body temperature returned to normal. When he searched through the locker room, Tamir wasn't there. He wasn't in the sauna, or the pool. Like a cloud of steam, he had vanished.

17

Before going up to the hotel room, David ordered a drink at the bar. What if Tamir was lying? What if he were setting up the settlers with his no-arrest story? If so, David would be leading his friends into a trap. The moment the bombs exploded, Shapiro, Shimshon, and Joey would be arrested. Three of Arafat's henchmen would be out of the way, and the security services would be applauded for stopping the Jewish terrorists before they caused more havoc. David would be given another assignment outside the country and everything would be just dandy. Furthermore, if Tamir's promise turned out to be phony, he too could sit in prison until an early pardon was arranged. The main thing was that the Service be protected at all costs. Every agent knew this. It was better to jeopardize oneself, than to damage the organization which was so critical to the country's defense. That's what his commanders had taught him.

"I can't go through with it," he said to his wife after describing his meeting with Tamir.

"Why would Tamir lie to you?" she asked.

"Because of what happened to Danny. Maybe he senses I'm wavering. The man has radar. This way, he's counting on me to go through with it, and he'll bust the settlers too."

After weighing the pros and cons, they both agreed that he should tell Gal the whole story. David knew it was the right thing to do. But he was nervous. It could boomerang back on the force. If his confession were leaked, it would incriminate the *Shin Bet*, and perhaps even bring a suit against Tamir for entrapment. David had a lot to think about during the long, pre-dawn drive back to Pincus. One thing for sure, it bothered him that he was being followed. Even though the trail car kept in the distance, he knew it was two of the Company's boys. Just for fun, near Shilo he turned off the main road into the Arab village of Turmus Aya. Morning prayers were ending and Moslims were coming out of the local mosque. Before making a U-turn, he drove close enough into town to draw their attention. Within seconds, stones started flying. The agents who were tailing him drove straight into the ambush. They had no choice but to stop and open fire. In the rear view mirror, David saw the Arabs start to flee. Unescorted, he drove the rest of the way back to Pincus.

The first thing he noticed was that the *mezuza* on his doorpost was hanging at a different angle. At first he walked into the house, not giving the matter much thought, but then he decided to check. Sure enough, someone had taken out the microphone and put in a genuine parchment. The same switch had been made all over the house. Either Tamir had another agent working on the *yishuv*, or he had arranged for some phony Bezeq inspection to get a guy into the house. David had been with the Service long enough to know when an agent was being left out in the cold. Tamir wasn't taking any chances. Well, two could play that game, he thought, unfastening the fake *mezuza* around his neck and flushing it down the toilet.

When he walked back outside, he met Joey on his way home from morning prayers. The wide-eyed *baal tshuva* grabbed David's hand and led him toward the sheep pen in a deserted corner of the *yishuv*.

"The surveillance has already begun," he said with a serious, no-nonsense expression.

David held a finger up to his mouth. He picked up some stones and threw them into the sheep pen to get the animals to bleat. He didn't see anyone in the area, but he was certain that their conversation was being recorded.

Joey nodded and smiled like it was all a big game.

"An Arab *mashtap* who Shimshon knows has located the houses in Ramallah. Cars have been identified and morning routines have been verified. Some other team is handling that job. I don't know who they are. Shlomo is playing his cards close to his vest. Our job is in Shechem."

David threw some more stones into the pen.

"The explosions are meant to cripple, not kill," Joey whispered. "Shlomo told me to stress that."

David nodded. "The devices will be ready. You just tell me when."

"It's set for the *shloshim* of the two girls who were killed. That way, everyone will be sure to get the connection."

"That's a week away," David observed.

Joey nodded.

"Is there a meeting?"

"They will let me know tonight."

"Just be careful," David warned him. "There are a lot of *shtinkers* in the field."

"That's what Shimshon says."

David's heavy feeling returned when he sat down with Gal. He was counting on the rabbi to stop the whole plan before it got out of hand. But the settler leader acted as if nothing special were brewing.

"How's Danny?" he asked.

"Feeling better every day. Hopefully, in another few weeks, we will be able to take him home."

"*Baruch Hashem*," Gal said. "It's enough time away from your studies."

"I didn't know you and my dad were acquainted," David said.

"Yes. It turns out that way. I really didn't remember."

"He says you spoke for hours."

"Wherever I go – taxis, buses, on the street, people

recognize me and talk. And every week, there's a different reporter. Unless the discussion is about some point of Torah, I usually don't remember."

He spoke casually, as if the meeting with David's father had been like all the others.

"Maybe he doesn't know I'm a *shabaknik*, David thought. "Maybe it's just my paranoia."

If Gal did know, why would he endanger the others? Was it some kind of test to make David choose between his job and a far deeper calling? True, David's life would have to be different, now that he knew there was a Creator who had saved his son's life. If G-d wanted the Jewish people to live by the Torah, then you had to be an egotist not to. David was prepared to keep kosher and to give up the beach on *Shabbat*. But in the same way that he couldn't betray the good people of Pincus, how could he betray the *Shin Bet*? He knew he had to be careful. It was no secret that the settlers felt persecuted by the provocateurs who had betrayed them in the past. If David told Gal, and Gal leaked the story, the *Shabak's* image would be dragged through the mud. Surely, Tamir would be forced to step down. And while David didn't feel any great personal affection toward the head of the service, he respected the position he held.

No. He couldn't tell Gal. If he already knew by himself, fine, but the information wouldn't come from him.

"I think you should know that some people are planning to take matters into their own hands," David said.

The rabbi's eyes gazed beyond David as if he were glass, as if he were envisioning a world from a long time ago...

"That's understandable," he replied.

"Why don't you stop them?" David asked.

"I'm a rabbi, not a policeman," he answered.

David nodded. That was true. That's why they had special forces like his.

"Why don't you stop them?" Gal asked. His eyes refocused on David and seemed to peer all the way down into the younger man's soul.

"Who am I?" David answered. "No one listens to me."

"No one listens to me either," the rabbi solemnly observed.

David felt tongue-tied. He couldn't bring himself to spit out the story. Frustrated, he stood up, planning to leave.

"What if the government rose up to save Jewish life?" he asked, pausing at the door of the study.

"Then the rules of *milchemet mitzvah* apply and everyone who participates is doing a *mitzvah*," Gal answered.

The rabbi stood up. He walked toward the door.

"One other thing," he said. "In the *Gemara*, it is written that birds carry our words into the air and bring them to places beyond our control. When I lived in Hevron, my telephone was tapped. I wouldn't be surprised if the *Shin Bet* is listening in even now. You were in military intelligence, you should know."

"Explosives," David corrected.

"Oh, yes, explosives. I thought your father mentioned intelligence when we spoke."

For a moment, David felt dizzy. "I guess that's what I told my parents so that they wouldn't worry."

The rabbi nodded. He smiled at David with his all-knowing eyes. The *Shabak* agent smiled nervously back.

"He knows," David told Rita when they met later that day.

"You told him?"

"I didn't have to. He's known all along."

When they got to Danny's room in the hospital, he was sleeping.

"What are you going to do now?" she asked, as they gazed at the boy.

"I haven't made up my mind," he answered.

But he had. For one thing, he was going to make sure that Achmed Kibril would never do any more dancing.

18

It didn't take long to ready the charges. They were simple devices that David put together after visiting a few hardware and electrical supply stores. He found the right magnets in a boating store in Tel Aviv. When the explosives were assembled, he stored them delicately in a crate filled with foam stuffing, as if they were valuable *etrogim*. He kept the battery packs in an empty suitcase at home. In the meantime, Shlomo Shapiro had done his homework, carefully tracing the daily routine of their targets. Two other Arafat henchmen had been put under surveillance as back ups, in case something went wrong with the original plan. A week before the scheduled attack, Shimshon drove David and Joey through a test run of their route. They practiced rigging a car engine by wiring a red light bulb to the motor in place of the charge. Though their assignment was Shechem, David convinced Shimshon to show him the tapes of Ramallah, in the event they ran into a foul-up. The good-natured Shimshon was happy to do it, never suspecting that David was planning to pull off the job all alone.

That was the decision he came to. He couldn't bank on Tamir's promise that there wouldn't be any arrests. So he decided to do it alone. A government agent carrying out orders. It was as kosher as you could get. That way, none of the settlers would get into trouble, and the world would be cleansed of some evil.

Tamir knew the plan of the settlers down to the tiniest

detail. Tapes of their conversations took up five shelves in headquarters. He knew their targets, their back-ups, and the license number of the cars they would drive. He knew that *Motzei Shabbat* was the date they had chosen to pull off the strike. And he knew that a few days after the bombings, after David was flown out of the country, the police would arrest the settlers involved. Everyone would think that Dor had escaped. In America, Danny would recuperate in a hospital in Boston, and the family's true identity would never be known.

Even though all bases were covered, the *Shabak* chief was nervous. On Thursday night, one of the yeshiva students from Pincus got married. At the wedding celebration, David took the hand of Yehoshua Gal and led him away from the dancing. Though two secret agents were mingling with the guests, the recording equipment couldn't pick up the targeted conversation. Dor clutched the rabbi's arm and spoke with him directly in front of the band's powerful speaker. In the communication room in Gilo, Tamir could only hear the pulsating music.

"Where's the lip reader?" he shouted.

As if hearing Tamir's roar, David led Gal back into the dancing.

"I can't get a fix on their mouths," the lip reader replied from the wedding. "They are moving too fast."

Tamir paced back and forth in front of the monitors. His rising blood pressure told him that something was wrong. Something was not going according to plan. As he gazed at the celebration on the screen, the closeness between the rabbi and student upset him. Either Dor was the most convincing agent he had, or he had surely crossed over. The shine in his eyes and the passion with which he clung to the rabbi were more than an agent just doing his job. And all the while, Tamir couldn't make out a word they were saying.

That's why the chief of Israeli security spent a

sleepless night. So did his busiest agent. At midnight, two days before the scheduled attack, David drove off to the *Kotel* in the car he had rented. In the rear-view mirror, he could tell he was being followed. He parked outside the Old City Wall and, toting a shopping bag, he passed through security without drawing a glance from the soldiers on duty. But when the buzzer sounded, they told him to stop.

"What's in the bag?" one asked him.

"Just a flashlight," he said.

He laid the high-powered flashlight on the table and passed through the security gate once again. This time the metal detector was silent.

His first stop was the bathroom. The agent who was waiting outside had no idea that the Hasid coming out of the men's room was David. Washing his hands at the fountain in front of the Wall, David kept an eye on his tail. When the agent grew nervous and hurried into the bathroom to see what was taking so long, David backtracked to the entrance to the Western Wall tunnel. Using the key he had duplicated from Shlomo, he unlocked the gateway and vanished inside, locking the entrance behind him. Switching on the flashlight, he ran in a dash along the ancient corridors and sprinted along the long *Kotel* tunnel. Using another key, he unlocked the trap door leading up to the Moslem Quarter. Quickly, he hurried along the cobblestone path, looking like any Hasid eager to get out of the dark, threatening quarter. Rita drove by in the car she had rented as he was heading toward Meah Shearim. David climbed in the car and took off his large black hat.

"I'm worried," she said.

"Don't be," he assured her with a smile.

"You sure you'll be all right?"

"*B'ezrat Hashem*," he answered.

The charges and batteries were in the trunk of the car.

Rita climbed out and waited for a taxi to take her back to the hotel. David slid over to the driver's seat.

"See you for breakfast," he said.

It was a beautiful Jerusalem night, the kind where the lights of the city and the stars in the heavens seem to merge. David drove along the Ramallah bypass road, passing the junction where Danny was wounded. Turning north, he headed toward Shechem.

Amos Tamir had his mouth filled with corn flakes when the telephone rang. Flakes burst from his mouth like shrapnel when they told him the news. Car bombs had exploded in Ramallah and Shechem. The three men who had danced on *Kever Yosef*, and who had vowed to dance on settlers' graves, would no longer do any more dancing – unless they could grow back new legs. The professionally-rigged charges had blown them away.

The Arab uprising in the country became another page in history. Not a rock was lifted, not a bottle thrown. Dozens of high-ranking Palestinian policemen fled the country and opened up grocery stores in London and Paris with the monies they had managed to steal. Civil war broke out throughout Palestinian territory, as terror groups fought for control. Arafat found refuge in Bagdad. After six months of internecine slaughter, the Supreme Palestinian Council implored Israel to intercede. Palestinians lined the streets and waved white handkerchiefs of welcome when *Tzahal* returned to Aza, Ramallah, and Shechem. The yeshiva in Joseph's Tomb reopened with double the number of students.

Shlomo Shapiro, Shimshon, and Joey continued with their lives without ever being questioned. Amos Tamir was forced to resign in a storm of political pressure. The bomber was never found.

David Dor was transferred to Boston as planned. But a new assignment never came. After a few months, he was quietly dropped from the service. A year later, the family returned to Israel with a healthy Danny and a new baby boy. From the Ben Gurion Airport, they took a cab to Ramat Aviv. The next day, they drove home to Pincus.

OPERATION HALLEL

The chief of staff, the generals, nuclear physicists, and rabbis stood staring at the panoramic screen in the IDF's Strategic Military Control Center. The computerized screen spanned a wall in the war room which had been code-named "*Magen David*" because of its star-shaped design. Up on the screen was a satellite map of the world. Israel was a small red light in the center of the globe, like a heart amidst the organs of the body. Other lights were flickering on the screen from all over the northern hemisphere. New lights flashed on over Nevada, Utah, and New Mexico. Each light marked the launching of a nuclear warhead from an underground silo. Russia had started the massive attack only a minute before with a wave of missiles which were now on their way over Turkey and arcing steadily closer toward Israel. Bombers were streaking toward the Mediterranean. None of the bearded men in the room seemed surprised when the United States joined in the air strike. America's participation in the UN coalition against the tiny Jewish State had been predicted for weeks, ever since the mass arrests of Jews in America. The Arab oil embargo had crippled the world economy and left Americans angry and cold. Until Palestine was freed, the Arabs were refusing to export their oil. On the pretext of safety, American foreign-service personnel had been evacuated from Israel. Once again, the Jews had been set up for slaughter.

On the screen in the war room, lights were flickering now over Pakistan, France, England, and Germany.

"It's seems like every uncircumcised dog with an

A-bomb wants to get a crack at us," Yehuda growled, throwing up his hands in dismay.

For a moment, everyone laughed, even the rabbis. In fact, Yehuda, the world-famous air-force commander was the only non-religious officer in the underground center. The secret bunker had been renicknamed "The Covenant Room" because all of the bearded, skullcapped men present believed that this was the place where G-d would reaffirm, before the eyes of the world, the ancient Covenant He had made with Abraham, bequeathing the Land of Israel to the Jews. Yehuda believed it, too, in a deep non-religious way which he couldn't define nor express. He was a simple man, a soldier's soldier, born with an ardent love for his land and his people. In war after bloody war, he had risked his life on the battlefield and in the skies. Both Jews and Arabs called him the Lion of Yehuda. Now, once again, he had stayed on to fight, long after many others had left, because he knew, in the way only a military specialist could know, that Israel's great victories over much vaster forces had been caused by something more than military prowess and weaponry. Yehuda had sensed, almost mystically from his very first battle, the presence of some unseen helping hand.

All of the eyes in the room were watching him now. Lights had flashed on over China and from submarines scattered throughout the seven seas. Yehuda gazed at the tense faces around him. They were all good solid soldiers. Many were graduates of *Hesder yeshivot*. Others were Russians who had spent years in Siberian jails. Several of the bearded men had been his soldiers before they had become *baale tshuva* during the great religious revolution in Israel. Seemingly overnight, the nation had returned to the Torah. After the last elections, when the majority of the Knesset became religious, most of Yehuda's contemporaries had fled. The people he had grown up with, the builders of the country, had become a tired and spiritually empty minority – all of the socialists, liberals, democrats, professors, and writers who had lacked the final faith to continue the struggle against what seemed like insurmountable odds. The young people had abandoned the country with them, the children of the kibbutz generation who had yearned for peace at all costs. The orphans of Rabin Square had fled the country for the more peaceful plazas of L.A. and New York when the religious parties took over.

Yehuda himself had his share of doubts. There had even been moments of fear. Not fear of dying. His battle scars proved that he didn't fear death. His fears came from not understanding what was happening to his country. His mind couldn't comprehend the great religious upheaval. He simply couldn't fathom the fervent practice of a law and tradition he had never bothered to learn.

Yehuda glanced down at the one man who remained seated in the war room – the eighty-two year old Chief Rabbi. Neither the Chief of Staff of the army, nor the Minister of Defense would make a decision without his assent. Unlike the uniformed men in the room, the Rabbi wore a long black coat, black hat, and *tefillin*. An old, fraying Psalm book lay clutched in his hands. He never bothered to look up at the screen. He didn't have to, he said. Everything had already been written. Yehuda had waged a fierce battle against the Rabbi's inclusion amongst the Joint Chiefs of Staff. Military decisions and strategy demanded real combat experience, he argued. But the country's new ruler couldn't be convinced. "Torah scholars increase peace in the world," he maintained.

Judah aimed the remote control at the large screen. The image changed to the star-war map of nuclear launchers in outer space. A storm of atomic warheads were arcing through the heavens from American and Russian space stations. Yehuda looked down at the white-bearded Rabbi.

"I think it's about time we did something, sir."

"Call Jerusalem," the old Rabbi whispered.

Yehuda glanced at the digital clock on the screen. The countdown clicked down to five minutes and twenty seconds until the first missiles would reach Israel's borders. With a steady, battle-tried hand, he picked up the red telephone on the table. Even now, after two years, it was difficult for Yehuda to accept that his country had a King.

"*Hallel*," was all the quiet voice answered.

All eyes in the war room were focused on Yehuda as he hung up the phone.

"Operation *Hallel*," he repeated.

There was a spontaneous cheer in the room, a burst of applause and confident embraces. Amidst all the tumult, the Chief Rabbi continued on with his prayers.

Yehuda shuddered. For the first time in his entire army career, his palms began to moisten. In the past, his brilliant strategies had crippled enemy forces. His pilots had paralyzed Syrian missiles and Russian-built tanks. His special units had executed stunning assassinations in Iran, Tunis, and Iraq. He himself had piloted bombers and rescue missions since the earliest days of the State. He had parachuted behind enemy lines to lead attacks on terrorists bases in missions that were never reported. But Operation *Hallel* was something much different. Operation *Hallel* was madness.

"This is national suicide!" he screamed at the Rabbi. "Those aren't Scud missiles headed our way – they're nuclear bombs!"

"You have a job to do," the Rabbi calmly answered.

"Whoever heard of a military plan dependent on prayer?"

Yehuda glanced around in hope of enlisting support. All of the eyes and beards in the room were staring at him. He drew back his shoulders, and once again aimed the remote control at the screen. The scene switched to a view of the Temple Mount. Yehuda paused. Everyone held their breath.

"What are you waiting for?!" somebody yelled.

Suddenly, the paratrooper commander, and onetime kibbutznik who had moved his family to Hebron, jumped Yehuda from behind and grabbed the remote control from his hand.

"If he won't do it, I will," he said and pushed on a button.

Up on the screen, a gigantic explosion rocked the ancient Mount. The golden dome of the Moslem shrine was blown to smithereens. Arabs took off in a run. A cloud of gold dust spread over the *Kotel*. The war room resounded with cheering. It was the same cry of victory that Yehuda had shouted when the Old City had been captured a generation before. Across the room, Israel's highest ranking general raised a shofar to his lips and gave a piercing blast.

"They're all madmen," Yehuda thought.

His friends who had abandoned the country had been right after all. The government of Israel had been captured by crazies.

Yehuda grabbed back the remote control from the paratrooper commander. He flicked the screen back to the map of the world. Nuclear missiles and bombers were zeroing in on the tiny Jewish State, yet his colleagues in the war room were clapping their hands.

"Switch it back to the Temple Mount!" they demanded.

With the clock counting down to three minutes, Yehuda returned to the scene in Jerusalem. Four separate views of the Temple Mount appeared on the screen. The Moslem shrine had vanished. In its place, the Foundation Stone jutted up from the earth like the peak of a mountain, as indestructible as the Covenant which G-d had sworn to Abraham on the very same spot. Yehuda remembered the Bible story from his school days on the kibbutz. His teacher had called it a fable. His parents maintained that religion was a dinosaur of the past – the opium of the Jews of the ghetto. And that's what he had passed on to his son, Shimson. Where was the boy now, Yehuda wondered? Hiding with his gentile wife in Mexico City, or rounded up in some detention camp in L.A.? When the boy had fled the country, a piece of Yehuda had died. His other son, his Uri, had been killed in a war. His wife, bless her soul, had dropped dead from heartbreak. The only thing which Yehuda had left was his allegiance to *Tzahal*.

His pilot's eyes were glued to the screen as Israeli tanks smashed into the Temple Mount courtyard. Another cheer went up as the voice of the tank commander came loud and clear over the radio.

"Har HaBayit b'yadanu!" he shouted.

On screen number two, hundreds of yeshiva students were running up to a corner of the Mount. They came in swarms, singing and dancing, as if drunken with fervor. Their words, the words of the *Hallel*, sounded over the war room's speakers.

"The sea saw and fled... the Jordan turned back... the mountains skipped like rams...."

On screen number three, a team of *Levites* and *Kohanim* were erecting an altar which a flatbed truck had driven into the Temple Mount courtyard. A jeep sped onto the scene, towing a trailer behind it. The ramp of the trailer swung open. Precious time was ticking away as a *Kohen* tugged on a rope and led out the pure red heifer which Technion geneticists had bred.

And now, up on screen four, the King's limousine sped toward the Western Wall where thousands of people had gathered.

Yehuda flashed the screen back to the space map. Startled eyes watched as the rainbow of lights arcing over the earth began to flicker and fade. One by one, they disappeared from the screen. Another wild cheer filled the war room.

"Screen scan!" Yehuda ordered.

"Screen functions normal," the chief technician answered.

"Computer check!" Yehuda barked.

"All systems normal," the programmer affirmed.

"There's got to be some mistake," Yehuda mumbled as missile after missile vanished in outer space.

"There's no mistake," the Chief Rabbi said softly.

One by one, American and Russian space stations exploded.

"We didn't do that," Yehuda said.

"Why don't you get a drink of water, Yehuda," the old Rabbi said kindly.

"I'm all right, sir," the lifetime soldier answered.

The clock read one minute and counting. On the world map, the remaining warheads were converging on Israel from all over the globe. On the Temple Mount, the praying was becoming more and more frenzied. Multitudes sang out in unison, *"Why should the nations say, Where is their G-d? Our G-d is in heaven. Whatever He desires, He does."*

The words of the prayer echoed over the holy city. Masses thronged toward the *Kotel*. Jews from all over Jerusalem joined together, pressing forward to glimpse the King as he pushed his way to *Har HaBayit*. "David, King of Israel," they shouted as he approached.

He reached the site of the outer courtyard and gazed up to Heaven.

"My vows to the Lord I will fulfill in the presence of all His people," he sang. *"In the courtyards of the House of G-d, in your midst, Jerusalem, Halleluyah!"*

The men in the war room were all strapping on their *tefillin*. An army commander, a *Chabadnik*, walked over to

Yehuda and invited him to don a pair too. The kibbutznik gazed down at the black boxes and shook his head no.

"Are you sure," the Hasid asked.

"Yes, I'm sure," Yehuda answered.

"You needn't feel embarrassed," the Hasid persisted.

"Leave him alone," the Chief Rabbi ordered.

The *Chabadnik* withdrew. Of all the battles which Yehuda had faced, the battle he was fighting right now in his heart was the fiercest. How could he change a whole lifetime of belief? Even if he wanted to, he couldn't. He was that kind of man. Principles were sacred, whether right or wrong. If he had championed misguided ideals, he would stand up to the punishment. Wasn't his presence enough for them? He was there, just like the rest of them, standing in the war room beside the Chief Rabbi. He had devoted his life to his people – with all of his heart, with all of his soul, with all of his might. That was the religion he knew. If that wasn't enough for them, or for G-d, so be it.

"We can still knock out Moscow and Berlin with our A-bombs," the air-force commander insisted.

"No," the Rabbi answered.

"We can't just do nothing," Yehuda protested.

"Pray with the others," the soft voice replied.

"I can't," Yehuda said.

"Try. *Hashem* wants to hear. It's your voice that's missing."

Yehuda felt faint. In all of his sixty-five years, he hadn't prayed once. He didn't know how. He didn't know even to whom. Up on the Temple Mount, ashes from the slaughtered red cow were being sprinkled over the crowds of *Kohanim*. The sight was too much for the man called the Lion. Feeling his legs weaken, he collapsed into the chair beside the Rabbi. The world's stockpile of nuclear warheads were approaching the borders of Israel, and the leaders of the Jewish nation were sacrificing a cow on the

Temple Mount altar! Camera crews rushed in for close-ups. Yehuda felt dizzy. Was the innocent slaughter of animals the enlightenment which the Jewish people were supposed to project to .the world?

"Perhaps we should respond more conventionally," Yehuda suggested.

"No," came the quiet reply.

"As a back-up."

The Rabbi didn't answer.

On the Temple Mount, the smoke of incense rose in a column up to the sky. Before all of this witchcraft began, Yehuda was beginning to believe. He had felt himself wanting to believe. The faith of the men in the room was so powerful, Yehuda had started to feel it too. But sacrificing animals was simply too much. His reasoning mind said no – these maniacs had to be stopped. There was nothing else he could do. He reached into his belt to draw out his gun. He would hold the Chief Rabbi hostage and activate the nuclear devices which the Israelis had secretly built in Moscow and Berlin. But before he could grab the old man, a hand clutched his arm and dragged him into a circle of dancing that had spontaneously began in the war room. The generals, commanders, and army chiefs of staff were all holding hands in a circle and singing:

"All the nations surround me. In G-d's name I cut them down. They surrounded me like bees. They were extinguished like a thorn fire."

Once, in his youth, Yehuda had danced like this. On the kibbutz, around an Israeli-night campfire, with his strong, robust comrades, he had sung songs of Zion. Their youthful faith had seemed invincible too, like the faith of the men in the war room. Now, as he danced in a circle, clutching hands imbued with belief, a transfusion of faith charged through him, cleansing him of his doubts. Before the dancers had completed their first circle, Yehuda was singing along with them.

"I shall not die, for I shall live and relate the deeds of the Lord. G-d has chastised me, but unto death, He has not handed me."

The words of their song formed on his lips as if he had been chanting it in synagogue for years. A great elation washed over him.

"Open for me the gates of righteousness. I will enter them," he sang. *"I will give thanks unto G-d."*

Everyone sang and stared up at the screen. As the first wave of bombers reached the shores of Tel Aviv, a wall of rain clouds appeared in the sky. Jerusalem vanished in an impenetrable fog. In the lead French bomber, the dials on the instrument panel were spinning wildly in circles. The mysterious fog darkened the cockpit. An unworldly thunder shook the plane like a toy. The terrified pilot tried to swing the giant bomber around, but the steering was jammed. Screams of Russian and German pilots crackled over the speakers in the star-shaped war room. The clock clicked down to zero. The dancing ended. Eyes stared up at the map. When the lights on the screen overshot Israel and continued on toward Cairo, Damascus, and Amman, pandemonium broke out in the war room.

Yehuda picked up the bearded man next to him and gave him a kiss. Radio communiques bursted over the control center's receivers. A dispatch from the Golan Heights reported that a storm of hailstones bigger than basketballs had paralyzed Syria's tank force. Tidal waves had overturned enemy battleships and submarines like toys. An earthquake registering 9.2 on the Richter Scale had devastated Jordan, and twenty divisions of the royal army had plummeted into the earth.

"I can't believe it," Yehuda said, but his own eyes were seeing that the words of the *Hallel* were true....

"This is the Lord's doing; it is marvelous in our eyes. This is the day that the Lord has made. Let us exult and rejoice in Him."

Within minutes, the cities of Cairo, Damascus, Baghdad, and Tehran disappeared from the map. Half the country of Libya fell into the sea. Amidst the celebration in the war room, only the Chief Rabbi noticed that something was wrong. Somehow, a slower, out-of-date aircraft from Poland had kept straight on target. It appeared over Mevasseret Zion and roared noisily toward Mount Moriah. All eyes turned toward Yehuda.

"How'd it get through?" someone yelled.

"Bring it down!" another demanded.

"It's too late," Yehuda answered.

The throng at the Temple Mount gazed up into the Jerusalem sky and watched two small dots grow bigger. They stood there, unwilling to believe, until, seemingly all at once, they realized what the falling dots were.

"Bombs!" someone shouted.

People scattered in every direction. In the war room, even the face of the Chief Rabbi was pale. Yehuda looked around the room for someone to do something, to say something, to pray something, to sing. But nobody moved, nobody spoke, as if something had gone terribly wrong.

"Do something, G-d," Yehuda quietly prayed.

The first bomb landed by the *Kotel* with an earth-shaking THUD. The impact caused a deep crater, but the explosion never came. The other bomb landed with a THUNK a short distance away. The stones in the Western Wall trembled. For an eternal moment, everyone waited without taking a breath – the thousands clinging to the ground at the *Kotel*; the men in the war room; the millions of viewers on TV. Only the King remained erect at the Wall.

"They're not going to blow up!" Yehuda screamed.

It was almost as if the people at the *Kotel* could hear him. Everyone stood on their feet and raised their hands to the sky. Their cheer resounded all over the world. Crowds rushed forward to peer down the craters at the bombs which didn't go off. The Chief Rabbi collapsed, exhausted in his chair, not sure himself if this last miracle was the Finger of G-d, or plain Polish ineptitude.

"The bombs have mysteriously failed to explode," an American TV reporter explained to his satellite viewers. "A freak technical failure has saved the city of Jerusalem today. Unusual weather conditions, thick fog, and a chance summer hailstorm, have paralyzed the world's nuclear arsenal and spared the indestructible Jewish nation."

"The hell with unusual weather conditions," Yehuda exclaimed.

On the screen in the war room, the CNN reporter continued his eyewitness coverage.

"Scientists from the Cape Kennedy Research Center in Florida are saying that planetary disturbances which transpired over two billion light years ago are the cause of the startling events," he explained.

"*Shtuyot!*" Yehuda said loudly. "G-d did it all. G-d saved us. It was Him, plain as day!"

He turned to the Chief Rabbi.

"Can't they see it?" he asked.

A kind, wise smile spread over the Rabbi's face.

"It's hard enough for our own people to see it," he answered. "What do you expect from the *goyim?*"

ON EAGLES' WINGS

This day, as always, Mervyn Levy woke up at six, in time to catch the morning *minyan*. For over fifty years, he had said the same morning prayer, "*Modeh ani...* I render thanks unto You, living and everlasting King...."

Quietly, so as not to disturb his sleeping wife, he rose out of bed and tiptoed to the bathroom to wash. It looked like another splendid South African day. Light filtered in from the bathroom skylight and sparkled over the hanging ferns and marble counters. Birds chirped happily outside. The only reminder of trouble was the faint aroma of smoke blowing in through the window.

Mervyn dried his hands with a soft, monogrammed towel. The reflection in the mirror was mildly depressing – darkening bags under his eyes and a paler shade of grey in his hair. He adjusted the black skullcap on his head, ran an electric shaver back and forth over his suntanned face, and stepped outside the bathroom to say the morning blessings.

Gunshots sounded in the distance as he dressed. Away from the aroma of soap in the bathroom, the smell of the fires was stronger. He gazed out of the mansion's second story window to make sure everything was quiet around the high-voltage fence which surrounded the house. The Doberman and German Shepherd snoozed peacefully out on the lawn, not bothering to lift up their heads as Johnson, the white security guard, walked by on his rounds. In the distance, the cloud of smoke which had blackened the Johannesburg sky for the last three days looked ominously closer.

Mervyn walked into his upstairs study. Volumes of holy Jewish texts, many worn with use, filled the shelves of his library. Plaques and certificates which he had received for a lifetime of philanthropy and fundraising covered the walls. Mervyn turned on the radio and tuned in on the chimes of the BBC News.

The announcer's polite British accent belied the gravity of his report. In Johannesburg, the rioting blacks had overtaken the President's residence, and were holding him captive until their demands for a rebel government were met. The eastern district of the city was ablaze from the night's rioting, and masses of rampaging "*shocks*" were heading toward the northern suburbs, battling soldiers with the rifles that Marxist subvertists had smuggled into the country.

The announcer's calm, civilized reporting continued. The rioting tribes were overpowering the South African soldiers with the sheer force of their numbers. To Mervyn's chagrin, they were progressing toward the suburbs of the affluent whites. The airport road was still open, and thousands of citizens were fleeing the country each hour. All highways entering the city were open, but motorists were being advised to drive elsewhere.

Mervyn switched the station to Radio South Africa. The voice of the Defense Minister was typically cool, promising to bring the situation under control. Other than that, the world stock market was active, and South African sugar cane was selling well in France and England.

Mervyn walked across the hallway to his son's empty bedroom. The view from the boy's window looked out toward the city. Beyond the sparkling blue swimming pool and tennis court, smoke billowed in the air over the Johannesburg skyline. The twenty-year-old youth was in Israel, and Mervyn never stopped worrying about his safety. He had left home, contrary to his father's wishes, to study in a Yeshiva in the volatile West Bank. While

Mervyn was pleased that the boy was learning, he feared that the impressionable lad would come under the influence of some radical rabbi and decide not to come home. Their daughter, too, was in Israel, volunteering on a religious kibbutz. Every day, the first thing the Levys looked for in the newspaper were the reports from the Middle East. Both he and his wife were terrified that their children would be the victims, G-d forbid, of an Arab attack. Every week, in letters and phone calls, Mervyn urged the kids to come home. Gazing about the boy's room, he felt it was hopeless. Pictures of Israeli warplanes and tanks covered the walls, alongside posters of Masada and Jerusalem. Looking at them made Mervyn uneasy. He had never been a Zionist. He loved the Holy Land itself, and he donated money to several religious schools in Jerusalem, but he could never support a government in Israel which didn't uphold the laws of the Torah. In addition, the Israelis hardly behaved like a civilized people, and a decent living couldn't be found. It would take the Almighty Himself, or at least the *Mashiach*, to bring him to Zion. This was what his rabbis had taught.

The black cook and the houseboy were nowhere in sight as Mervyn walked downstairs to the kitchen. He picked up the phone and dialed the synagogue. Since the outbreak of the rioting, before driving over to pray, he called to check that the road was all clear. As he waited for an answer, an explosion in the distance shook the foundations of the house.

"Hallooo," said a deep African voice at the other end of the wire.

"Who is this?" Mervyn asked.

"It ain't the rabbi," the voice, like jungle drums, answered.

Mervyn could hear the laughter of "*shocks*" in the background.

"I want to speak to the *shamash*," Mervyn demanded.

"You're next, Jew," the ugly voice said and hung up the phone.

Mervyn's wife appeared in her bathrobe and slippers. "What was that explosion?" she asked.

"The rioting," he answered.

"What's the matter?" she asked, noticing his pale white complexion.

"They've taken over the *shul!*"

"Who?"

"The *shocks*."

"Oh my G-d, no," she gasped.

It was practically their personal synagogue. Mervyn had donated the money to build it.

"How do you know?" she asked.

"One of them answered the phone."

Rose Levy walked to the window. The dogs were up and around now, racing along the perimeter of the fence, jittery from the explosion. Their noses pointed in the air, sniffing at the ashes in the wind.

"Where are the servants?" she asked.

"I haven't seen them," Mervyn said.

He opened the window and called to the security man whose company guarded the house day and night. His report confirmed Mervyn's suspicions. The servants had left with their suitcases and Mervyn's Mercedes early that morning. Sure enough, when the Levys checked through the house, several radios, cameras, and pieces of silver were missing, along with the valuable car.

"It's like rats leaving the sinking ship," Rose said. "If we were smart, we would leave too."

"Nonsense," the businessman answered.

"There's nothing here for us now," his wife insisted.

"What are you talking about? Our whole life is here. Our house, our friends, my business."

"Most of our friends have left the country," she argued. "Our house is like a palace that no one comes to visit. You can't even get to work. They've taken over the synagogue, and our children are six-thousand kilometers away in Israel. Oh, Mervyn, let's join them."

She looked at him pleadingly.

"We will join them when G-d wants us to," he said.

"Please, Mervin. We have all the money we need. Even if we can't take it all out of the country, so what? Who cares about the business? Who cares about the house? I want to be close to our children."

Mervyn didn't answer. He was tired of discussions about living in Israel. In a matter of hours, the riots would be squelched, and life would return to normal.

He retreated to his study to phone the police. Until the authorities drove the "*shocks*" from the *shul*, he wouldn't be able to *daven*. He didn't have his *tefillin* at home. They were in the cabinet in *shul* where he left them each day after the morning prayers.

Finally, the police station answered.

"Hallooo," the same deep tribal voice said.

"Police?" Mervyn asked.

"That's right. This is the pooolice."

Immediately, Mervyn hung up. The police station was less than a kilometer away from his house. Quickly, he opened his wall safe and pulled out two guns. His wife watched from the doorway. He had taught her to shoot in the range he had built in the basement.

"Please, Mervyn, please, take me to Israel," she urged.

"We'll go to Israel when G-d wants us to," he insisted. "Meantime, our life is here."

He placed a heavy Magnum in her hand. Unable to face the look in her eyes, he turned away and dialed the security services. He breathed easier when a white voice answered the phone. Mervyn requested that two additional guards be sent to his house, but they didn't have a single man free.

"I'll pay you double," he offered.

"Not even triple," the man said. "We are all hired out."

Two other security services told him the same. Finally, he managed to hire an extra guard for one-thousand *rand* a day.

"I thought you had brains," his wife said. "But this is committing suicide. Is that what G-d wants?"

"G-d wants us to trust in Him, and He'll take care of the rest."

Just then, the telephone rang. It was a collect call from Israel.

"It's Jerry," Mervyn said. Rose ran to pick up the phone in the kitchen.

"Hello, Jerry. Can you hear me?" Mervyn yelled.

"*Shalom*, Dad," the boy answered.

"Where are you?" his mother asked.

"In the yeshiva."

"Thank G-d you're all right," the mother said.

"Why shouldn't I be all right? It's great here. But I hear you have problems. Why don't you pack up and come to Israel?"

"Nonsense. Everything is fine here," Mervyn insisted.

Just then, a bullet shattered the living-room window. A sliver of glass grazed Mervyn's cheek. Instinctively, Mervyn dropped down to the floor.

"I'm worried about you, Dad. I heard on the radio that the rioting is getting worse."

"You're mother and I are fine," Mervyn replied.

Drops of blood trickled over the telephone. A bullet hole graced the oil painting on the far wall. "How is your sister?" he asked.

Jerry said she was fine. They had spent *Shabbat* with each other in Jerusalem. Interference on the line jumbled the rest of his answer.

"Jerry, do you hear me?" Mervyn shouted. "You're mother is sick with worry about you two. We want you both to come home."

"Israel is my home," the youth said.

Before Mervin could argue, the connection was lost. Rose found her husband sitting on the floor, wiping the blood off his cheek.

"Sweetheart, what happened?" she asked in alarm.

Her husband didn't answer. He crawled across the room and switched on the radio. According to the latest report, the Defense Minister had fled the country. The revolting tribes had taken over the Union buildings, and a fierce battle was being fought at the airport.

"Please, Mervyn, let's leave the country right now," Rose beseeched.

"We'll go when G-d takes us," he answered.

He reached for the telephone and dialed the security service to find out why the new guard hadn't come.

"Hallooo," the voice answered.

Trembling, Mervyn hung up the phone.

"I'm going to pack," his wife said.

Mervyn raised his head to the window in time to see the security man, Johnson, open the front gate and run off. The guard dogs ran off down the street after him. The cloud of smoke was closer now, only a few streets away. Quickly, Melvyn ran downstairs, unbolted the heavy front door, and raced outside to relock the gate. Like a soccer forward, he scampered back into the house, triple-locked the door, and raised the voltage of the electric fence. Suddenly, a voice called out from outside the house.

"Levy? Are you in there?"

Mervyn peeked out the window. An army jeep was parked at the gate. A soldier held a megaphone to his lips.

"*Shalom*, Levy," the soldier shouted. "An airplane is waiting to take you to Israel. We're from the Israeli army."

"Go away," Mervyn yelled back.

"We have orders to evacuate all Jews from the area," the soldier replied.

"Orders from whom?"

"Orders from the Prime Minister of Israel."

"I take my orders from G-d," Mervyn yelled back.

Angrily, he closed the windows and shutter.

"It may be our only chance," his wife said. She stood beside their suitcases, all packed to leave.

"It's the Satan," Mervyn mumbled.

He strode past her, and returned upstairs to his study. Determined to carry on as usual, he opened the business file he had been reviewing the previous night. If he couldn't drive to his office, he would continue to work at home. In a few hours, the South African army would have the situation under control. Nervously, he reached over and switched on the radio.

"Hallooo," the jungle voice said. "*AMANDLA!* The people will govern!"

Mervyn switched off the set. He picked up the telephone, but the line was dead. Rose stood staring at him from the doorway. They had been married for thirty years. Before she could speak, a great rumble, like thunder, sounded outside the house. Lightning seemed to flash in the sky. The lamp in the room blinked off and on. Melvyn rushed to the window. A tank had smashed through the electric security fence. It parked in the yard, leaving a trail of trenches in the manicured lawn. The tank hatch flipped open, and another soldier appeared.

"Levy!" he called through his megaphone.

Mervyn stared out the window.

"Let's go with them," Rose pleaded, appearing at his side.

"No," he answered adamantly.

"Levy! We've come to take you to Israel. The roads are all closed. It's your last chance."

"I'll go to Israel when G-d comes and takes me," Mervyn yelled out. "Now get off of my property!"

The soldier shook his head and dropped down out of sight into the tank. The hatched closed. The tank lurched into gear, spun a neat circle, and drove off, chewing up more of the Levy front lawn.

"Why, Mervyn?" his wife asked with tears in her eyes. "Tell me why."

"G-d won't betray us," he answered. "He'll send the *Mashiach*. The Almighty will answer our prayers."

Rose thought he was wrong, but she didn't know what to say. She loved him. She admired his earnest belief. But she was frightened. She didn't possess his ardent convictions. Her husband was ready to die for his religious convictions – hers were less strong. She wanted to be with her children, to see them married, to see them have babies of their own.

An explosion shook the mansion. The gas burner in the villa down the street had blown up, and the three-story home was ablaze. Rose looked out the window. Rebel soldiers were converging from every direction.

"They're coming!" she said.

Mervyn handed her more bullets.

"What good will these do?" she asked. "There are thousands of them."

"We'll have to shoot as many as we can. Maybe we can scare them away."

Another roar shook the house. This time it came from above. A ferocious wind stripped the leaves off tree branches outside. Mervyn rushed to the staircase leading up to the roof. He swung open the metal door. A gust almost knocked him over. An army helicopter hovered above the house. A Star of David was painted on its tail. A rope ladder unravelled in the sky and dropped down to the roof. Once again, a soldier held a megaphone to his lips.

"Let's go, Levy," he called. "This is your final chance."

"Please, Mervyn, please," Rose said, pulling at his arm. She grabbed a hold of the swaying ladder and tried to drag him toward it. "If not for my sake, for the sake of the children."

"Levy, hurry!" came the call from above.

Mervyn didn't answer. He stood on the rooftop, praying. "Please, G-d, come and save us. Please, G-d, come and save us," he repeated again and again.

Rose couldn't budge him. The blacks were running up the street. Within moments, they would reach the mansion.

"Climb up the ladder!" the soldier ordered.

Mervyn ignored him. He continued to pray. Beside him, the ladder jerked out of Rose's grasp.

"Mervyn!" she yelled at her husband. "Open your eyes! G-d sent you a jeep. Then a tank. Then a helicopter. What more do you want?"

Gunshots whistled through the air. The helicopter flew up and away. The blacks were charging into their yard now. They smashed into the house.

"They're coming! They're coming!" Rose hysterically shouted, but her husband continued to pray.

He saw them burst onto the roof. He saw them grab his wife before she could shoot. He heard her wild scream. They slammed the metal door, trapping them with no hope of escape. Mervyn didn't even raise his gun. He only kept praying. Even when they grabbed him, he still kept on praying for the Almighty to save them. A black arm grasped him around the neck. As the air left his body, he closed his eyes and heard Hebrew voices.

"I must be going to heaven," he thought.

Then, once again, he felt a great whirlwind around him and heard the roar of a thundering chariot. A commotion of voices burst out all around him, all speaking the sacred tongue. He opened his eyes expecting to see a vision of angels and the gates of *Gan Eden*, but he was still on his roof.

It was the blacks who were shouting in Hebrew!

"They're Ethiopians!" he realized. "Jews!"

Sure enough, they were Israelis! A special team which the *Mosad* had sent to rescue the South African Jews!

The helicopter swooped back over the house, dangling a rope through the air. Two heavy vests landed on the rooftop with a thud.

"*Maher!* Quickly," one of the black soldiers ordered.

Forcefully, he strapped a vest around Mervyn. Another soldier snapped a hook closed, and Melvyn was hoisted off his feet into the sky. He spun in small circles as the rope whisked him hydraulically up toward the aircraft. Its automatic fire kept the real rioters at bay on the lawn. Up and up he swirled. Israeli soldiers reached down to pull Mervyn into the ship.

"I'm not going to Israel until...." he began to argue, when a punch silenced his protests at last. Rose was lifted aboard next to her unconscious husband. As gunshots ricocheted off the cabin, the helicopter rose away from the house and from the burning city below. Not until the Levys had been flown to a military base forty kilometers away and transferred to an Israeli Air-Force plane did Mervyn awaken.

"Where are we?" he asked.

"On a plane to Israel," Rose told him.

Mervyn stared out the window as the powerful jet raced down the runway and soared into the air. Below them, the South African plainlands disappeared under clouds of black smoke.

"G-d answered your prayers, Mervyn," Rose said with a smile.

Mervyn glanced back out the window. Tears of happiness welled in his eyes. They were on their way to Israel. The Almighty was bringing them home.

TINOK SH'NISHBAH

O nce upon a time, not so very long ago, hospitals in
Israel weren't as well staffed as they generally are
today. In the euphoric years right after the War of
Independence, Israelis brimming with a new optimism and
hope started to have lots of babies. It was one of those
wild, busy days at Jerusalem's Hadassah Hospital. All
morning long, expectant mothers with bellies rounder than
wine barrels had been arriving at the maternity ward.
Young Sarah Rodriguez ran from one bed to another, trying
to keep pace with the rush. The poor, inexperienced nurse
felt she might give birth herself any moment from the
pressure. Sixteen nervous and screaming women were in
various stages of labor when the senior nurse took sick and
collapsed onto a vacant bed in the corridor. Suddenly, the
twenty-six-year-old *olah* from Argentina had to double-up
on the job. That meant another eight bellies to care for.
The frazzled girl was less than a week on the ward, fresh
out of her Hebrew *Ulpan*. Women in every corner were
calling out for her aid, and she could barely understand
what they were saying.

"What a *balagan*," she thought to herself.

When another pregnant woman waddled into the ward
holding her belly, Sarah stood frozen. What was she going
to do now?

In the waiting room down the corridor, husbands sat
biting fingernails. Others paced back and forth like
prisoners in jail. Still others stared catatonically at the wall
clock. Only *Rav* Hillel sat calmly, studying a page of
Gemara. At the young age of thirty, he was streaking

through the *Shas* for the third time. His eyes darted over the page without seeming to read the dense script. In truth, he knew it by heart. He had memorized several tractates before taking his *Smichah* exams.

Occasionally, Hillel glanced up at the Mormon minister who was pacing the floor in front of him. They had arrived at the hospital just minutes apart. The man had nervously introduced himself, explaining that he and his wife were expecting their very first child. Hillel remembered his own excitement four children before. From time to time, the Mormon would smile timidly at Hillel, looking toward him for encouragement. From their brief conversation, it was obvious that the man felt uncomfortable with his novice Hebrew, and perhaps he felt uncomfortable about being in a Jewish hospital, the way Hillel would have felt out of place in a gentile hospital in some foreign land. Hillel considered getting up to speak to the man, but he knew that the *mitzvah* of studying Torah was greater.

At that very moment, the flustered Sarah Rodriguez was slipping the identity bracelet of Hillel's new son onto the tiny foot of the minister's baby boy. Similarly, the name tag of the gentile baby ended up on the foot of the Jew. After all, mistakes can happen, especially on a busy day.

A week later, Hillel's baby flew off to America with the Mormon minister and his wife. The minister's blond cherub of a baby went home to a crowded Jerusalem apartment and a joyous circumcision. Of course, from the very beginning, there were signs that something was wrong. For one thing, Hillel's baby refused to nurse from the breasts of the gentile. And the blond hair and blue eyes of the minister's baby never turned brown. But who ever thought that such a mistake could occur?

Hillel returned to the *Beit Midrash*. In Salt Lake City, Utah, Hillel's son, Paul, suffered through eight terrible months of vomiting and diarrhea. The baby rejected all of the non-kosher food that was fed him. Finally, after a blood exchange and intravenous feeding, little Paul accepted a bottle and Beachnut and embarked on an exceptionally precocious childhood. At the age of two, he had the vocabulary of a four-year-old child. By the time he was four, he could read a newspaper and memorize the entire front page. He was enrolled in a Mormon elementary school, and after a week in first grade, he was promoted to the third. When the learning proved too slow, the teacher met with Paul's father to discuss the boy's future. Not wanting to make the child feel like a freak, they decided to let him stay in third grade. To keep pace with the speed of his studies, a private tutor was hired. By the boy's eighth birthday, he had mastered Latin and had read the entire canon of Mormon, Protestant, and Catholic works. Arithmetic, literature, and the sciences seemed to bore him. Instead of playing with friends after school, he spent all of his time at the library. Languages, philosophy, and theological studies enthralled him. By his thirteenth birthday, Paul was fluent in Latin, English, German, Russian, and Greek. In addition, he had read all of the works of Plato, Aristotle, Kant, Tolstoy, Shakespeare, and the philosophers of England and France. Clearly, the lad was a genius. When asked what he wanted to be when he grew up, the studious teenager would immediately answer, "I want to be just like my father."

On the other side of the world, in Israel, things were not going so grand for Hillel. He himself was progressing wonderfully, already the *rosh yeshiva* of a prestigious school, but his son, Yosef, was a source of grave disappointment. The boy refused to study. He refused to sit and learn. Worse, Hillel was beginning to believe that the problem was medical. After all, he had sat coaching his son patiently, night after night, but the words of the *Chumash* and *Mishna* simply refused to stick in his brain. The boy was unable to memorize a line. The sweet songs of King David fell on deaf ears, and the last place you could persuade him to go was to synagogue. To Hillel, the blond, curly-haired boy was a sphinx. He loved listening to rock-and-roll on the radio. Playing soccer, he bounded over the field like a gazelle. He could sleep peacefully until ten in the morning when everyone else in the house was up by six. While Hillel's other children were content to wear hand-me-downs, Yosef would don only new clothes. He didn't get along with anybody in the house, or at school. When asked what he wanted to be when he grew up, he would answer – a movie star. His father, who had never been to a movie theater in his life, could only sigh and pray that one day the boy would have an awakening.

At the age of thirteen, Hillel's real son, Paul, was given permission to learn Hebrew. It immediately became his favorite language. Within a year, he had read the entire *Tanach*. The following year, he breezed through the *halachic* works of the *Rambam* and *The Guide for the Perplexed*. He discovered a great beauty and design in the Hebrew language. In the Old Testament, he felt a stirring sense of inspiration and drama. In Jewish law, he uncovered a profound wisdom which non-Jewish theologies seemed to lack.

At the age of fourteen, Paul graduated high school. Three years later, he graduated from Harvard University, finishing number one in his class. He did his Masters in Divinity at Yale, and continued on to receive doctorates in Philosophy and Language at Cambridge and the Sorbonne. His father and the whole Mormon world were stunned when he had himself baptized and adopted the Catholic faith. His first sermons as a priest were dazzling, overwhelming in scholarship. He spellbound his audiences with his encyclopedic knowledge of comparative religions.

Before very long, the archdiocese of New York offered him an ecclesiastical position. He wrote speeches for the archbishop until the diocese awarded him a cardinalship of his own. With his dark, intense looks and staggering intellect, the young Cardinal Paul brought a new, revitalized look to the Church. He appeared at fundraising dinners throughout America and was a frequent guest on coast-to-coast talk shows. He was photographed with Presidents, Prime Ministers, and Kings. He was filmed in hospitals, prisons, coal mines, and famine-ravaged villages in Kenya. Paul was thirty-years-old when *Time Magazine* named him Man of the Year.

Back in Jerusalem, in a doctor's waiting room, *Rav* Hillel flipped the *Time Magazine* back down on a table. Something about the cardinal's piercing black eyes made him look back down at the picture on the magazine's cover, but he failed to notice the familial resemblance between himself and the clean-shaven priest. Even the identical birthmark they shared on their foreheads failed to attract his attention. The doctor informed Hillel that he had ulcers. Hillel knew why. His son Yosef was living in Eilat, managing a resort hotel. For years he hadn't worn a *kippah*. Hillel's failure in educating his son burned a seering hole in his stomach. Already, Yosef had been married and divorced, and with all of the Swedish and German tourists in Eilat, Hillel was afraid to think what might happen next. It was his life's greatest pain. *"And you shall teach them diligently to your children."* How he had tried. Night after night, he had abandoned his own studies to sit with his son. But what could he do? His other children were brilliant, but Yosef had a *goyisha kup*.

Once the boy entered the army, his father lost all control. By the time he finished his service, he looked like a plucked chicken – no *peyes*, no *tzitzit*, no *kippah*, no *tefillin*. Now he called himself Joe. On his forearm, he had a tattoo. Instead of going to yeshiva, he enrolled in college.

That was when Hillel's ulcers began. After a semester, Joe dropped out and moved to Tel Aviv. One night, he was arrested with drugs. Another time, he was caught stealing. When he flew off to Greece, Hillel had mixed feelings. He didn't want the youth to leave Israel, but maybe he would discover himself overseas. Postcards arrived from Paris, New York, and Los Angeles. Eventually, he came back to Israel. One afternoon in the religious neighborhood of Bayit Vagan, a hippie showed up on the doorstep. For a moment, Hillel didn't recognize him.

"It's me," Yosef said. "The black sheep of the family."

Hugging the youth broke Hillel's heart. Not because of the embarrassment it caused in the neighborhood. Not because of the whispers in the rabbinic court where Hillel now served as a judge. For the sake of the boy, Hillel felt sad. Looking at him with his fleece of blond hair and gold earring, Hillel felt he didn't know him. He didn't understand who he was, as if he weren't his offspring at all.

On the other side of the Atlantic, when a few aging bishops expired, Cardinal Paul became the Church's number-one man in America. He was more than a religious figurehead. He was a celebrity; brilliant, witty, handsome, young – the new symbol of Western religion. This was his public image. Privately, in his personal life, Paul felt empty inside. He felt his life was a painful charade. Outside, he would smile for the crowds, but inside he was crying. The rituals, the prayer services, the speeches, the sermons, they were all a great masquerade. Inside, he felt as wooden as the statues surrounding him. His heart felt like stone. He played his part like an actor in a play because he didn't know what else to do. He didn't know where else to find a real connection to Heaven. Like the god they believed in, the Christian and Catholic religions lacked life. In all of the liturgy, only the Psalms of King David spoke in his heart. Strangely, it was the Old Testament and Hebrew that he loved. They were like mistresses which he kept on the side, secret passions, treasures that he visited late at night when no one was watching. Like a Shakespearean actor, he acted out his role, donning the cloth, performing the rituals, while clandestinely longing for G-d in his heart. When an invitation came from the Vatican to join the bishopcy there, Paul didn't hesitate. He was tired of America and its show business ways. He longed for seclusion, for solitude and peace, to discover a truer path to his Maker.

In Israel, the dreaded day arrived. Hillel answered the telephone.

"Hi, Dad," Joe said. "I'm calling from Cyprus. I married a *shicksa*."

The words pierced Hillel's heart like a saber. His ulcer roared like a lion inside his belly. When he hung up the phone, he tore his shirt in mourning.

"He isn't our son," he said to his wife.

Joe's newest wife was from Finland. Fortunately, the couple decided to live there. Her father owned a successful restaurant, and Joe was brought in to manage. Hillel refused to be broken by the horrible disgrace. He erased the boy from his mind and continued on with his rabbinical career.

Not far away, just across the Mediterranean, as if swept up by fate, Paul was rising upward and upward in the Church's world canon. Upon arriving in Rome, he was granted a term of isolation. He lived in a small room without companionship or love, writing scholarly treatises and poetry. Often, he would stay up the whole night reciting Psalms. He spent days on end pouring over the ancient Jewish texts in the Vatican library. Frequently, he met with the Pope, and the two learned men would spend hours discussing philosophy and theological issues. Before long, Paul became the Pontiff's closest advisor. Once Paul found the nerve to ask the Pope if he believed the historical accuracy of the Gospels. For a moment, the older man didn't reply. "I believe in their message," he answered. The royal robes and staff of his office were like an armor, making further heretical questions impossible to ask. So Paul kept his doubts to himself. Though he had longed for isolation, he found himself once again in the center of public life, next in line to the aging and ailing Pontiff.

Years and wars and rulers passed like old newspapers discarded in the wind. On the eve of the historic visit of the Pope to Jerusalem, the revered saint fell ill. Since the United Nations was pressing to make Jerusalem an international city, freed from Jewish rule, the Pope's visit was filled with meaning. Paul had been the architect of the trip, convincing the Pope of its great importance to the Church, whose light had been dimmed ever since Israel's miraculous rebirth in the land of the Bible. Receiving a piece of Jerusalem would put Christianity back on the map.

The world held its breath as the Pope lingered for days on his deathbed. His last wish was that Bishop Paul continue on in his stead to Jerusalem. Thus, the rabbi's son was appointed Pope Paul the Eighth. Amidst great piety and pageant, the World Ecumenical Council buried its old leader and inaugurated its new. The next day, Pope Paul the Eighth flew off for his dramatic confrontation in the Holy Land.

Paul was filled with excitement as he soared on his way to Israel. Not only were the eyes of all the world focused on him, he was also returning for the first time in his life to his birthplace. With great pride, his father had always told him that he had been born in Jerusalem. Not surprisingly, the city held a special place in his heart. Still, when he burst into tears at the first sight of Israel, even before the aircraft landed, he was taken aback. Certainly, he had cried when the Pope had died, but not like this.

Tears streamed out from his eyes uncontrollably. His entourage on the plane watched the new Pontiff in reverence and awe. To them his reaction was proof that Jerusalem was their city too.

Reporters from all over the world were waiting at the Ben Gurion Airport. Dozens of television cameras were aimed at Paul as he stepped down the ramp to the runway. All over the world, billions of people watched as the new Pope fell to his knees and kissed the Holy Land. Hillel, now Israel's Chief Rabbi, stepped forward to help the Pope to his feet. Their eyes met. The Pope stared into the old rabbi's kind eyes and trembled. For a moment, he felt he was going to faint. Never had he met someone so holy. Without even exchanging a word, he knew he had to speak to this man.

"Please come to our house for dinner," Hillel said before the crowd of politicians rushed over to grasp the Pope's hand.

Not knowing why, Paul leaned forward and embraced the old man. The photograph of the two religious leaders hugging like father and son made front pages all over the globe. In fact, one reporter described the historic meeting between Judaism and Christianity as a father and son reunited after a long separation of years.

"G-d willing," Paul answered in Hebrew.

Then the Israeli Prime Minister and President were upon them, and the Pope was whisked off to a round of speeches and high-level talks. Only three days later did the Pope have the opportunity to see the Chief Rabbi again for an intimate talk at his home.

His aides waited downstairs with the limousine as he entered the modest apartment alone. The rabbi's wife opened the door and stared at the visitor with an uncharacteristic directness. For some unfathomable reason, she couldn't remove her eyes from his face. It was true that the Pope didn't show up in Jerusalem every week, but with a woman's intuition she felt something more.

The Pope smiled nervously under the old woman's scrutiny.

"I'm sorry," she said with a blush. "For a moment, I thought you were somebody else."

"I often feel like somebody else," he replied with a smile.

"Please come in," she said, stepping aside.

Almost instinctively, the Pope reached up to touch the *mezuza*. From the entrance to his study, the rabbi noticed the gesture.

"*Baruch haba,*" he said, welcoming his guest.

It seemed only natural that they hug once again. Sitting alone in the study, they spoke together in Hebrew. Conversation came easily with a remarkable rapport as if they were long-lost friends.

Paul conversed freely in Hebrew, as if it were his native tongue. His eyes moistened as he gazed at the bookshelves that lined every wall in the study. A love of Torah filled the apartment like light. Their conversation jumped from subject to subject, from politics, Judaic-Christian tradition, the Holocaust, and details of Talmudic law. Paul found himself envying the rabbi's certainty and faith. Concepts which he had wrestled with all of his life, like the coming of the Messiah and the future world of souls were taken for granted by the learned Jewish sage.

The rabbi's wife called them to dinner. When the Pope inhaled the aroma of the chicken soup, he almost passed out. It was the most delicious dish he had ever tasted in his life. Tears welled in his eyes eating *matzah* balls. The old Jewish couple stared at him in amazement.

"I'm sorry," Paul said. "This whole experience is a bit overwhelming. I was born in Jerusalem, you know. In a way, it really is like coming home."

"When is your birthday?" the old woman asked.

"The tenth of June," the Pope answered.

"What year?" the Chief Rabbi asked.

"1950."

"Really?" the rabbi responded, glancing at his wife.

"My father was giving a series of lectures at Hebrew University," Pope Paul continued. "We left for America a short time later so I never got to see the land."

"Was your father a tall man with curly blond hair," the Chief Rabbi asked.

"Yes, he was," the guest answered.

"I think I may have met him... at the hospital on the very day you were born."

Hillel tried to remember the day clearly, but, thank G-d, after ten children, the details of each delivery were vague. The only thing he remembered sharply was the page of *Gemara* which he had been learning in the waiting room while his wife was giving birth.

"I'd like to make a request," the Pope said. "Tomorrow, I will be returning to Rome. Wherever I go on my travels, I am followed by officials and crowds and police. I would like to spend some time alone at the Western Wall before I go back. Is there any way you can arrange it?"

The rabbi thought for a moment, then smiled.

"Have you heard about the holiday of Purim?" he asked.

"Of course," the Pope said.

"Maybe we can begin its celebration a little early this year. You look to be around my height. I will lend you some of my clothes and everyone will think you're a Jew."

At once the Pope agreed. He had been wearing a costume all of his life. For a few hours, he would simply be changing roles. The rabbi led him into his bedroom. The clothes fit him exactly as if they were his. With the somber black coat and hat, he looked like any other *Yid* on the street. He stared at his reflection in the mirror and laughed. Even the old rabbi had to chuckle.

"All you need now is a beard," he quipped.

His wife had already thought of that. From a box buried deep in the closet, she pulled out a white fluffy beard which one of her sons had worn many Purims ago. Good-naturedly, the Pope put it on. Everyone was ready to enjoy a good laugh, but when they looked in the mirror, nobody could even manage a smile. Standing in front of the mirror were twins. Identical doubles. The Pope and Israel's Chief Rabbi. Hillel was speechless. They looked exactly alike – the same eyes, the same nose, the very same birthmark on their foreheads. They stood side-by-side, staring at each other in the mirror. The old Jewish woman looked expectantly on, waiting for the two men to realize what she had already guessed. Slowly the old rabbi turned toward his look-alike guest. His wise, understanding eyes penetrated to the depths of the other man's soul.

"My son?" Hillel questioned. "Can it be?"

"*Abba?*" Paul mumbled in amazement.

The two bearded rabbis embraced. Paul's mother burst into tears. Paul turned to her, not knowing how to respond. A great sob shook his body as he hugged her happily in his arms.

"*Eema,*" he whispered. "Oh, *Eeemmma.*"

"My baby," she cried. "You've come home."

The press conference the following morning took the world by surprise.

"I have decided to resign from the Papacy," Pope Paul declared. "I am giving up the Church to become a simple Jew. Jerusalem must never be divided. It must remain the eternal capital of Israel. This and only this will bring lasting peace to the world."

The entire Christian world was stunned. Jews danced in the streets. The Arabs threatened *Jihad*. Pope Paul the Eighth stayed in Israel where he was born. His circumcision ceremony was broadcast around the world. The next day he was *bar-mitzvahed*. Within a month and a half, he was married to the daughter of an influential rabbi. With the passing of time, he grew a big fluffy white beard of his own. And the other baby? The real son of the minister. What ever happened to him? Nobody knows. He divorced his third wife, dropped out of sight, and vanished from the face of the earth.

EHUD

Ehud was a happy man, truly content with his lot. He had a lovely wife, three lovely children, and a lovely house in Ramat Gan. He had a good job and good friends. He liked and respected all people, and all people liked and respected him. He was friendly, optimistic, and always tried to see the good side of things, believing that everything that happened in life was for the best. He did whatever he could to help people, and he avoided quarrels and fights, believing that peace was life's most precious value. He was a smart man, an educated man, but humble, never thinking he was better than anyone else. He had his opinions, but he respected all points of view, except for the radical. He kept to the middle path in life and followed the rule, "Do unto others what you would have them do unto you." He wasn't a religious man, practicing rituals and the like, but he lived a very moral, principled life.

One quiet evening, while Ehud was reading his newspaper, there was a knock on the door. A man stood outside. He was a tall man, a big man, with a nondescript face. He might have been a Gentile, or an Arab, or a Jew.

Ehud greeted him with a smile and a pleasant hello. The man seemed surprised that Ehud didn't recognize him.

"The other day in town, I lent you twenty *shekels*," he said.

Ehud didn't remember. He thought and thought, but he couldn't remember a thing. It wasn't like him to forget, but the man seemed quite certain. It wouldn't be polite to argue, Ehud thought. It was only twenty *shekels*. And apparently he had given the man his address. Ehud apologized for forgetting, gave the man twenty *shekels*, and said goodnight.

The very next night, he returned. The same man. He appeared at the door while Ehud's wife, Tzipora, was cooking dinner in the kitchen.

"I came for my television," the man said.

"Your television?" Ehud asked.

"The television set that I lent you," the man said. "I want it back. My children don't have a TV to watch."

"What will my children watch?" Ehud asked.

"I'm sorry, but that isn't my problem," the man replied.

"But the television is mine," Ehud protested. "I bought it, and I have a warranty to prove it too."

Ehud walked to the cabinet where he kept all of his papers in alphabetically arranged files. But the television warranty wasn't there. He searched through his old bank statements, phone bills and medical records, but the warranty was nowhere to be found. Embarrassed, he returned to the door.

"For the moment, I can't seem to find it," he said.

"That proves it then," the man said. "I'm sorry, but I don't have much time, and I really don't want to fight. Please give it to me now."

Ehud didn't want to fight either. For one thing, the man was bigger than he was, and more principally, Ehud didn't like fighting. Fighting was barbaric. Fighting was cruel. Perhaps the man was too embarrassed to admit he was poor. And maybe the man's children really didn't have a TV to watch. If so, the situation truly wasn't fair. After all, Ehud's children watched every night. It was, Ehud finally decided, the right thing to do. So he walked to the den, pulled out the television plug from the wall, and to the cries of his startled children, he carried the set to the front door and handed it to the man, feeling in his heart that he was doing something noble, something majestic, something good.

When the man left. Ehud sat down with his unhappy children to explain why it was so important to have done what he did. Everyone in the world was equal, he told them, and it was important for everyone to share all alike. When there were differences between people, there was envy, and envy led to fighting, and fighting brought an end to peace. Just as they had enjoyed watching television, so would some other children now. Ehud's wife stood listening in the doorway, a soft smile on her lips. This was the reason she loved her husband so much. He was so caring, so open-hearted, so good. More important than the television was the example her husband was setting for the children, and the valuable lesson they would learn.

"But what will we do now?" the older boy asked.

"Read," Ehud said. "From now on, I'll read you books."

The very next evening, Ehud sat in his armchair, reading a book to his children, almost awaiting a knock on the door. When it came, he sprang up and hurried across the room.

"Good evening," the man said. "I came for my clothes."

For a moment, the two men stared at each other. Ehud sensed his wife and his children behind him, watching to see what would happen.

"They are upstairs in the closet," Ehud said.

He invited the man inside. He felt he was being tested. To see if he could really practice what he believed; that all men were brothers; that everyone was equal; that his claims on the world were the same as all other peoples, without firsts or seconds, better or worse.

Ehud led the man upstairs to his bedroom. Maybe, he reasoned, the man really didn't have any clothes besides the same very nice suit he wore every night. Maybe he had no job, and no money to buy what he needed. Ehud opened his closet, took out his clothes, and spread them out on the bed: pants and shirts, sweaters and jackets and shoes.

"A suitcase would help," the man said.

Ehud gave him two. The man filled them both. Ehud wasn't worried. He was glad. He had a job. He could always buy more clothes. And even with all the man took, Ehud still had more than he needed. Magnanimously, Ehud helped him carry the suitcases downstairs. With smiles on their faces, Ehud, his wife, and his children said goodnight to the man at the door.

The next night, the children were waiting at the windows, but the man didn't come.

"Where is he, Dad?" one son asked

"I don't know," Ehud answered.

"I wish he would come," the girl said. "I like him. I think that he's fun."

His wife also seemed disappointed. She had even prepared something for the visitor to eat. Ehud felt glad that they all liked the man, but when the man didn't come, he felt unquestionably relieved.

But the very next day he was back.

"He's coming! He's coming!" the boy called from his post at the window. The little girl ran to the door. Ehud greeted him with a cordial hello.

"I've come for my house," the man said. "My family wants to move back tonight."

Ehud's voice stuck in his throat. He felt dizzy. He felt weak. Giving up his house was too much.

"He wants to take our whole house, Mommy!" the little girl yelled, running to tell her mother.

Ehud felt his sons' eyes upon him, watching to see what he would do.

"It isn't your house," Ehud said.

"Yes it is," the man answered.

"We bought it. We have a deed," Ehud insisted.

"I have a deed too," the man answered, and he reached in his pocket and pulled out a deed. "The people you bought the house from weren't the legal owners. I lived here before with my family and have the original lien."

How could it be, Ehud thought? Hadn't he received the house from its original owners? Quickly, he examined the man's deed. Superficially, it seemed all in order; including the right address and plot number, the name of the builder, the seal of the notary, and signatures of lawyers and witnesses. Once again, Ehud felt faint. Little white dots swirled in his brain. The man had to help him into a chair.

"I'll bring you some water," Tzipora said.

She returned with two glasses and offered one to the man.

"The deed seems all in order," Ehud said. "But I'm not a lawyer. Of course, on something like this, I'll have to have legal advice."

"I really don't care for lawyers," the man said. "I'd much prefer to solve this ourselves. Lawyers always get ugly, and I really don't want to fight."

"Of course we don't want to fight," Tzipora said. "But..."

"I'll handle this," Ehud said. He stood up from his chair and told his children to go up to their room.

"We want to listen," his older boy said.

"Let's give him the house. Dad," the younger added. "We can all live outside in my tent."

Ehud looked at his wife.

"We could go to my mother's," she said.

His wife really meant what she said. Ehud's heart moved toward her with a surging of love. She was so beautiful. She was so pure. He remembered how happy he had been on their wedding day to have found a partner who believed in all the principles that he cherished.

It was true, Ehud reasoned. They could go to her mother. It wasn't as if they would be out on the street. And maybe the man didn't have his own home or anywhere to live. And it was also true that lawyers could get ugly. And it was only a house. There were other houses. What did it matter where they lived? It was only walls, floors, and furniture. The main thing was that everyone should live somewhere and that there shouldn't be a fight.

Ehud reached into his pocket. With trembling fingers, he handed over his key. In the morning, he would decide what to do about lawyers. Now the important thing was for his children to learn the great lesson of kindness and fairness and peace.

He told his family to gather what they needed for the night. He collected his important papers, including his mortgage and deed to the house, a change of clothes for work, pajamas, his toothbrush, and the small handgun in his bedside table, which he was afraid to leave in the house lest the man's children find it. He handed the man his mother-in-law's phone number in case he had any problems. Then, carrying two small bags, he led his wife and his children out from their home.

The next day, Ehud was typically busy at the office. He spoke to his lawyer, but there was nothing to do on the phone, except to schedule an appointment for some time later in the week. For the moment, Ehud decided not to go to the police.

Life at his mother-in-law's apartment was crowded, but the elderly woman seemed happy with the unexpected visit. That evening, Ehud was trying to distract himself with the newspaper when he heard a familiar knock on his mother-in-law's door. Tzipora glanced up from the television. Husband and wife exchanged looks.

"He's back!" the girl said, running to open the door.

Tonight, the man was dressed in one of Ehud's nicest suits. He stood in the doorway and said with a big happy smile.

"I've come for my wife."

His wife? Had Ehud heard right? Tzipora?

Slowly, Ehud stood up. Again he felt dizzy. Again he felt weak. His mind struggled to reason. Of course every man deserved a wife. But Tzipora was his wife.

"But I married her," Ehud said.

"I married her too," the man answered.

"I have a *ketuba* to prove it," Ehud argued.

"So do I," said the man.

"Her ring," Ehud gasped.

"Anyone can buy a ring."

"But we have pictures from the wedding."

"Pictures can be faked."

"Our children," Ehud said. "What about our children?"

"The children are mine," the man answered.

Ehud trembled. He was speechless. He was afraid to talk, afraid to reason. He would say white, and the man would say black. He would say up, and the man would say down. Both things were true. But his wife. He looked at his wife. His beautiful wife. She too was silent. She too was confused. Why belong to one man? Why not belong to two? Why should she be Ehud's wife and not someone else's? All people were the same, weren't they? And weren't all men brothers?

"I'm afraid I don't have much time," the man said. "Are you coming, Tzipora?"

Ehud looked at his wife. He knew she was his. More than that. She was him. He didn't need a deed or a document to prove it. She was like a piece of his body. She was like his heart. Would he give the man his heart? That was what the man wanted. He was demanding that Ehud give up his heart. Ehud grasped the gun in his pocket. Slowly he raised it into the air. He intended to point the gun at the man, but he couldn't. Instead, he pointed it at himself. He closed his eyes, and he fired.

That was the lesson that Ehud taught his children that night.

ORDERS ARE ORDERS

F or the third time that day, Izzy was looking through
the snapshots his wife had sent him when a rock
richocheted off the guard tower. Outside in the dimming
twilight, he couldn't see a thing. It wasn't the first time
that a rock had hit the tower during his three months on
the isolated Samaria hilltop. Arab kids had nothing better
to do than throw rocks at Jewish soldiers. To be on the
safe side, the young Israeli tightened the strap of his
helmet. Orders were orders. And in the army, safety came
first.

His gaze turned back to the pictures. How happy his
son looked at his first birthday party, as if he understood
its significance. Izzy had asked for a special leave to attend
the celebration, but since he had only one week remaining
in his *Hesder* army service, the request had been denied.

"Pang!" "Pang!" "Pang!"

Smashing against the metal guard tower, the rocks
sounded like bullets. Down below, at the crest of the hill,
on the other side of the sheep pen, a group of dark figures
had gathered. Izzy stuck his rifle out the window in
warning. Just to be sure, he called his two buddies, who
were out patroling the area in a jeep. Some people thought
the settlers were irresponsible for staying put on remote
hilltops like these during the *Intifada*, but Izzy didn't
agree. Israel was the land of the Jews, and a Jew had the
right to live wherever he chose. It was the job of the
government and the army to protect its citizens, whether
they lived in Netanya or Hevron.

To his way of thinking, the situation was absolutely

absurd. So what if a Jew wanted to live in a cabin on a desolate hill in the heartland of biblical Israel. Why should the whole world make such a fuss over it? Why should it bother foreign presidents and kings? Didn't they have better things to worry about than what a handful of Jews were doing on the other side of the globe?

The twenty-one year old soldier tried his best not to think about it too much. Instead, he studied *Gemara* whenever he could. He spoke to his wife every day. In a week, he'd be finished with being away in the army, and he could get down to being a father to his one-year old boy.

When a brick smashed through the thick plastic pane of the window, Izzy instinctively ducked. Down on the hillside, a mob of Arabs was advancing his way. Across the dirt road, on the roof of the small wooden cabin, an Arab youth was hauling down the Israeli flag. As luck would have it, the settler who lived on the one-man *yishuv* was off at a wedding. Besides the barking dog, Izzy was the only defender on the remote, windswept *givah*.

Figuring he may need some back-up, he phoned his friends in the jeep, but they were being stoned too.

"We're on our way," they told him.

Rocks pounding the guard tower reverberated like popcorn popping in a microwave oven. Izzy fired off a few shots in the air to warn off the attackers, but the Arabs continued to advance on the tower. Like the good soldier he was, he wouldn't fire at them until he received a direct order. His rabbis had taught him that the government of Israel was holy, the Israeli army was holy, and so was its chain of command. Calling his *Mem-kaf*, he described the situation and requested permission to shoot.

"Hold on," the young voice said. "I've got to check with the *Mem-mem*."

The *Mem-mem* wasn't certain. The truth is, he wasn't much older than his soldiers, and the orders to shoot weren't clear. With sensitive peace negotiations in progress, and a quasi cease fire in effect, he didn't want to be the one to blow the Middle East situation sky high.

"Tell him to hold off until I get word from the *Mem-peh*," he told the *Mem-men*.

The *Mem-peh* said he would call the *Magad*. After ten minutes of busy signals and crossed connections, the *Magad* was put on the phone.

"Why should I stick my neck out on this one?" he thought. "It's the *Machat's* headache, not mine."

"Affirmative. I understand the situation," the busy *Machat* said. "I'll speak to the *Mefaked HaUgdah* and get back to you on the double."

"*Tov, tov,*" *Mefaked HaUgdah* said with a sigh. As far as he was concerned, he didn't know why the army had to babysit every troublemaker who wanted to live on a mountaintop in the West Bank. But since the rules about opening fire were reissued every week, depending if negotiations were stalled or progressing, he figured he had better forward the call to the *Aluf HaPekud*.

The *Aluf HaPekud* didn't have an answer. He wasn't in a hurry to make headlines. If he messed up, he'd catch all the blame. Besides, he was an army man, not a politician. So he decided to call the *Ramat-kal*.

The army's Chief Officer wasn't about to put his future career on the line when cameras from all over the world were focused on *Tzahal*. But since a soldier was in danger, he got through to the Defense Minister as fast as he could.

"I've got a soldier being bombarded by stones on a hilltop near Shechem. Can I give him a green light to shoot?"

"What are you asking me for?" the Defense Minister answered. "Call the Prime Minister."

"You call him, that's your job."

With a deep sigh, the Defense Minister called the man whom the nation had elected to bring security to the land.

The Israeli Prime Minister took a moment to think. This wasn't a time for gut reactions. He had to keep the whole complicated picture in mind.

"Get me the President," he said to his aide.

"Our President, sir?" the aide asked.

"No, not our President. The President of the United States."

The President of the United States wasn't in the Oval Office. He wasn't in the White House. He was on a two day vacation, playing golf.

"Tell him to wait," the President said as he lined up a putt. Biting his lip, he eyed the hole and took a few practice swings. Then, concentrating on the flag, he swung the putter forward and watched as the tiny white ball streaked over the Florida green. The ball curved along a slight slope and headed straight for the hole.

"Get in there, baby!" the President shouted. But the ball hit the rim of the cup and bounced over the hole, coming to a stop a few golf clubs away.

"Damn!" the President swore, shaking his head.

"The Israeli Prime Minister," his aide said, holding the phone out.

"Yeah, yeah, in a minute," the President answered, striding over to his ball. Once again, he lined up the putt. This time, the curve broke in the other direction. Focusing between the cup and the ball, he gave the putter a flick. Once again, the ball hit the lip and bounced out, coming to rest only inches away.

"Damn it!" the President moaned.

With his golf cap, he wiped the sweat off his brow. After a few sips of cold water he looked around for his aide, who was standing at his side with the telephone.

"Hello, Mr. President, *shalom*," Israel's Prime Minister said.

"Yeah, *shalom*," the President answered.

"How are you, sir?" the Prime Minister asked.

"I'm on vacation," the President answered.

"Yes, sir, I know, sir. I'm sorry to bother you, but I have a soldier under attack and I want to know if he can open fire."

"Open fire? In the middle of peace negotiations? Are you people nuts?"

"We are trying our best, Mr. President," the Prime Minister said.

"What's the matter with tear gas?" the President asked.

"The wind blows it away."

"Then use rubber bullets."

"No one is afraid of rubber bullets these days."

"Then start making concessions. On both sides. With a little flexibility, we can wrap this thing up."

"With your help, Mr. President, I am sure that we will."

Sweating, the Prime Minister set down the phone. Immediately, he had the Defense Minister back on the line. "The orders stay the same," he told him.

"The same?" the Defense Minister asked in an uncertain tone.

"That's right. The same!" the Prime Minister barked.

"Sorry for the question, Dov, but exactly what does that mean? You know as well as I do that the orders change every week."

"They don't change every week," the Israeli leader fumed. "The government's policy is clear. Orders are orders. A soldier is not to open fire unless his life is clearly at stake."

"Yes, sir," the Defense Minister answered. Even before he hung up the phone, he gave the command to call the *Ramat-Kal*.

The Ramat-Kal called the *Aluf HaPekud*. The *Aluf HaPekud* called the *Mefaked HaUgdah*. The *Mefaked HaUgdah* called the *Machat*. The *Machat* called the *Magad*. The *Magad* called the *Mem-peh*. The *Mem-peh* called the

Mem-mem. The *Mem-men* called the *Mem-kaf.*

Without further hesitation, the *Mem-kaf* rang up the guard tower.

"Izzy, do you hear me?" the *Mem-kaf* yelled over the wire. "Izzy are you there? Do you hear me, Izzy? Izzy, are you there? Do you hear me? Izzy, are you there?"

THE JACKASS
THAT BRAYED

The floor rumbled when Meir walked inside the small, hillside caravan. The ceiling sagged in places. Ants, flies, and scorpions visited throughout the summer. Wind and rain poured in from every window in the winter. The kitchen faucet dripped without compassion. The toilet-flush took ten minutes to subside. And the shower splashed cold water in unpredictable spurts. Yes, the caravan had problems, but the young Shoshana settler loved it. In fact, he hardly paid attention to the deficiencies at all. The caravan was Meir's first home with his new bride, and he was as happy as could be. The two tiny rooms were his palace. It didn't matter to him that when his wife gave birth in another few months, they would have to put the crib in the dining area, next to the refrigerator, which was too big to fit in the kitchen. Meir wasn't troubled in the least. Other settlers managed. They would manage too. The important thing was that they were living in the hills of Hevron, on one of the *g'vaot* that had sprung up literally overnight. They were defending the Land, holding down the fort, waiting for all of the Jews to come home.

He swung open the flimsy caravan door and stepped out into the cool morning air. The soldier up in the guard tower looked down and nodded *shalom*.

"*Boker tov*," Meir responded in his warm, open manner. "Wait, I'll bring you some juice."

The soldier didn't refuse. As his luck had it, he was stationed in Shoshana for a month of reserve duty. Though most of the soldiers on guard duty in Shoshana weren't religious, and though their opinions often opposed the ideology of the settlers in the tiny circle of caravans high in the hills of Hevron, everyone ended up liking Meir. You couldn't help it. His friendliness was contagious. His door was always open, and soldiers were always welcome to use the telephone or to enjoy some fresh, homemade cake. Meir himself served in a tank unit, and word had gotten around about his exploits in Lebanon, how he had rescued a wounded soldier and carried him back, under fire, to safety. Now he hurried back to the caravan, and with quickness that characterized all of his movements, he brought the soldier a pitcher of juice.

Already the fury of Hevron, the trucks and honking horns, the bustle of the Casba and market drifted up on the wind, carrying with it the scent of tobacco and spices. Shoshana looked down on the ancient Jewish city from its perch on the hill. Israeli flags waved over the cherished Tomb of the Patriarchs, and over the small *Avraham Avinu* settlement in the city. On the hill across the way, Tel Romeida's cluster of caravans sat huddling together like a wagon train guarding against Indian attack. No doubt, Meir thought, Shoshana's seven caravans appeared just as vulnerable from the Tel-Romeida side of the hill. The settlers lived each day on a miracle. A dirt road ran beside Meir's caravan, and Arab shepherds herding their sheep could reach up and knock on his bedroom window as they passed. If G-d hadn't been watching, the lone army guard tower wouldn't have helped. Even Meir's parents, hardened Zionists from the early days of the State, thought their son was crazy for living there.

Meir was in charge of communications in the area. The settlers kept in contact through cell-phones and radio. A van made hourly rounds around Hevron and up to the settlement city of Kiriat Arba and back. Even though surrounded by seventy-thousand Arabs, Meir didn't carry a gun. Did a man carry a gun in his own house? Hevron had been the home of Abraham, the father of the Jewish people. The first piece of land he had purchased in the Holy Land was in Hevron, recorded in the Bible for all the world to see. Hevron was the first capital of David's kingship. Jews had lived there for three-thousand years until the Massacre of 1929 wiped out the Jewish population. Now Jews were returning and rebuilding. For Meir, it wasn't a matter of politics. It wasn't even a matter of history. Hevron was simply his. He felt it in his bones, in his blood, in the air he breathed. It was like all of the Land of Israel – a part of his body, as integral to him as his heart. When reporters came to ask questions, he had nothing elaborate to say. The Arabs? He didn't hate them. They were people. G-d had created them too. But when they wanted to kill him; when they wanted to injure his wife and his children and tell him he couldn't live in his very own land; yes, he wasn't embarrassed to say that he hated that.

Today was Meir's day off, a day to work on his garden and on the upkeep of the *yishuv* – the caravans, the plumbing, the water tanks and emergency generator – something always had to be fixed. The tiny patch of garden, two-meters square, was Meir's great joy. He had planted it with *shoshanot*. Beautiful red and yellow roses. From skinny twigs, they had grown and blossomed atop the barren hillside, turning the words of the Prophet to reality; "*And they shall build the waste cities and inhabit them. They shall also make gardens and eat the fruit of them. And I will plant them upon their land, and they shall no longer be plucked up out of the land which I have given them, says the Lord, thy G-d.*"

Was there a better reason in the world to sing, Meir thought, and he sang. He sang songs of Carlebach. He sang songs of Zion. He sang of the redemption and of the return to the land. He gazed at his five healthy rose bushes and the big round flowers that grinned like happy faces in the sun. The soldier in the guard tower heard Meir singing and smiled. Meir's pregnant wife, Sarah, smiled in the caravan doorway. For her, living in Shoshana wasn't easy. It was a hard life, sometimes a scary life, but it was worth it to hear Meir sing.

The young couple were eating breakfast and listening to the radio news, when the soldier in the tower yelled out, "Meir!" In a second, the alert settler was standing outside, poised for action.

"Your roses," the soldier said with a frown.

Meir glanced at his garden. A jackass stood in the small patch, his front legs squashing two tulip bulbs. His mouth opened wide and he chomped a rose off of its stem. Meir watched the beautiful flower disappear down the animal's throat. "HEE HAW," the beast brayed. Meir yelled out and ran toward the jackass. The creature gave a small hop, then stood, unmoving, indifferent, prehistorically dumb.

"He only ate one bush," the soldier said, walking over.

Meir stared at the naked bush in anguish. The jackass licked its lips. It was big as jackasses go, with an escort of flies, a flea-bitten hide, and a noticeable stink.

"The roses will grow back," Meir's wife said, hoping to calm him.

"Sorry I didn't see him sooner," the soldier said.

"It's good it wasn't a terrorist," remarked Johnny, the American settler from his caravan doorway. He was forever finding fault with the army security in the area.

Meir still hadn't spoken. "What are you going to do?" his wife asked.

"I say let's kill it," Johnny said.

Like many American settlers, Johnny opted for the instant solution. He was a product of microwave ovens and disposable dishes. Meir wasn't as rash. Though he wasn't a Torah scholar, Meir reasoned that before any punitive action could be taken, he had to deliver a warning. Johnny, for all of his well-meant idealism, had been influenced by too many cowboy movies.

Meir walked over to the jackass, raised his shoe, and gave it a kick on the rump. The startled beast brayed, bolted, and loped off down the dirt road. Meir ran off after him.

"Be careful," Meir's wife called.

Meir followed the jackass along a narrow path which wound through an olive grove to a fenced yard and a two-story house, seven times the size of Meir's caravan. The jackass stopped in front of a feed trough and brayed, wanting some water to wash down Meir's roses. The settler knocked on the carved wooden door and waited until the owner appeared, an Arab about fifty-years old, wearing the long white gown and head gear of a well-to-do Moslem. He stared expressionlessly at Meir, as if this was a daily occurrence – a Jew on a social call at his door.

"Is that your jackass?" Meir asked.

The Arab's eyes shifted quickly to the animal and returned expressionlessly to Meir. He paused, as if deciding whether to answer or not.

"He ate a rose bush of mine."

The Arab shrugged, as if to say what could one do? Jackasses ate bushes. That was a part of Allah's great plan.

"I don't want your jackass eating my roses again," Meir warned. "Tie him up. Keep him in your yard. Do you understand?"

The Arab nodded. This time with a smile. Meir couldn't tell if he was being friendly or laughing, but Meir trusted him about as far as he could lift up and throw the mule.

That was on Sunday. On Tuesday, Meir came home from work to find his wife silently preparing lunch in their corridor kitchen.

"What's the matter?" Meir asked.

"The jackass came back," she said. "He ate another two of your rose bushes before the soldiers could chase him away."

Meir slammed open the caravan door. It rebounded off the wall and yanked the screws off a hinge. The settler's heart sank when he saw his small garden. Only one rosebush was spared. Like a picky eater, the jackass had nipped off the tasty flowers, leaving the thorny stems. Meir leaped down the embankment to the dirt road and ran off toward the home of the four-legged vandal.

"Be careful," his wife called once again from the window.

The jackass was taking an afternoon nap, snoozing in the sun as if he had just finished a sumptuous Sabbath repast. Around its neck was a rope tied to a tree. The smell of pungent tobacco wafted outside as the Arab opened the door of the house.

"Your jackass ate another two of my rosebushes," Meir informed him.

The Arab looked over at the innocently sleeping animal. "It cannot be," he said. "The jackass has been tied up all day."

"It ate my rosebushes," Meir repeated.

"Perhaps it was someone else's animal," the Arab said. "After all, jackasses look alike."

Meir felt the Arab was playing with him.

"But, of course, I am sorry all the same," the Arab graciously added.

"I don't care if you're sorry," Meir said. "The fact is my rosebushes are gone. If I find your jackass back on my property, you'll never see him again. Understood?"

"That isn't your property," the Arab said bluntly.

For a moment, Meir couldn't answer. He felt that someone had snuck up from behind and bludgeoned him on the head. In the dark eyes of the Arab, Meir could feel centuries of hate. He knew there wasn't a way to answer the man, for the real answer rested on Divine truths too ethereal to explain. But even on the practical side, the Arab was wrong. The Shoshana settlers had returned to land owned by Jews throughout the time of Turkish rule up to the Massacre of 1929 when Arabs burned the houses on the site and murdered the Jewish residents who hadn't had time to flee.

"Perhaps," the Arab said, "your roses wouldn't be eaten if you lived somewhere else."

"Just walk away," Meir thought to himself. "Just walk away," he repeated until his feet obeyed the command.

At the gate, Meir stopped. Softly, he warned the man again, then turned and walked away, back to his caravan home. But the very next day, Meir was driving some women up to the *Kiryah* to do their weekly shopping when he received a radio call in the van.

"This is Meir," he answered, steering around a steep Hevron turn.

"I'm sorry, Meir," said the soldier on the other end of the wire. "But the jackass just ate the last of your roses."

Meir's foot hit the brakes. His fist crashed down on the horn. Arab children gathered on the street to see what was causing all of the noise. Meir jerked the vehicle into first. The van lurched forward, scattering the children. A sharp U-turn later, he was racing back down the hill, swerving through traffic, pounding on the horn, while the kerchiefed women in back hung on for their lives.

A soldier stood by Meir's caravan, holding his M-16 in one hand and a rope tied around the jackass's neck in the other.

"I made sure he didn't get away," he said.

"Top notch security work," Johnny said, walking over.

Meir was furious. Shaking. Even his wife kept her distance. He stared at the naked branches where once his beautiful roses had bloomed.

"Now will you kill it?" Johnny asked

"They will grow back, Meir," his wife said, but even so, she wanted to cry, knowing what the garden meant to her husband.

Meir asked Johnny to drive the women up to Kiriat Arba. He took the rope from the soldier and began leading the jackass away.

"Where are you going," his wife nervously asked.

Meir didn't answer.

"Sure you don't want me to come with you?" Johnny asked.

Still Meir kept silent, not giving away his plans.

"At least," his wife said, "Take a gun."

Meir kept walking. He wasn't angry at the jackass. What did a donkey know? And he wasn't even so angry at the Arab. What for that matter did the Arab know? The lies that Arafat told him? Meir was angry at something else. He was angry at his country. At its weakness. He was angry at himself.

He led the jackass down the incline to the city, past the shops of spices, nuts, and grains; past camels butchered and hanging in windows; past cripples and carts pulled by horses to the Arab blacksmith who worked in a hole in the wall near the Casba.

"How much will you give for the jackass?" Meir asked.

The blacksmith glanced at the young bearded Jew and studied the animal. He offered twenty-five dollars. Meir said one hundred, knowing from experience that anything was worth at least four times a Hevron first offer. Finally the blacksmith agreed to fifty. He paid Meir in cash. In dollars. From a roll in his pocket that must have totaled two thousand.

With the money in hand, Meir returned to the yard of the jackass's owner and knocked on the door.

"Your jackass ate the last of my rosebushes," Meir told

him. "So I sold it. Here's your money."

The Arab didn't reach out his hand. He looked at the dollars, then spit on the ground. With a look of contempt, he closed the door without saying a word.

Meir dropped the money on the doorstep and walked out of the yard.

Several hours later, two Israeli police appeared at Meir's caravan door. A group of Arabs, including the municipal administrator, had complained to Israeli police headquarters that Meir had killed the man's jackass. Meir explained what had happened; how the jackass had eaten his roses; how he had delivered two warnings; how he had sold the animal and given its owner the money. The policemen wrote down the information, ate the piece of chocolate cake which Meir's wife served, and left in a friendly manner.

The next morning, the policemen came back. The jackass's owner denied receiving money from Meir. The Arab municipal council was threatening to close all shops and businesses unless Meir was taken into custody. The story had already appeared in all the Arab papers, and the police wanted to avoid any escalation of tension in the town. It was simple, Meir said. He would take them to the blacksmith who had purchased the jackass. Sarah, his wife, followed them out to the police car and watched them drive off. Meir was cheerful. His depressions didn't last long. Driving with the police, he felt glad that after two thousand years of exile at the mercy of the gentiles, in Israel the policemen were Jewish.

The jackass was still in the shop of the blacksmith. But when the Israeli police started asking questions, the blacksmith forgot all his Hebrew. He told the police that he had never met Meir in his life.

"He's afraid to tell the truth," Meir said. "He's afraid of what they'll do to him. That's the jackass, right there."

"I've had that jackass for years," the blacksmith

countered.

The police didn't know whom to believe. On the one hand, they knew that the Arabs couldn't be trusted. But on the other hand, they believed that religious settlers like Meir were fanatics and threats to the status quo. One thing was certain. The jackass himself wasn't talking. Because they had no real evidence against Meir, they were forced to let him go.

An edgy Meir returned to Shoshana to find a crowd of newspaper and television reporters outside his caravan, interviewing Johnny. Cameramen were taking photographs of the garden and scouting the grounds of the settlement as if to uncover the carcass of the infamous beast.

"Why did you kill it?" a reporter asked Meir.

"Is it buried nearby?" another wanted to know.

"What right do you have to live in Hevron?" a woman asked in English.

Photographers snapped pictures. Microphones were pushed in his face. A television camera from ABC News in America was pointed at him like a gun.

Before Meir could answer, a hand grabbed his arm and dragged him away from the crowd. It was Johnny. As he pulled Meir into his caravan, Meir saw the great, bearded face of Caleb Cohen, the leader of the Hevron settlers, as he battled his way into the center of the microphones.

"This is a blood-libel," he boomed. "Not only against one innocent Jew. This is an attack against the Jewish people's right to live in the Land of Israel."

Word came that hundreds of Arabs were gathering in front of the Hevron police station, demanding the dismantlement of the Shoshana settlement. Not wanting to miss the action, the reporters scattered like roaches to their cars. For all of his supposed extremism, Caleb Cohen was right. It seemed that all the brewing tension of the Middle East had surfaced in Meir's backyard.

The charismatic leader strode into the caravan followed

by another half-dozen settlers. They converged around the dining-room table. Cohen immediately grabbed the telephone, calling for an on-the-spot meeting of the Hevron Settlement Council

Silently, Meir's wife set glasses, juice, and cake on the table. Settlers kept arriving, piling into the caravan until the walls seem to bulge. After a heated discussion, two emergency resolutions were passed. The settlers in the caravan would refuse to surrender Meir to the police, and that very night, a group of families would be sent to occupy abandoned apartments in the heart of the Arab Casba.

The command room in the *Avraham Avinu* settlement down the hill called on the radio. The Arabs were rioting at the police station. Thousands of them. The army was battling the crowd with tear gas and rubber bullets. The scattering Arabs had regrouped and were headed up the hill to Shoshana. Sure enough, a convoy of army command cars and jeeps were now arriving outside. Dozens of Israeli soldiers jumped off the vehicles to form a protective barricade around the small enclave.

Johnny burst into the caravan. "The Apaches are coming from all directions," he said.

Outside the window, Meir could see the Arabs swarming up the hill. A barrage of tear gas caused them to run.

"Not only that," Johnny continued in his excited, broken Hebrew. "I just got a call from America. My parents saw me just now on TV."

There was a knock on the caravan door. It was the Hevron army commander calling for Meir. He had orders to take him to the police. Caleb Cohen opened the door and answered him angrily. Meir wouldn't be handed over until all Hevron Arabs living in former Jewish houses were expelled.

"It's for Meir's protection," the commander said. "For

the protection of all of you. If this protest gets bigger, I can't guarantee your safety."

"That's your problem," Cohen said and shut the door.

A great clatter shook the roof of the caravan. Dust swirled up from outside and for several seconds Shoshana was enveloped in a cloud. An army helicopter swooped down and landed by the children's playground, which had been donated to the settlement by a wealthy Mexican Jew. Another salvo of tear gas kept the second charge of Arabs at bay as the Israeli Minister of Defense jumped out of the chopper and ran to the caravan door. The settlers immediately let him inside.

The Defense Minister surveyed the twenty bearded faces in the caravan, smiled, and spoke straight to the point, like a general barking out orders to troops. The settlers all listened respectfully. After all, they were his soldiers too. They all served in the army and fought in their country's wars. To the settlers, the army was holy, a guardian of the Jewish people like the Torah itself.

"Meir has to turn himself in," the Defense Minister explained. "Only for questioning. Not to arrest him. Only to quiet the crowd outside and the brewing political storm."

"Question him here," Cohen insisted.

The Defense Minister smiled. He and Caleb were friends. Many times before they had come face-to-face, and a mutual respect had developed between them.

"I don't need to question him, Caleb," the Defense Minister said. "I just want it to look like we're doing something. Riots have broken out in East Jerusalem and two Arabs were killed. There are television cameras outside from all over the world."

"I'll go with him," Meir said, not wanting to be the cause of an international crisis. Not because he was afraid of the rioting Arabs outside. Rather, he didn't want the world to see Jews fighting Jews. And he knew that if he didn't go peacefully, the army would have to take him and the caravan of settlers by force.

"It's not your decision," Cohen said. "Today it's you; tomorrow, it will be someone else. This is directed against all of us."

The vote which was taken resulted in a deadlock. Cohen glanced at the rabbi sitting in silence in the back of the room. Ultimately, they would agree to do what the Torah demanded.

"Meir is right," the scholar said. "It is better for Meir to go through the formality of questioning than to parade Israel's internal disputes before the gentile world."

While a nervous Sarah looked on, Meir walked outside with the Defense Minister. A press conference was convened on the spot. The smell of tear gas was suffocating. The Defense Minister coughed when he spoke.

"We are taking the suspect in for routine questioning," he said. "As to the legality of Jewish settlement in the area, an investigation is being conducted to determine if Shoshana is in line with stated government policy."

Meir was whisked away into the helicopter, up over his caravan and garden, up over the hills of Hevron, away from his teary-eyed wife. He stared out the aircraft's window at the clear blue-and-white Israeli skies, gazing at the biblical valleys and mountains he loved. They soared into a breathtaking view of Jerusalem as it must have looked to the angels. The helicopter set down by the Knesset, and from there, it was a short drive to the courtyard of the Russian Compound and Jerusalem's municipal jail.

That night in Hevron, four Jewish families moved into abandoned Casba flats that rich American Jews had purchased from Arabs willing to sell. At the United Nations in New York, the world bloc of Arab, European and third-world countries demanded Israel's immediate withdrawal from the occupied territories. When Israel's ambassador took the podium to respond, all but eleven nations walked out. It wasn't the first time it had happened to him.

"Israel will not give up Jewish territory for any jackass, no matter what language he speaks," the ambassador quipped to the near-empty hall.

Also that night, while Syrian troops were put on alert 5 kilometers from the Golan Heights border, the frightened Arab blacksmith gave the world-famous jackass a slap on the rump, and the beast hopped out of his shop. An hour later, sometime after midnight, the animal was back home at his feed trough, braying to be fed. The terrified owner awoke from his sleep, put on a robe, and ran outside. Quickly, he herded the jackass into its shed, grabbed a small hand axe, and WHACK, WHACK, he chopped at the creature's terrified head. The sound of the animal's bleating echoed from the shed. After six vicious blows, the beast still hadn't fallen. The perspiring Arab chopped again and again. Finally, the sturdy ass quivered and collapsed into the puddle of blood on the ground. Sweating feverishly, the Arab hacked his beast into pieces, and with the help of his wives, he buried the jackasses appendages and head in the shed.

The next morning, Meir had just finished praying in his jail cell when guards came to whisk him to court.

"The Defense Minister promised it was only for questioning," Meir protested.

"The Defense Minister is in charge of the army," a guard answered. "This is the Israeli police."

Meir's heart sank. The Israeli police was the strong-arm of the political left. The judge read out the three counts against him: destruction of private property; illegal settlement on government land; and plotting to blow up the Tomb of the Patriarchs in Hevron.

Meir gasped. The Tomb of the Patriarchs was the second holiest Jewish site in the world, next to the *Kotel*.

"You've got to be kidding," Meir said.

"If you choose to make a statement," the judge coldly said, "I will remind you that you have the right to be represented by council."

"No Jew in his right mind would blow up the Tomb of the Patriarch's," Meir said.

"No Jew in his right mind would live in Hevron," the judge answered.

"Abraham lived in Hevron," Meir said. "David lived there. Jews have always lived there."

"Would you care to show me their deed?"

"Yeah," Meir answered. "It's written in the Bible."

"It's also written in the Bible that snakes talk and that Jonah was swallowed by a whale. If you are convicted, my young friend, you can expect to sit in prison for the next seven to thirty years."

The judge smiled, stood up, and walked out of the room.

By the time Meir returned to the prison, several hundred settlers had gathered to cheer him as he emerged from the police van. Caleb Cohen pushed forward to meet him.

"Where's my wife?" Meir asked.

"She's staging a hunger strike outside the Knesset," Cohen said.

"They've charged me with plotting to blow up the Cave of the Patriarchs," Meir told him.

"That's a new one," Caleb answered. "You've got to give them credit for that."

A guard tugged on Meir's arm. Johnny appeared at Meir's side.

"Don't let them break you," he said. "Remember, they sent the *Alter Rebbe* to prison on trumped up charges too."

"That was Russia," Meir said.

A jab in the back propelled him back into the fenced courtyard.

In Tel Aviv, at the same moment that the settlers were demonstrating outside the Jerusalem prison, the Peace Now Movement had joined with the Society for the Prevention of Cruelty to Animals to stage a demonstration of their own. People shouted peace slogans and waved signs reading "Settlers out of the West Bank," "Jewish People Love Animals," "G-d Created Jackasses Too."

Far across the ocean, the UN Security Council passed a resolution condemning Israel and demanding immediate withdrawal from the territories. The United States refrained from using its powerful veto. In Israel and throughout the world, pressure was mounting against the religious Jews who had returned to build communities in the cities and plains of their forefathers. For, as the rabbi of Hevron explained to Meir in prison, the wrath of the nations and of the protesters in Tel Aviv was not directed against the jackass's murder, nor even against the Jewish settlements that dotted the West Bank like pinheads on a map. Their anger was directed against the settlers' claim to their past, which the return to Hevron and Jerusalem and to Shilo made all too disturbingly real. For if the Jewish people's claim to the Land of Israel were true, in the way the settlers claimed, not based on mere historical ties to the land, but on G-d's love for his Chosen People – if that claim was right, then Christianity, and Islam, and Buddhism, and Socialism and Capitalism were all wrong – and that was a proposition that the world was not yet prepared to accept.

At the Prime Minister's office, a telephone call from the United States President had convinced the Israeli leader that strong action was needed against the settlers to pacify the enemies of the isolated Jewish state. The Israeli cabinet had met, debated, quarreled, and voted, and army bulldozers were already on their way. Racing to beat them was a convoy of buses filled with settlers heading for the showdown in Shoshana. But in their hearts, everyone already knew that the settlers wouldn't fight the army. They were, perhaps more than anyone else, patriots to the end. They would be dragged out from caravans by their arms and pulled down from caravan roofs by their legs, but not one settler would raise a hand to strike his fellow Jew.

In his jail cell, Meir prayed that G-d would watch over Shoshana and save his cherished caravan from being squashed like a soda can under the wheels of a huge army bulldozer. All he could do now was pray. What would be, would be. If necessary, he would build a new settlement. He would begin a new garden. He would plant new roses.

In Hevron, the scene wasn't pretty, but all was not lost. Before the army could close off the roads, several hundred determined Jews gathered in Shoshana for the stand-off. Barricading themselves inside the caravans and chaining themselves to fences and pipes, they refused to surrender. Israeli policemen and soldiers surrounded the embattled *givah*. The Hevron army commander ordered the settlers to evacuate the area immediately. Otherwise, they would be thrown out by force. The settlers refused. For hours, the tense stalemate prevailed. The Prime Minister hesitated giving the order. What Israeli politician wanted to throw Jews out of their homes in Israel? That's what the gentiles had done to the Jews for thousands of years. But in the face of Arab rioting all over the country and fierce international pressure, the order finally came. Soldiers rushed forward to evict the settlers. Special women soldiers were sent in to drag out the wives and young girls. Settlers were dragged and carried and pulled down from roofs. No one fought. No one hit a soldier. Still, it took close to two hours to haul away all of the passive resisters.

Finally, only one settler remained. Calev Cohen. He was holed up alone in a caravan that no soldier dared to approach.

"I've got a bomb with fifty kilograms of TNT strapped to my waist!" he announced from the caravan window. "If anyone tries to force me to leave, the bomb goes off."

The area was immediately cordoned off.

"I want a radius of thirty meters on every side!" the army commander called out through a megaphone.

Settlers and soldiers alike were herded a safe distance away. Photographers and TV cameramen sought vantage points further up the hill. The Prime Minister was alerted. On television sets all over the world, viewers held their breaths.

In truth, Calev Cohen didn't have a bomb on him at all. He was stalling for time, that was all. In Jerusalem, activists were trying to get a court order that would stop the evacuation. And Johnny, the imaginative American, had asked Cohen to give him a few hours to see what he could do.

"This is the land of the Jews!" the settler leader screamed out at the army commander when he tried to persuade him to come out.

"What are you going to prove by blowing yourself up?" the commander called out. "This isn't Masada."

"The Romans chased the Jews out of Masada," Cohen yelled back. "And now *Tzahal* is continuing their work. The shame!"

When word came that the high court had refused to hear the anti-evacuation petition, even the most ardent settlers seemed crestfallen.

"The only true law is the Torah!" Cohen called out in response. "And G-d gave this land to the Jews!"

When the Defense Minister arrived and tried to personally convince Cohen to surrender, the stubborn settler yelled out, "You'll go down in history as a traitor to *Am Yisrael!*"

The stand-off continued all through the night. That was enough for G-d to hear Meir's prayers. Just after dawn,

when weary-eyed soldiers and settlers alike were sipping
on hot cups of coffee, the owner of the jackass trudged up
the hill, pushing a wheelbarrow. Johnny followed behind
him. Cameramen hurried forward. In the wheelbarrow was
the jackass's head. Its eye was still open, as if it too wanted
to see what would happen.

"I killed the jackass," the Arab confessed.

The army commander stared at him dumbfounded.

A cheer went up from the settlers. They all rushed the
givah. Soldiers stood watching, waiting for an order that
never came. The families of Shoshana returned to their
homes. Calev Cohen emerged from his caravan, wrapped
in *tallit* and *tefillin*. Settlers lifted him onto their shoulders.
In Shoshana, the Jews had light and gladness and joy and
honor.

"How did you do it?" Meir asked Johnny when he
returned home to the caravan that he loved.

"I made the Arab an offer he couldn't refuse," the
former American answered, using a line from a popular
Mafia movie.

"What kind of offer?" Meir was curious to know.

"I showed him my M-16 and told him that either his
head or the head of the jackass was going to be in the
wheelbarrow. So he picked up his skirt, ran to the shed,
and dug the beast up. You have to know how to talk to
these people, that's all."

Out of embarrassment, and out of a fear for his life, the
Arab ran away from the city of Hevron. Years later, Meir
moved to Gush Katif to build hothouses for his roses.
Meir's innovations in horticulture won him worldwide
success. His roses were exported all over the globe. And
as fortune would have it, the down-and-out owner of the
jackass showed up one day looking for work. Meir was
never one to hold grudges. He was happy to give the Arab
a job. Johnny was right – you just had to know how to talk
to them.

THE GREAT AMERICAN NOVELIST

This is a story about the Great American Novelist, Ephraim Lane. For readers who like their work made easy, the whole story is a metaphor, like the *Book of Hosea*, for the Jewish people's wanderings in foreign pastures.

Ephraim Lane was born with the name Ephraim Lansky. In his youth, he was a voracious reader. By the time he was six, he could quote long passages from Hemingway, Faulkner, Fitzgerald, and Wolfe. When he was thirteen, he shocked his parents by refusing to have a *bar-mitzvah*. Judaism, he claimed, was lousy fiction. All human beings were chosen, he said. In the spirit of rebellion which was to characterize his future, he vowed to use his talents to erase all differences between gentiles and Jews.

Ephraim attended an elite boarding school in New England. He partied through four years at Harvard, and fought valiantly in the Marines. His first novel about the Second World War, written in his young twenties, and published under the more American-sounding E. Lane, was an explosive worldwide bestseller. The passionate account of manhood, trial, and fear was not just another copy of Hemingway, like so many books of the time, but the dawning of a brilliant new light.

His next piece of fiction was shorter and far more complex. The allegory about a society gone corrupt received good reviews but failed to attract an audience. Like the strong-hearted fighter he fancied himself, he pulled himself up from the canvas and published his third work, a literary satire of Jewish life in New York which put his impish grin on magazine covers all over the country. A try at a Hollywood screenplay, a loud bout of drinking, a publicized marriage and speedy divorce sent the young author back down to the mat.

The film of his screenplay flopped. A collection of short stories was practically ignored. Ironically, many years later, when Lansky became required reading in courses in American Literature, the collection was considered a classic. He wrote a fine, miniature novel about baseball, and an uninspired tale of a writer with a middle-age crisis. For years he seemed to be forgotten. At literary parties, he was invariably the center of some ugly, drunken brawl. Critics said what a shame. But Lansky surprised them all. With some great secret strength, he sat himself down at his typewriter and pounded out the bestselling book of the decade – a savage satire of a Jewish mother who destroys the lives of her children with guilt.

Throughout the summer, on beaches and subways, everyone was reading Lansky's book. More readers rushed out to buy it when the Jewish community called the writer a self-hating Jew. The paperback edition broke all records for sales. Lansky's second marriage to a curvy Swedish masseuse, four inches taller than he was, made all the society pages. All of his works were reprinted, and any article he wrote, whether on politics, women, space travel, or fishing netted him gold. In the very same year, he won the Book Critics Award, the Pulitzer Prize, had a child with his Swede, divorced her, moved in with a famous, black, soul singer, went through spring training with the Dodgers, starred for three weeks in an Off-Broadway play which he directed and wrote, had a small heart attack, and walked out of the hospital with his nurse.

In interviews, he talked about repentance and giving up marijuana and booze. He split up with his singer, bought a house up in Maine, and took the summer off to rest from his heart attack and relax with his much younger nurse. In September, he forwarded three-hundred manuscript pages and a note to his publisher, saying that he was thinking of scrapping the rest of the book. It was a powerful Kafkaesque intrigue, set in a Soviet prison, the story of a loyal party worker exiled for being a Jew. Even conservative critics had to take off their hats. "A metaphor of the soul imprisoned by a fantasy of hope and poetic despair," the *New York Times* critic called it. The Jewish community turned to embrace him. Prophetically, the plight of Soviet Jews became an international struggle. On the eve of his nomination for the Nobel Prize, E. Lane, born Lansky, stood in the doorway of his snowbound Maine cottage and announced his engagement to his housekeeping nurse. On the pinnacle of his great success, a *Newsweek* reporter braved his way through the snow to ask Lansky what he hoped to do now.

"Drink beer, watch TV, and have as many children as I can," the writer said with a laugh.

In short, in his forty-eighth year, the novelist became an American legend. Pictures, posters, and stories about him appeared everywhere. He was either loved or hated wherever he went. When his wife ran off with a rock star, Lansky bought an island off Tahiti and lived there without electricity or plumbing for months. Then suddenly, he abandoned the role of the hermit and came home to run as an independent candidate for the governorship of New York.

Perhaps his defeat, or his chain of busted romances, or the prospect of turning fifty was responsible for his change. Or perhaps all of the whiskey and night life were simply wearing him down. Whatever the reason, the seemingly indefatigable novelist sunk into a lasting depression. The occasional pieces he published, while still graced with genius, were flat. Instead of writing about the world, he wrote about himself. Even his most faithful readers grew tired with the subject. His publisher tried to release his old sellers in fancy new jackets, but the public wasn't fooled. Ephraim became forgotten like a racehorse laid out to stud. His fourth marriage to a Japanese poet passed without fanfare. The petite Oriental barely came up to his shoulders. "Ephraim Lane has finally found a woman with whom he can feel like a man," his first, or was it second, wife said. Their betrothal lasted a little under a year. In the meantime, two stinkers were published bearing his name, a fat novel about a South American revolution which substituted detail for depth, and another collection of essays, short stories, and solipsistic pieces which almost no one bought.

Lansky's career seemed to be over. But people forgot the old prizefighter inside, the crafty veteran lying on the ropes, blocking punches, waiting to catch his breath until he could score the big knockout. They forgot that to get to the diamond you had to bore through the coal. Ephraim hadn't thrown in the towel. True, he knew he was falling. He recognized that his talent wasn't the same. He lacked the quickness, the energy, and the stamina of his prime. Yet he kept on punching, unwilling to give up the electrifying roar of the ring.

That's when he decided to make a great comeback. First, he gave up the booze. And the drugs. And the women. He returned to his cottage in Maine. He hired a black man for a housekeeper, disconnected the telephone, and wrote. He wrote every morning until one. In the afternoon, he would nap and take a five mile jog. Evenings, he spent with his kids. A half a year later, he had given birth to a book. A fable of King Solomon. A Solomon who the world misunderstood. An irreverent, autobiographical portrait of the King as a man and a writer with a thousand wives and a passion to savour every experience under the sun. It was as one critic commented, "A portrait of the artist as a young man." Almost everyone loved it. Only feminists and rabbis complained. *The Secret Diaries of Solomon* became the only book ever banned by the American Congress of Rabbis. His life, they claimed, was a public campaign to annihilate the Jew in himself. Some questioned if his parents were Jewish at all.

Lansky took up the fight. "There is no G-d," he claimed. "The Jewish people are racists! I am ashamed of my Jewishness," he pronounced. "If I could grow back my foreskin, I would."

Another writer explained Lansky's new battle cry by noting, "The man has a genius for keeping himself in the press."

Thus, on the eve of his fiftieth birthday, Lansky embarked on his historic world mission: CAMPAIGN FOR PEACE – TO TAKE ISRAEL AWAY FROM THE JEWS.

His idea was unquestionably outrageous. Lansky's essay, published in *Esquire*, called for the transfer of the Jews of Israel to Alaska. There was, first of all, plenty of room, he maintained. Additionally, it would be a boom to the state's slumping economy, for if anyone could turn tundra to gold, it was the people who had caused the desert to bloom. "The Israelis are all heading for America anyway," he wrote. "We might as well stick them all up in Alaska where there is plenty of room for their taxis."

Most people took the magazine piece as a satire. A few nervous Eskimos protested. "Keep The Jews Out," their signs in Anchorage read. But what started as a joke seemed to snowball. A few respected Jewish intellectuals wrote articles of praise and support. Lansky's proposal, they claimed, deserved serious thought. Why only talk about giving up the West Bank? Perhaps the solution to the conflict lay in giving up all of the land. Why talk about transferring the Arabs? Transfer the Jews instead.

The White House issued a categorical no. But the Parliaments of both England and France discussed the issue in heated debates. Arabs in the U.N. demanded that the Security Council vote on the matter. Almost magically, Lansky's new tome appeared. His nonfiction fact-finder on Israel, *Obstacle To Peace*, became an overnight bestseller. Suddenly, the author was a Middle East analyst without ever having set foot in Tel Aviv.

"Why should I?" he said. "I can be just as good a Jew in New York without oppressing other peoples' rights."

Invitations arrived from the Vatican, the PLO, and the Peace Now Movement in Israel. Harvard awarded him with an honorary doctorate. And he would go on to win the Nobel Prize – not for Literature – but for Peace.

Lansky had risen to heights of which he himself hadn't dreamed. From a modest boyhood in Brooklyn to the whirlwinds of world news. And for some unknown reason, his destiny kept calling.

Once again, his photograph was printed in all of the papers. Ephraim Lansky on his knees, kissing the ring of the Pope. For a week, he had been a guest of the Vatican. He had sat with the celebrated Church father for hours, arguing over politics and religion, world history, and sex. When the Pontiff stepped out on his balcony to greet the cheering thousands, the Jewish writer was at his side.

"I love you," the novelist yelled out to the world. "I love all people! All of you are my brothers!"

The roar from the crowd was tremendous. The Pope leaned over and whispered, "Tell them you love *Yoshke*."

"I love *Yoshke*!" Lansky yelled.

The crowd's reaction was deafening. Their roar shook the foundations of Rome. On television screens all over America, the Jewish writer could be seen yelling, "I love *Yoshke*," again and again. A week later, he was baptized. In the Jordan River, on the Jordanian side of the border. The

Pope and the King of Jordan were present, along with hundreds of cardinals and bishops and journalists from all over the world. Jordanian soldiers surrounded the area, and Soviet anti-aircraft missiles were poised in alert. Westward, across the scorched valley, atop a Judean mountain, an Israeli sharpshooter had the novelist square in his sights. The silver-haired Lansky was dunked, and a new savior was born. Draped in a white robe, with water dripping from his head, he came up from the Jordan like a pot-bellied prizefighter emerging from the ring.

"Will you be continuing to Israel on your mission of peace?" a journalist asked him.

"Not in this direction," he said, pointing across the valley. "Not over illegally occupied land. If the Israelis are ready to meet me, it will be in New York."

The Pope hung a crucifix over Lansky's neck and kissed him on both of his cheeks. The Jordanian King shook his hand. The peacemaker flew back to Rome with the Pope. "I just want to be a simple monk," he told reporters. Thus began a surprisingly long seclusion. For the writer, the monastery was truly a godsend. Like his winter in Maine, it was a chance to get away from the whiskey and women. In five short months of seclusion, Lansky finished his seventeenth book.

He had enjoyed writing by candlelight in the small, spartan room. He had truly worked hard, writing day after day, with only a break now and then to drive into Rome to spend a night on the town. His last chapter was nearing completion when there came a knock on his door. Brother John had arrived with a message. The writer's agent had phoned from America. Ephraim's mother was dying, and she wanted her only child to come.

Lansky took off his brown monk's frock and sash, and changed into a suit. Carrying a briefcase with his manuscript inside, he boarded the first plane to New York. He phoned the Miami hospital when he landed and learned that his mother was still fighting for her life. Another jet took him south. At the airport, a limousine was waiting. When he finally got to the hospital, the shriveled, old woman was still breathing on her own. He set his briefcase on the floor and leaned over the bed.

"Momma," he said.

She opened her cataract eyes. "Come closer," she whispered.

Ephraim bent down over the once strong woman, now a mere wisp in her hospital gown. With her last remaining strength, she raised herself up on her elbows. Her throat rattled and she spit straight into his face – all of the saliva which she had been saving for days.

"*Shagetz*," she said.

Then her strength gave out and she collapsed dead on the bed.

Lansky's autobiographical, *Born Again* was his biggest bestseller ever. The rabbis put him in *herem*, excommunicating him from the Jews. Lansky said he didn't care. Not about the condemnation, and not about his success. He felt exhausted and horribly depressed. He felt soiled, as if, no matter how hard he scrubbed, the spit of his mother wouldn't come off.

The author felt empty inside. What more was there to accomplish in life? Vanity of vanities, all is vanity. What did it all come to? Interviews and photographs, money and fame. And the truth was that Solomon had written it with far more style and grace.

He began to suffer from blackouts. His sleep was disrupted with nightmares like newsreels from his past. He went to a neurologist, an astrologist, and a shrink. He went to clear out his mother's apartment and found himself moving in. He hid from the world in the penthouse condominium overlooking Miami Beach. Day after day, he searched through the closets and drawers, hoping to find the piece of his life that was missing. For weeks he didn't pick up a pen. He had nothing to write. Nothing to say. He felt impotent. Finished.

The gun shop didn't open until eleven. He paid the taxi driver and walked around the block. Cubans hung out on doorsteps. There was a smell of sweet rice in the air. Like Hemingway, he had decided to blow out his brains.

He took the shotgun back to the apartment. Even his death would be a poor copy of a writer far greater than he.

"I lived, and I died, and my whole life I lied," he started to scribble.

He took the shotgun to bed with him, but he couldn't pull the trigger. For the first time in his life, he was scared. He rode the elevator down to the lobby and walked out to the beach. The night was black. Waves rumbled and roared onto shore. Even Virginia Woolf, a woman, was braver than he was, he thought, as he gazed out at the mocking sea. His belly screamed for a drink. Hours later, the telephone kept ringing and ringing. He awoke in a stupor.

"You've won the Nobel Prize," his agent said from New York.

"For literature?" the writer asked.

"No," came the reply. "For peace."

Lansky accepted the award dressed in black tails. The King of Sweden placed the medal in his hand. The two men had more than the medal in common. The King had married the writer's second wife. The auditorium was packed to the rafters. Eletronic flashes twinkled like stars. The prize winner stood at the podium and waited for the murmur to end. A hush fell over the hall.

"Your majesty," he began. "Distinguished panelists, guests, friends, and family. Brothers the world over. I am truly sorry, but I cannot accept this award."

A sound of surprise filled the hall.

"I cannot accept a prize for peace when there is none. Today, as I speak, the fighting continues between Arab and Jew, between Irish Catholic and Protestant, between white people and black. I cannot accept a prize for peace when my own heart is filled with a lust for war. A war against hatred. A war versus oppression. A war combatting racism, military occupation and the exploitation of the downtrodden and poor. To earn this prize for peace, one must first have ended war. Ladies and gentlemen, the battle lays waiting before us. The battle has not yet begun. Let us wage war together so that one day we can all live in love."

The applause was unending. Lansky returned the medal to the Swedish monarch, winked at his wife, and walked off the stage. He pushed his way past reporters, claiming, "I have nothing more to say." By the following morning, the whole world had heard how the writer had rejected the prize.

Overnight, the Jew who had turned his back on his people became the world's symbol of peace. Interviews wearied his days. What did he think about the conflict in Ecuador, Belfast, and Afghanistan? In truth, he didn't think about them at all. But he made up winded answers. Politics was all a big sham – what did it matter what he said?

All of the speeches soon bored him. The honorary doctorates held no appeal. The partying wasted his strength. His eyesight was waning, sleep came in spurts, he often passed gas at inopportune moments, and he was unable to write a full page without tiring.

So when Arafat phoned, he was ready.

"I understand we have things in common," the terrorist said.

"What's that?" the writer asked.

"We're both not schoolboys anymore."

"That's true."

"And I'm writing a book," the Arab confided.

"Get a good agent," Lanksy advised.

"Perhaps you could help me?"

"Perhaps," the boxer in Lansky answered as if the two men were sparring.

"We have something else in common," Arafat said.

"What could that be?"

"We both hate the Jews," the terrorist added.

The blow hit below the belt. "I don't hate Jews," Lansky answered.

"That's right," Arafat replied. "Neither do I. But nevertheless, my people must be freed."

"All people must be freed," the peacenik agreed.

The terrorist invited him to Gaza. With his incomparable showmanship, Lansky called a press conference and announced that he was flying to the Middle East to join Arafat in his struggle to liberate Palestine. The Israeli agent who was posing as a photographer could have assassinated him with no trouble, but the order never came. So Ephraim flew off to Gaza. A long black limousine was waiting out on the runway when he stepped off the plane. Four razor-thin Arabs toting machine guns escorted him into the car. Immediately, he was frisked and blindfolded. His protests were greeted with silence. Finally, one of them said, "We are not going to hurt you, so you can shut up. But remember, to us, this isn't a game."

Lansky felt frightened. It was true. His own life had become one big charade. He had forgotten that other people still took their lives seriously. Seriously enough to kill or be killed for it. So he sat quietly for the rest of the ride. The blindfold wasn't removed until he was sitting in somebody's living room. It was a westernized home with a big color TV. Bodyguards still surrounded him. They stood tensely waiting, as if Israeli agents might burst in at any moment. Finally, Arafat came into the room.

The PLO chief had been right when he said that they had some things in common. Both men were plump, aging fighters with a demonic gleam in the eyes that loved a good brawl. They were both superb actors, ratings survivors in a world which transformed news into show biz.

"You must be very hungry," the terrorist said. "Allow me to introduce you to an Arab tradition – Middle Eastern hospitality."

Lansky smiled. He didn't mention that it was a tradition that Ishmael had learned from Abraham the Jew. The spicy meal had been prepared in advance. Arafat sipped tea. The writer drank wine. The old grandmother who brought in the food was the only woman Lansky had seen since he had descended from the plane.

"How do you like Gaza?" Arafat politely asked.

"I wouldn't know. I haven't seen it yet."

"I apologize for the blindfold. Security concerns warrant our caution."

"Security against what?"

"Against you. I really don't know you, do I? Perhaps this is just another one of your games. Perhaps you are working for Israel."

"Or perhaps I'm serious," the writer said.

"Perhaps. We shall find out. Why did you come? Tell me."

"Why did you invite me?"

"That's true. I did. I thought that maybe you truly believed in our struggle."

"I do."

"I am prepared to kill Jews for our struggle. Are you?"

Lansky paused. He smiled. "Is this lemon chicken?" he asked. Arafat nodded. Lansky left the question unanswered. Calmly, he sipped on his wine.

"While killing is an inescapable component of history, I have come, in my later years, to appreciate the value of peace."

"Have you come here to persuade me to make peace with the Zionists?"

"No."

"Then why did you come? For the publicity? To write another book?"

"I don't need publicity, and I'm weary of writing books."

"Why then?" the Arab asked.

Lansky stared back at the beady eyes, the scruffy beard, the dirty-looking face, and kefiah which had become a symbol of terror and hate.

"To prove to the world that there is a Jew who is ready to say that his people are wrong."

Arafat smiled. He leaned closer to Lansky as if he wanted to whisper something which he didn't want his attendants to hear. Lansky bent closer. With a smile, the Arab spit in his face.

A lot of spit. Thick with the juice of the chicken which he had been eating. The Jew felt like choking. The image of his dying mother flashed through his brain. He picked up a napkin and wiped off his face. The stink made him feel sick. He was trembling.

"You didn't invite me all of the way here just to spit in my face," he said, summoning all of his self-control.

"Yes I did," the Arab replied. "And to tell you that you are a lying, whoring, pig."

Lansky stood up from his chair. "Then there's nothing further to say," he said.

Laughing, Arafat rose. The bodyguards laughed with him. That was the moment. Lansky lunged forward and punched Arafat square in the chin. It was a crunching right hand that sent Arafat spinning. The speed of the blow caught the Palestinian leader completely off guard. He toppled back over his chair and thudded to the floor. The bodyguards were stunned. Seconds passed before they pounced on the Jew. Arms pinned him to the wall. Fists landed in his belly. Only when Arafat yelled out in Arabic did they reluctantly let go. Their dizzy leader wobbled to his feet. He held onto his chair for balance. Then he smiled and laughed.

The punch seemed to have won Arafat's trust. From that moment on, there were no more tests. Lansky was adopted into the fold. He sat in on their meetings, trained with their soldiers, and was constantly photographed at Arafat's side.

In Lansky's spare time he wrote a short text which he titled, "On Revolution." Revolution, he wrote, was the harbinger of all progress and change. Though there was no direct mention of the Arab-Israeli conflict, in a chapter on the virtues of terrorism, Yasir Arafat was listed with Yehuda the Maccabee, Robin Hood, and George Washington.

Most of his time, Lansky devoted to training. He spent two weeks on the sand dunes of Gaza, running and shooting and hurling grenades. After that, he was transported via Syria to Lebanon, where he hung out with the Hizballah. Whatever suspicions the Arabs had about the fat old Jew in their unit disappeared when he jumped off a mountain peak on his first hang-glider flight.

Lansky barely had strength for the rigorous routine of guerilla training, but he was determined to persevere. He stayed away from the Arab women as he had been warned. Several months passed. When Lansky told Arafat that he wanted to take part in an action, he balked.

"You are more important to us as a writer," Arafat said.

Lansky insisted he wanted to fight. To play a real part in the struggle. To martyr himself if he had to. To show people that he was ready to die in the battle for peace.

"Do you really hate the Zionists so much?" the terrorist ask.

"No," Lansky answered. "How can you? You have to admire them. Throughout history, people have tried to slaughter the Jews and they're still around. And truthfully, to put my life on the line for justice, I can't say that I'm ready. Who really knows what's just in this world? I've lived a good life. I've done everything one man can do. But now I want to take the fight to the end, to face the only real truth a man ever can – his own truth – to stand face to face with death and not be afraid."

The Arab didn't comprehend a word that Lansky said, but he decided to go ahead and use the stupid Jew in a dangerous suicide mission. It was a strike inside Israel that the PLO had been planning for years. Seven terrorists were to infiltrate Israel. They were to rendezvous and travel south in a truck transporting vegetables to the Beer Sheva market. Once in the city, they would drive to the university campus and open fire with machine guns and grenades. Lansky was chosen to be one of the team.

The letter he wrote on the eve of the mission wasn't one of his best. The style was confusing, wordy, and abstract. Israel, the symbol of justice and truth, had failed, he insisted. Good had become evil, and evil had turned into good.

It was a two kilometer hang-glider flight from the South Lebanese mountains to Israel. On a dark moonless evening, Ephraim Lansky soared upon eagle's wings to the Holy Land, just like the prophets had promised. Like a biblical vision, he soared from the north until he embraced the cherished soil. His landing was perfect with hardly a scratch. A short scurry through the valley brought him to the truck which would carry him south. Armed with an Uzi and hand grenades, the writer turned terrorist set off on the mission.

The rest of the story is history. Lansky's picture made every front page in the world. "WRITER FOILS TERROR ATTACK!" the *New York Times* headline read. On the outskirts of Beer Sheva, an anti-terrorist squadron was waiting to meet the truck. Lansky jumped off seconds before the fireworks started. One RPG missile sent the truck up in flames. All six of the terrorists were killed in the blast. Only the writer escaped. Lansky, the double agent – Israel's secret spy. Overnight he was a hero to Jews the world over. Even rabbis took off their hats. And every other writer was stunned. Lansky had created a new form to the art. Life writing, he called it. His book, *Double Cross*, appeared in print within two months. Told with his old genius for action, it was the day-to-day diary of his PLO adventure. The dedication read: For My Mother.

The Prime Minister of Israel and the Minister of Defense sat at his side at the press conference.

"Like the history of our people," Lansky said, "I have wandered. Through strange and foreign pastures, I have strayed. But now, like the people of Israel, I have come back to my homeland, to stay."

He refused to say more. He was sneaking up on sixty. His back hurt from the leap off the truck. Hemorrhoids too long ignored were taking revenge. All he wanted was to see a doctor and rest. Israeli warplanes struck at Hizballah bases in Lebanon. Arafat's headquarter's were bombed but the terrorist leader escaped. The next day, wearing a bandage under his kefiah, he called the Jewish writer a dead man. The Mayor of Jerusalem gave Lansky the keys to the city, and the Israeli Police gave him around the clock guards.

Ephraim Lansky had become a Jewish legend. But like all other heroes, Lansky had a flaw. After only a month of retirement and the life of a simple Jew, he grew tired of the daily trips to the neighborhood grocery, cups of black coffee at sidewalk cafes, and the razor-thin *International Herald Tribune*. For the first time since the Beer Sheva ambush, he agreed to a public appearance, the dedication of a new Humanities Building at Hebrew University. Receiving an honorary doctorate, he announced the creation of a scholarship fund in the name and memory of his mother.

During his speech, the girl was sitting in the front row of the audience. At the crowded cocktail party, she appeared at his side. The writer naturally assumed she was Jewish. It never entered his mind that she could be a young Arab co-ed. She said she was a literature major and they spoke briefly about books. Later that evening, when he arrived at his Jerusalem hotel, he lingered some moments in the lobby. Almost instantly, she walked in the door. Gallantly, he invited her up to his room to give her an autographed copy of his latest bestseller. It happened so fast, he was helpless. With a swift, practiced movement, she opened her purse and slid out what looked like a nail file.

"Greetings from Yasir," she whispered.

With a powerful thrust, she imbedded the knife in his stomach. In the reflection of the mirror, he saw his own murder.

"A film to the end," he thought, watching himself fall to the floor.

His knees went weak, like a fighter caught off guard with an uppercut to the belly. Hitting the canvas, he felt his heart explode.

The girl felt sure he was dead. Leaving the blade in his body, she panicked and fled. On a hunch, the lobby guard detained her downstairs. The hotel security agent found Lansky bleeding to death in the elevator on the seventeenth floor. Bending over the unconscious writer, he pounded furiously on his motionless chest.

Meanwhile, in the Sam Goldman Wing of the Hadassah Hospital, in the Ray and Sandra Shapiro Operating Room, a man critically wounded in a car accident was pronounced brain dead on the table. When word came that an ambulance was on its way, the deceased was kept artificially breathing. In the ambulance, the old fighter seemed to be out for the count. Someone kept pounding him on the chest, and someone kept breathing air in his mouth, but his ticker had stopped, and the prize-winning brain was composing its epitaph. After an hour of surgery patching up his wound, the battery of surgeons in the Betty Freidman Transplant Theater debated if there was any point in trying the difficult transplant. Ephraim's soul had left his moribund body. It was hovering up by the ceiling, screaming at the doctors below.

"Keep working, you jerks!" it yelled. "Keep working! Don't give up now!"

Lansky was damned if a skinny Arab girl would get the credit for doing him in.

"Put in the new heart!" he shouted, but the doctor's paid no attention.

Lansky had to admit, for a guy that had experienced everything in life, this was a novel sensation. On the operating table, with his chest split apart like a melon, his soul had flown out of his body. At first, the reporter in him had watched in fascination. He saw and heard everything which was going on the room, yet he was no longer attached to the world. A lifeless, overweight, white-haired old man lay on the operating table below, while his thoughts floated in space by the ceiling. But when the ceiling disappeared and he felt something grab him, pulling him into the heavens away from the earth, Ephraim felt scared. Seeing his mother, he cried out for help. But she didn't answer. In the distance, he saw a great light like a fire, more glowing than millions of stars. In the brilliant reflection, all the sin of his life filled up his being with a horrible darkness. He tried to put on the brakes and turn back before he plunged into the flaming abyss, but there was nothing to hold onto.

"*Shema Yisrael,*" he cried out. "*Hear O Israel, the L-rd is our G-d, the L-rd is One!*"

It was too late. A gigantic book hurtled his way from out of the heavens. It was a tome carved in marble, like a tombstone, engraved with all the misdeeds of his life. It would crush him, smash him, obliterate him the moment it struck. The collision seemed inevitable, inescapable, imminently real.

"Oh G-d, I'm so sorry," the doomed novelist moaned.

Suddenly, he felt a searing pain in his heart, an excruciating tug, a torturous shock to his being. An oxygen mask squelched his terrified scream. From out of the heavens, he heard an echoing refrain: *"A new heart I will give you... a new heart... a new heart."* With a tremendous whoosh, his soul flew back to his body.

"Adrenalin!" a surgeon commanded.

A team of surgeons stood around him, masked and wearing gloves. He watched as hands raised his heart in the air and flopped it down in a pan. A respiratory machine kept him breathing. On the operating table beside him lay a dead man. A Jew with a beard. He was looking at Lansky and smiling. Hands lifted his still-beating heart out of his chest. Blood splattered on Lansky's face, but he didn't feel the drops.

When the writer opened his eyes after the marathon operation, the first thing he saw was a woman. She was matronly with a *shetel*, like photographs of Lansky's great grandmother. Her face was kind and ascetic.

"Oh no," Lansky thought. "She's the guy's wife."

She sat praying by his bedside for hours. Her husband had been a *Chabadnik* who wanted to do *mitzvahs* down to the last. After the week of *shiva*, she returned straight to the hospital. The reborn writer glanced groggily down at the angelic young boy at her side.

"This is David," she said in simple English. "The others are at home."

"Who is taking care of them?" Lansky asked.

"My sister."

"How many are there?"

"Eight," she answered.

He had eight too. From five or six different wives. That made a family of eighteen.

"I know my husband would want you to have this," she

said, leaving his *tallis*, *tefillin*, and prayerbook on Lansky's bedside table.

He thanked her. What more could he say? What was a heart worth? A hundred-thousand bucks? A million? He'd send her a check when he recovered.

If he recovered. The doctors said they couldn't be sure. It would take some time to determine if his body accepted the foreign organ.

At first it was frightening, living with another man's heart. Often, the former loud and boisterous showman was afraid to open his mouth to speak, lest the smallest exertion cause his aorta to explode. Maybe his change of heart was due to the new heart he had received from the Hasid. Or maybe it was due to his encounter with death. Whatever the cause, something had changed him. The world famous egotist became quiet, humble, and meek. When they brought him his first real meal of food, he asked, "Is it kosher?" He asked the hospital rabbi to teach him how to put on *tefillin*. And he sent a message to the Hasid's widow, wondering if they had a spare Bible.

A young teenage lad brought Lansky a Bible that very day. It was the Old Testament, translated into English, with a commentary explaining the text. Putting a *kippah* on his head, the writer picked up the world's all-time bestseller. He spent hours engrossed in the Biblical drama which he had never bothered to read. But somehow, he felt disappointed, and he didn't know why. Then he realized. He had hoped that the wife of the Hasid would bring the book herself. Strange, but he missed her. He remembered her soft smile and warmth. She was nothing like all the other women he had known, but he found himself dreaming about her all the same.

When he was allowed out of bed, he sought out the hospital synagogue and sat reading Psalms. He felt an inner need to make peace with G-d. To thank Him for the life he had received. And to make amends for all of his past.

He knew he was recovering when his urge to write returned. At first, he wrote letters to the woman. She visited when she could, but with so many children at home, it was hard to get away. When he asked her to marry him, she blushed like a girl. He told her that he wanted to study the Torah. To sit in a yeshiva and learn. She was glad, she told him, but she also wanted him to continue to write. G-d wanted him to use his talent, she said.

His first book, *Back To Life*, outsold them all. Interviews interfered with his Torah studies, but his new wife encouraged him to talk. Everyone had a mission, she said. And his mission was to bring people closer to G-d.

His second book, *The Transplanted Jew*, was a history of the Jewish people, told with the author's inimitable flair. For a work of nonfiction, it had a respectable sale, though it was by no means a runaway hit. His next book, *The Jewish Heart*, a serious scholarly text, didn't even make the bestselling chart.

Lansky didn't care. He was happy. He was content to learn a page of *Talmud* in the morning, nap in the early afternoon, write for a spell before dinner, and spend the evening with his wife and eight kids. Seeing the bearded, skullcapped Hasid, no one would have recognized him from the past. Visitors to Jerusalem who saw the devout figure walking through the Old City on his way to the *Kotel* and nightly midnight prayer would never had guessed that he was none other than the flamboyant, hell-raising writer.

Ephraim Lansky died seven years later. After his funeral on the Mount of Olives, his wife revealed that he had written another book, an autobiography. Published posthumously, *Life in The World To Come* became the bestselling book of the decade. The old fighter had done it again.

BUSINESS AS USUAL

For the Jewish people, things always get worse before they get better. The wise man understands that the downswing of the pendulum is a sign that the upswing is coming. This is a simple law of nature. The darkest hour of the night comes just before the dawn. In the same manner, a high fever often precedes a cure. If this dialectic is so common, why do we forget the light at the end of the tunnel and succumb to despair? Because, when it comes to the Jewish People, the transformation from darkness to light can take two-thousand years.

The wise man knows that in the problem lies the solution. But this time, matters were completely out of hand.

Where was the rain? For more than a year, the heavens had been locked like a heavy steel door. Every day, eyes would gaze up to the sky. Winter had passed without a single cloud. Not even a drop of rain had fallen. Buckets had fallen over Egypt, Jordan, Damascus and Beirut, but the miracle of Israel had turned dry. Fertile fields reverted to desert. Crops withered before reaching market. The wealth of Israel's scientists couldn't figure it out. Wherever you traveled, you could see people stopped on the street, gazing up at the sky. When would it rain? The radio had ceased reporting the weather – it was always the same.

The Minister of Agriculture asked the Knesset to pass a law banning the public from watering their gardens. Immediately, the Society for the Beautification of Israel protested. Was the nation who had transformed the desert into a garden, to transform the garden back into a desert?

Did the Minister of Agriculture want to go down in history for that? Apparently not. He relinquished his proposal and ordered a comprehensive study instead.

It was another rainless day in Jerusalem when the Speaker of the Knesset read out the results of the Emergency Water Investigation. The massive study had cost the financially pressed government over 12 million *shekels*. The 1500 page report was the work of scientists, meteorologists, hydro-engineers, environmentalists, and a dozen Jewish Agency department heads. The hopes of the thirsty nation were focused on the Speaker of the Knesset as he set his reading glasses down on his nose. Speculation abounded. One plan proposed using a supertanker to bring a gigantic iceberg from the North Pole to Israel. Another plan recommended sending soldiers out all over the country with divining rods in order to discover underground wells. The Air Force was ready to do cloud-seeding, but there weren't any clouds to be seen from Mount Hermon to Eilat.

The report began with a long, dismal description of the crisis. After ten boring minutes, a Knesset member jumped to his feet and yelled out that the government didn't have to spend 12 million *shekels* to tell the parched country what every child knew. What was the report's conclusion, he demanded to know.

The Speaker waited for the chamber to grow quiet, then flipped to the end of the tome on his rostrum. "While many factors, including poor government planning, are responsible for the water emergency, the investigation committee has found that the greatest wastage of water in this country is caused by religious Jews through their practice of *netillat yadayim*."

A clamor erupted in the hall. In a rare display of unity, all of the religious Knesset members leaped to their feet in protest. "A blood libel!" a rabbi called out. The Speaker pounded his gravel. For a moment, order was restored.

The report continued, supporting its findings with mathematical proofs. To illustrate, two members of the Emergency Water Committee lifted a large, empty aquarium onto a table. Another committee member held up the type of *natlah* which religious Jews used to pour water over their hands. Demonstrating the procedure, he filled up the container with a liter of water and poured it out over his hands, back and forth three times until the *natlah* was empty. According to religious law, the ritual washing was mandatory upon awakening from sleep in the morning, before eating bread, after touching a normally covered part of the body, upon touching shoes, exiting the bathroom or shower, rising from a nap, leaving a cemetery, after a haircut or fingernail cutting, before prayer and after marital relations. With the mention of each activity, the committee member poured another bucket of water into the tank until it was filled. With three meals a day, three daily prayers, personal needs, napping, cemetery going and marital relations, the religious Jew averaged 15 hand washings a day. That was five times the daily hand washing of a secular Jew. Fifteen liters per day, times one million religious people, came to fifteen million liters of water per day. That amounted to four billion, 745 million liters of water per year.

There was silence in the Knesset as the sizable figure sunk in. Representatives of the Meretz party rose to their feet and began to cheer the report.

"We've said it all along!" one screamed out. "The religious are parasites! That's where all of our precious water is going! To Bnei Brak and Meah Shearim."

"What about you *goyim* washing your cars on the Sabbath?!" a long-bearded rabbi retorted. "What about all of those billions of liters to clean your stupid cars?"

Ushers and security guards had to interfere to keep the religious and non-religious apart. Above the uproar in the hall, the Knesset Speaker somehow managed to read out the recommendations of the report. All of the religious people in Israel would be compelled to wear plastic gloves, day and night, until the end of the drought. In this manner, they would be halachically exempt from the ritual of washing hands.

The Knesset Speaker raised his voice over the turmoil. "We call upon the religious members of the Knesset to put on the gloves that are being passed out to serve as an example to all of the nation."

"These gloves are worse than the yellow badge of the Nazis!" an *Agudah* rabbi yelled out. "I put forward a no-confidence vote in the government."

Another uproar burst out in the Knesset. The government depended on the support of the religious parties to preserve its slim majority. Amidst the fracas, the leader of the Sephardic party requested the Speaker's permission to read from another report. He held up a thick volume.

"It's called the Bible," he said.

He read a verse from the *Shema*.

"And it will be if you diligently obey My commandments which I command you this day to love the L-rd your G-d and to serve Him with your entire hearts and with your entire souls, that I will give rain for your land in its proper time, the early rain and the late rain, and you will harvest your grain and your wine and your oil. And I will put grass in your field for your cattle, and you will eat and be satisfied. Beware lest your hearts be swayed and you turn astray and worship alien gods and bow down to them. And the L-rd's fury will blaze among you, and He will close up the heavens, and there will be no rain, and the earth will not yield its produce."

The rabbi closed the Bible and said, "When the MK's from Meretz begin to keep the Torah, G-d will give us rain."

"Oh no," the leader of the secular Meretz party roared

back. "Rain is your department. That's why you've been getting *rebbe gelt* from the government all of these years, to keep the wrath of G-d at bay. It all goes to prove that all of your Torah study and prayer are worthless."

Objections were raised all over the hall. Suddenly, beards surrounded the Prime Minister. His government was in danger of falling. The pounding of the gavel could barely be heard over the screaming debate. Tempers flared. Knesset members started to shove one another. The *balagan* only subsided when word reached the assembly that a cloud had appeared over Jerusalem.

It was a small cloud – the kind of puffy white cumulus that kids are wont to draw. Meteorologists all said that it contained no rain, but for the drought-plagued country, it was a herald of hope. Everyone rushed out of the Knesset to cheer as the cloud sailed overhead on a gentle north wind. Traffic stopped all through the city as motorists rushed out of their cars to marvel at the unusual sight. Housewives hurried outdoors, and children ran out of schools to gaze up at the puff of heavenly cotton. Even the Arabs climbed up to their rooftops and cheered with great joy just as they had when missiles were falling on Tel Aviv. Work in the country stopped. Every head turned up toward heaven. Even on the lips of the staunchest communist there formed a silent non-sectarian prayer. On this day in history, the heart of the Jewish people was one.

Leisurely, as if it had all the time in the world, the cloud floated up north. A small El Al aircraft provided the nation with round-the-clock reports. Thousands of people followed the cloud by car up the Jordan Valley highway. Unexplainably, when the cloud reached the Kinneret, it stopped. Mysteriously, it hovered in the sky directly above the parched lake. The Chief Rabbi of Israel called for a national prayer. At noon the following day, everyone in the country was to say the same supplication.

Not to be left in the dust, the Knesset decided to join

the crowds heading north to the lake. A long line of air-conditioned Volvos drove up the *Biq'a* toward the Galilee. At the Zemach Junction, the throngs made way to let the politicians pass. Piles of dead fish, beer bottles, and Coke cans greeted them along the dry banks of the lake. Shofars were blown. Israel's famed Sephardi Kaballist gave the order and his followers began to parade around the depleted and shrunken sea. The Prime Minister put on a *kippah* and joined the procession in effort to protect his coalition. Knesset members followed in their cars. Everyone, even the outspoken leaders of the Meretz and the Arab parties joined the great march. The masses trekked behind them, seven times around the lake, *shofars* and trumpets blaring.

It seemed like everyone in the country was there. Roadways and hillsides were lined with hopeful faces, kibbutzniks and *haredim*, Russian *olim* and Jews from Ethiopia, old people and young. Come noontime, the roar of the nation's prayer was tremendous. The earth seemed to tremble. TV crews broadcast the religious happening live around the globe. When the first drops of rain started to fall, a cheer went up, not only in Israel, but in living rooms and bars throughout the world.

"It's raining!" a reporter cried, bursting into tears. "After nearly two years of drought in Israel, it is raining at the Sea of Galilee."

Soon, camera crews had to flee from the deluge. The puffy white cloud hovered over the lake and released an endless stream of rain. All day and night, the rain continued to fall. Scientist were speechless. In defiance of nature, the cloud hung over the lake without moving.

"It's amazing!" a BBC reporter declared. "People gathered on the surrounding hillsides, not more than fifty meters from the lake, are totally dry."

And so it continued. Tons of water poured down uninterrupted for days. It seemed that everyone in the country, religious and non-religious, came to see the incredible sight. Missionaries arrived from all over the world. There were Mormons from Utah, cardinals from Rome, Buddhists from Tibet, and Jews from America. The Christians said that *Yoshke* did it. The Arabs praised Allah. For a change, the non-religious in Israel were quiet. As the waters of the lake began to rise, the largest gathering of journalists that had ever covered a single event congregated along the banks of Tiberias. Falafel stands and kiosks sprouted up everywhere. Helium balloons shaped like the cloud were sold by the thousands. Pictures of the Kaballist rabbi appeared on T-shirts and postcards. Sworn atheists shelled out fifty *shekels* to purchase knitted *kippahs*. Umbrellas bearing the insignia of the Likud were handed out free to the crowd.

The downpour continued for forty days until the Kinneret overflooded its banks. Then, as suddenly as the rain had began, it stopped. The cloud rose up in the sky and vanished. Swimmers returned to the shores of the lake and boats once again sailed over its waters. The pilgrims who had come from all over the world folded and packed up their tents. Almost reluctantly, Israelis returned to their homes. Traffic backed up for kilometers as people rushed back to work. Horns blared, bumpers smashed, and drivers traded license numbers and punches. People forgot that only yesterday, they all had been friends. Almost overnight, life in the country returned to normal. Arabs went back to shooting Jews, the Meretz party introduced a bill in the Knesset to cut religious educational funding in half, and journalists flew off to report other world news. It was business as usual in Tel Aviv come *Shabbat*. Soon the only reminder of the great miracle was the gigantic cloud-shaped balloon which a Tiberias hotel owner filled with helium and suspended over the lake.

Sometimes it takes a drought. Other times it takes a war. The Kaballist rabbi said that the Almighty had many ways of uniting His people. Such is the path of redemption.

THE ENGAGEMENT

L istening to the lecture in the Yeshiva University classroom, Johnny's gaze was drawn almost mystically eastward. Across the street, a police car was stationed by the pizza parlor that anti-Semites had shot up two weeks before, slightly wounding two students. Over the drab brick buildings of Amsterdam Avenue, Johnny pictured the busy expressway leading out to Long Island where his engagement party was to be held that evening. As usual in his afternoon classes, the lecturer's voice grew dim in his ears. Magically, the New York cityscape vanished like a movie set that workers disassemble the day after filming is finished. Call it a daydream or a spark of something Divine, Johnny was back in the land of his forefathers, riding in an Egged bus on the road to Hevron. There, gazing out the bus window at the Biblical hillsides of Judea, he had realized that to be true to himself, he had to make Israel his home.

Remembering those two months in the Holy Land, Johnny felt the same shiver of love he had experienced on the bus. It was a shiver he had never felt with Linda, his fiance, the girl he was going to marry. What was it about vineyards and terraced hillsides that could affect someone in such a powerful way? It was something that words couldn't capture – the feeling that he had been there before, in a different lifetime, the feeling that he had found his way home. The land seemed to whisper, to call out, to sing with a voice of its own. Branches of olive trees seemed to be raised upward in prayer. Over these hillsides and down these same valleys, King David had strolled as a youth. Gazing out the bus window, Johnny felt that time had stood still. As if David was still grazing his sheep beyond the next orchard, around the next bend. The love that Johnny felt toward this land was beyond any doubt. Beyond any question. Not like his feelings towards Linda. Or towards New York. Or towards getting a Masters in Business. On that bus ride to Hevron, an unmistakable feeling of love had illuminated his being, creating him anew.

"More visions of King David today, Johnny?" the instructor of Talmud inquired. "Or perhaps I've interrupted you from building a new *yishuv* in Samaria?"

At first, Johnny didn't notice that the rabbi-professor was speaking to him. But then the laughter of fellow students shattered his revery, yanking him two-thousand years forward through time. With a cry of silent protest, his soul shrunk back into the oppressive four walls of a classroom in New York and his final month at Y.U.

"I'm sorry, sir," he said.

"Would you like to share your *tiyul* with us?" the teacher asked.

"No, sir," Johnny answered.

"Then would you care to summarize the argument that we have been discussing?"

Johnny looked around the room for the answer, as if it were scribbled on the forehead of one of his friends.

"I'm sorry, sir," he repeated.

"So am I," the instructor replied. "If you make a concerted effort to join us back here in America, you may still be able to pass this course and continue on toward a Masters Degree next year. Otherwise, you may find yourself in *Tzahal* faster than you think."

Once again, his classmates shared a good chuckle. A friend summarized the argument between Hillel and Shammai, two of the great rabbis of the Mishnaic era, even though neither had graduated from Y.U. The respected institution had been his home for four years – a place where a young Orthodox student could enjoy the best of both worlds, Judaism and America; *Shabbos* in *shul* and *Motzei Shabbos* on Broadway. Throughout his four years, Johnny had loved it. And Part II was just beginning – Columbia Business School, just a couple subway stops away. What he would lose in *Gemara*, he would gain in a leap up the ladder of corporate success.

"It isn't the end of the world," his realistic grandmother had noted. "Going to a *goyisha* school isn't such a terrible thing. After all, studying in Yeshiva doesn't put bread on the table."

When the afternoon class finally ended, Johnny hurried back to his dorm room and changed into his best Sabbath suit. Posters of Israel were scotchtaped to all of the walls. The engagement party was scheduled for eight o'clock that evening. Since his younger brother had smashed up his car, he had to catch a train out to Long Island. He had known his fiance, Linda, for years. They had practically grown up together in the same Great Neck community, attending the same *shul*, going to the same parties. Their parents were good friends. Johnny had never felt a great flame for the girl, but everyone said it was *birshert*, "a heavenly match." True, she was pretty, and her family was loaded, and she was crazy about him. But for his part, for someone who was getting married, he felt strangely unmoved.

"Love isn't like in the movies," his father said. "You have to work at it."

"If you don't love her now, you'll love her in time," his mother assured him.

As for his grandmother, she had a way with words that couldn't be beat. "Love, *shmov*," she said with a shrug. "Love doesn't put bread on the table."

Before he hopped into the subway heading downtown, he stopped into the now-famous pizza parlor to wolf down a slice.

"With olives, *nachon?*" the Israeli who owned the place asked.

"*Nachon*," Johnny answered.

Ever since he noticed that the owner used olives from Israel, Johnny had become hooked on pizza with olives.

"Going to a wedding?" the owner asked, commenting on Johnny's attire.

"I'm getting engaged," Johnny told him.

"*Mazel tov!*" the man said. "In that case, the olives are on the house!"

Sitting in the subway car, dressed in his Sabbath suit, Johnny started to squirm. Across the aisle, a row of Blacks, Hispanics, and Poles from the Bronx were all staring at him with cold looks of hate in their eyes. Ever since returning from Israel, Johnny made it a point to wear his *kippah* wherever he went, even on late-night subway rides back to Y.U. after seeing a film with Linda in the city. Opposite him, the train's passengers glared at him like attack dogs ready to pounce. The word "JEW!" seemed to flash in their pupils. Johnny realized that G-d, for the moment, had switched their kill buttons to off. If not for that Heavenly Kindness, they surely would have torn him apart to the bones.

That was one of the reasons why Johnny wanted to go live in Israel. *Intifada* or not, that was the home of the Jews. At least there, the Jews had an army. Johnny had spent a month on an army base in the Negev cleaning warehouses and washing down tanks. Wearing a *Tzahal* uniform had done more for his *Yiddishkeit* than all of his years at Y.U. After his summer in Israel, the difference was clear. America was great for Americans. Israel was the land of the Jews.

The problem was Linda. She wanted to live near her parents.

Johnny agreed that her parents were nice people. They were wealthy, they lived in a beautiful house, they gave

Linda everything she wanted. After the wedding, they would buy them a house and set Johnny up with a job in a top Wall Street firm when he finished his Masters in Business.

"Our children can be bar-mitzvahed in Israel," Linda agreed.

"I want my children to grow up in Israel," he said.

"Then find them some other mother, not me."

For months, he had dropped the issue completely. But now, as the train stopped at 72nd Street, and a man stepped into the crowded subway car holding a copy of the Hebrew newspaper, *Israel Shelanu*, Johnny was reminded of the sensitive subject again. For a split moment, their eyes connected in recognition, fellow travelers in a foreign land. Across the ocean, a car bomb had exploded in Tel Aviv, leaving three people dead.

"Is that the future you want for your children?" Linda would say. "Car bombs and wars?"

Johnny knew she meant well. Perhaps she was right. Maybe when things settled down, when peace came, or when Israel defeated the Arabs in an all-out encounter, maybe then his wife would consider making the move. Not that New York was a haven for Jews. The drive-by shooting at the pizza parlor on Amsterdam Avenue proved that a Jew wasn't safe anywhere. But attacks like that didn't take place every day. Linda's fears weren't groundless. He couldn't fault her for that.

At 34th Street, posters of Simon and Garfunkel were plastered all over Penn Station. In another week, they would appear at the Garden for a historic reunion. Sure, they had married *shicksas*, but man could they sing!

As usual, the train to Long Island was packed with an army of laptop and newspaper Jews. They were an army of lawyers, accountants, brokers, and businessmen flocking back to their suburban fortresses after a pressured day of work in the city. It wouldn't be long until Johnny joined

their ranks. He could picture himself now, riding on the
train with his Toshiba, Bloomingdale sport jacket, and
button-down shirt, heading home to Linda, a *hevruta*, and
a flick. It certainly wasn't the worse fate in the world. And
if he hit the jackpot on Wall Street, like Linda's father
assured that he would, Johnny could drive home in luxury,
listening to Torah tapes in his Jaguar after rush-hour traffic
had ended.

A taxi took him the rest of the way to Linda's. The
three-story mansion was lit up like a cruise boat. There
were spotlights all over the lawn. Lively, Hasidic pop
music filled the air. A fleet of expensive, sleek cars lined
the block. Johnny recognized his parents' modest Buick
sticking out amongst the Cadillacs and Lincolns. Linda
promised it would be a small affair, just for relatives and
their families' very best friends. Next week, they would be
having a separate party in the city for their classmates. But
from the line-up of cars on the street, it seemed like
Linda's father had invited all of his Nasdaq and Dow Jones
accounts.

Johnny paused outside on the street, feeling butterflies
swirl in his stomach. No doubt, the glass table in the foyer
had turned into a Mount Sinai of presents – silverware,
candlesticks, *kiddush* cups, *mezuza* cases, lithographs, Smith
Barney checks, and everything a young couple needed to
set up a *frum* Jewish house.

"Johnny's getting his Masters in Business at
Columbia," Linda's father would say a dozen times,
introducing him to each new account.

"Communication hardware," one guest would tell him.
"Internet is a thing of the past."

"Keep your portfolio mixed," another CEO would
advise. "Never put all of your eggs into one basket."

"My present to you, boy, is two words. Zenith Optics.
Its a sure-fire winner," a big smile would say, handing over
an envelope with stocks.

Johnny would nod his head and answer with his best Columbia Business School smile, "Yes, sir, thank you, sir, that's really good advice."

And of course, Linda would look beautiful. And his parents would be so proud. And his young brother would make faces while he recited the short *Dvar Torah* that he had prepared.

And all of the while, Johnny would be thinking of the car bomb in Israel and the fate of the wounded.

"Is something the matter?" Linda would ask.

"No, of course not," he'd answer. "Everything's great."

They would be happy. They would be rich. He would donate lots of money to Israel. When their son grew up, if things were quiet, they would make a big bar-mitzvah party at the King David Hotel.

As his future spread out before him, a bus rounded the corner and came down the street. When he saw it, the words of a Paul Simon song rang in his ears....

"Just get on the bus, Gus. No need to discuss much. Just get yourself free."

The bus stopped in front of him and the bus driver opened the door.

"Where to?" Johnny asked.

"Kennedy Airport," the bus driver replied.

Johnny turned back for one last look at the house. Linda stood in the brightly lit doorway, as if searching for a boat lost at sea. In her engagement gown, she looked like a queen.

"I ain't got all night, pal?" the impatient bus driver prodded.

Quickly, before Linda could spot him, Johnny climbed on the bus.

"Coming from a wedding?" the driver inquired.

"I'm getting engaged tonight," Johnny answered.

"Congratulations!" the bus driver said. "In that case, the bus ride is free."

Back down the street, the band continued to play... *"Once again will be heard on the mountains of Judea and the streets of Jerusalem, the song of joy and happiness, the song of the hatan and the kallah."*

Excited, a happy Johnny sat down on a seat. Outside the bus window, the hills of Judea rose up to greet him.

DAYS OF MASHIACH

E ven before the jumbo jet came to a stop on the runway, Dr. Elliot Miller unfastened his seat belt and jumped up from his seat.

"Where are you going?" his wife, Sandra, asked.

"I want to be the first one off the plane," he replied, pulling his carry-on down from the overhead rack.

"Please remain seated until the aircraft comes to a complete stop," the voice over the loudspeaker commanded.

Though the doctor normally respected regulations and rules, his excitement overcame him completely. He pushed forward down the aisle like a sprinter determined to win the race. To please his wife, they had remained in America as long as they could. But now the ingathering of the exiles was ending, and they were among the last Jews to come home.

"The Land of Israel!" he thought to himself. "Thank G-d, I finally made it!"

Using his elbows and shoulders, he fought his way to the front of the cabin.

"I'm a doctor," he said, when other passengers protested.

In truth, there were over one-hundred doctors on the planeload of affluent Jews, but the other new immigrants bought the excuse, figuring there must be some kind of emergency.

When the flight attendant swung the cabin door open, Elliot felt so overwhelmed, he nearly lost his balance. Ben Gurion Airport didn't look so different than other airports around the world, but there was an Israeli flag flying on the roof of a building. In the distance, the mountains of the Holy Land rose toward a biblical sky.

Elliot flew down the steps of the ramp. When his feet touched the runway, he collapsed to his knees and pressed his lips to the asphalt.

"I'm in Israel! I'm in Israel!" he thought to himself, feeling he was going to faint.

"Just what are you doing?" his wife asked, appearing behind him.

Elliot looked up and blushed.

"Kissing the Holy Land," he responded.

"Look at your trousers," she said. "You've got them all dirty."

"Who cares?" he replied. "We're in Israel!"

"Woopey doo," she answered sarcastically. "If you want to make a fool of yourself, do it when you're alone. People recognize me."

It was true. Wherever they went, people recognized Elliot's wife. The witty and attractive woman had become one of America's most well known personalities as the host of a nationwide TV talk show.

"Let's go, Joe," an airport worker growled, giving Elliot a kick in the butt. "Get into line with the others."

A pain shot up Elliot's spine, but he didn't protest. No doubt he deserved it, he thought. He should have made *Aliyah* sooner, with the *Mashiach's* first call. Grimacing, he stood up from the runway and wiped the dirt off his knees.

"How dare you!" Sandra declared. "You can't treat my husband like that! He's one of New York's leading physicians."

"This isn't New York, lady" the worker replied. "We've got so many doctors from America here, they're like sand in the desert."

Obediently, Elliot stepped into the long line of passengers that had formed on the runway. He wasn't going to let the kick in the rear get him down. He was finally in Israel, and he was grateful for that.

"Aren't there buses or something to take us to the terminal?" Sandra asked, as a Jewish Agency worker started to march the new arrivals toward the distant terminal.

"All the buses are busy with regular passengers," the Israeli retorted.

"And just what are we? Lepers?"

The man kept on walking, followed by the plane load of rich American Jews.

"This is preposterous," Sandra complained as she wheeled her carry-on suitcase along the sun-baked runway. "I'm going to do a story on this!"

"Just thank G-d we got here," her husband replied.

When they reached the terminal, they were told that the two Jewish Agency officials who had to stamp their papers had gone out to lunch. After waiting an hour, the long line of *Olim* started to move. It took another two hours before Dr. Elliot Miller and his wife reached the Absorption Desk at Ben Gurion Airport.

"Why are there only two officials working here to handle a flight of over four-hundred people?" Sandra asked pointedly. It was her beauty and wit, combined with her hard-hitting journalist style, which had propelled her to the top of America's media ladder.

"You should have come two years ago," an official answered. "In those days, the whole process took less than an hour."

"Are we being punished?" she asked with the assertiveness of someone accustomed to getting her way.

"Please, Sandra," Elliot said. "We're almost finished."

"I get the feeling that we are being punished, that's all, and I want to know why."

"Listen lady," the other official said. "If you are not happy with the way things are done here, you can go back to America. We've managed so far without you; we'll survive if you decide not to stay."

"Well, I never...." Sandra stuttered. "I knew Israelis had *chutzpah*, but this is the worst."

"Next!" the official called, stamping their passports and immigration cards.

That was only the beginning. They had to wait another hour for their luggage that was held up in some kind of strike. In front of a camera, Sandra was the sea of composure, without a hair out of place, but now her mascara was running down her cheeks with droplets of angry sweat.

"I told you we should have stayed in New York," she said with growing irritation.

"Be patient, darling. You promised you would give it a try."

"I am beginning to realize that I made a mistake."

"So did I," Elliot thought to himself with a sigh.

It was times like these, when Sandra had one of her tantrums, that Elliot thought about Miriam. In medical school, Miriam and he had been sweethearts. Miriam was quiet, gentle, with a happy smile on her face whenever he was around. There was never any question that she loved him. But then he had met Sandra at a party and everything changed. Sandra was exciting, flamboyant, the center of a crowd. Wherever she went, all eyes turned her way. Elliot lost his head. Abandoning the faithful Miriam, he ran after Sandra until she said yes. Instead of a life of marital harmony with Miriam, he married a woman who never really loved him.

"Why did you marry me?" he once asked her.

Like a surgeon wielding a scalpel, she answered, "You were the best thing I could find at the time."

As long as his medical practice flourished, Sandra played the role of his wife. True, her credit-card charges were staggering, but he put up with it because he enjoyed having a stunning woman at his side on their almost nightly outings to the theater and the finest restaurants in New York. But with the start of her fame and nightly talk show, the couple hardly met. They continued to live together, but with their busy schedules, they were like airplanes soaring by one another in the night. At first, they stayed together for their son, and then out of familiarity and convenience. After their son, Larry, left home for Europe, and her celebrity salary grew to be several times his, they found themselves with less and less in common. More and more, Elliot thought about Miriam. One lonely night, he even made some telephone calls to old medical school buddies, hoping to make contact. He surfed the Net for hours, searching for an address, but she, like his marriage to Sandra, had simply disappeared. Finally, in a chance encounter with an old roommate, he learned that she had married a non-Jewish lawyer.

"Boy was she crazy about you," his friend remembered. "She probably married a lawyer in spite, just to get doctors out of her mind."

That's when Elliot started to learn a little Torah. At first on the Web, to fill up his lonely hours at night. Then, at the urgings of an Orthodox cardiologist, he began to study with a *hevruta*. As far as religion was concerned, the subject left Sandra cold. She had her life. He had his.

But then, with the coming of *Mashiach*, everything changed. Spellbound, the world watched Israel's miraculous triumphs in war. Sandra got swept up in the fever. Ironically, it was the excavation work of the Arabs in the subterranean tunnels on the Temple Mount that ignited the flame. Digging up ancient remains on the Mount to erase traces of Jewish history, the Arabs uncovered the Ark of the Covenant and the Two Tablets of Law. Arab workers approaching the sacrosanct vessel were stricken with blindness. In the hospital, their delirious reports were leaked to the press. Hearing that the cherished Ark had been found, thousands of Jews stormed the Temple Mount. Amidst a roar of thunderous *shofars* and trumpets, the mosques on the Mount crumbled into dust and disappeared. Though the Jews hadn't fired one single shot, every Arab state declared war. Led by the Ark and *Mashiach*, the Israelis dealt a devastating blow to enemy forces. On television sets the world over, G-d reaffirmed His ancient covenant with the Jews. When the Temple Institute in Jerusalem set up an altar on top of the Mount, the Clouds of Glory returned. Day and night, the mystical cloud and pillar of fire hovered over the holy site like a Heavenly guard. Even a journalist as non-religious as Sandra was swept up in the awesome magnitude of the miraculous event.

Once again, as the forces of Israel threatened to wipe out the Arabs completely, the United States stepped in to negotiate peace. Quickly, a deal agreeable to all parties was made. The President called it a swap. It was as simple as that. The Arabs of Judea, Samaria and Aza were transferred to America, and the Jews of America were transferred to Israel. The Arabs received the million-dollar apartments and mansions of the American Jews, and the American Jews got to come home. That way everyone was happy. Except for Sandra. Like anything else, miracles on a daily basis become boring and mundane. Once the spiritual newness wore off, she realized that being a part of the world's greatest saga wasn't all glamour and fun.

"You mean we are going to live in the Gaza Strip?" she asked incredulously, as the Egged bus filled with new immigrants sped down the coastal road.

"Isn't it great?" her husband responded, with an excited smile on his face.

Looking around her on the bus, she noticed that everyone was smiling, as if all of these successful doctors, lawyers, and businessmen had taken some kind of hallucinatory drug. Not only the men, but the women were smiling as well. When the bus driver started singing "*Hava*

Negilla," everyone joined in the song.

The new *Olim* all cheered when the bus roared into Aza City. Staring out the bus window at the bombed-out neighborhoods and demolished buildings, Sandra was shocked. Did her husband really believe that she would agree to live here, when she could live in an elegant Park Avenue flat in New York? At the Jewish Agency building, which had served as a medical clinic that the Israelis had been careful not to destroy, they were herded into another long line. Once again, their immigration papers were stamped and they were handed a large cardboard suitcase called an *Erkat HaSochnut La'Oleh*.

"If anything on the list is missing, please let us knew," an official kindly said.

"When will we be able to go to Jerusalem?" Elliot asked him.

"There's a trip for your group planned for next Tuesday."

"Will we be able to see the *Mashiach*?" the eager newcomer asked.

"He stops by the Temple Mount every afternoon to oversee the Temple's construction. If you're lucky, you may be there at the same time."

Lugging their suitcases, they had to walk ten blocks through the war-torn city to their new home. Fortunately, a Jewish Agency worker was sent along to help them. His name was David Hirsh, a brain surgeon from California. He said that he had been in Aza four months and loved every minute of it.

"It's a chance to do my share," he told them with the same contented grin on his face.

"Don't you feel that your talents are being wasted?" Sandra wanted to know.

"Thank G-d, this country has brain surgeons to spare. In Aza, there are more doctors than patients. What we need now is Jews who are willing to do manual labor in order to make this great ingathering work."

Elliot admired his spirit. He too was anxious to help. His specialty was cardiac transplants, but if he was needed in Gaza Strip greenhouses to pick lettuce, he was ready to tackle the job.

Everywhere you looked, construction work was in progress. College students wearing athletic shirts from Harvard and Yale pushed heavy wheelbarrows, carrying debris away from demolished buildings. Vendors with *yarmulkes* and beards stood behind sidewalk booths, selling vegetables, fruit, baked goods, and fresh Mediterranean fish. Other workers, with decidedly American accents, help lower new sewage pipes into ditches.

"Most of the workers you see are from L.A. and New York. The old guy pasting up posters used to own one of the biggest department store chains in the States."

The poster was a picture of the *Mashiach* with the caption "DON'T WORRY!" the expression he had made famous during the war. With a big happy smile, the multi-millionaire Jew splashed a brush wet with glue over the sign. While Elliot was watching him work, a horse and wagon drove over and stopped by the sidewalk.

"Throw your suitcases in back and climb aboard, partners," the driver called out with a familiar Western drawl. Sandra recognized him immediately. It was Robby Roth, one of America's box-office favorites. "Welcome aboard the *Tshuva* Train!" the actor called out, tipping his cowboy hat to the newcomers.

"Robby!" Sandra called out, happy to see someone from home.

"Sandy!" the Jewish actor exclaimed. "America's prettiest interviewer!"

In times past, the two would have hugged, but Roth was religious now. Sensing it, Sandra backed off. Elliot asked Hirsh if he should pay the actor for his trouble, but Hirsh said the service was free.

"There's a shortage of cars in Aza for all the new immigrants, so the Jewish Agency uses these wagons to help people move in."

"You drive this wagon for the Jewish Agency?" Sandra blurted in wonder.

"Why not?" the movie star answered. "If the King of Israel can ride on a donkey, why shouldn't an actor from Hollywood drive a broken-down wagon?"

Their new home was a four-story building facing the Mediterranean Sea. Their apartment was on the top floor. A box of fresh fruit was waiting for them in the hall. By the time Sandra made it to the doorway, her heart was pounding from the long climb upstairs.

"There's a *mezuza* in the *Aliyah* Kit," Hirsh said. "Be sure to nail it up today. If you need something, give me a call. Welcome home and *Baruch haba*. I'll see you tonight at the Homecoming Barbecue out on the beach."

"If we need anything?" Sandra mumbled, staring at the devastated apartment. "Tell me I'm dreaming. Please, I beg you. Tell me I'm dreaming."

An entire wall of the living room had been blown away by a missile. The sea looked close enough to reach out and touch. Chunks of plaster hung down from the ceiling. Anti-Israeli graffiti was scrawled in Arabic over the still-standing walls.

"*When the L-rd brings back the exiles of Zion, we will be like those who dream,*" Elliot exclaimed, quoting a verse of Psalms. "Will you look at the view of the ocean!" he raved. "It's breathtaking!"

"Breathtaking?" Sandra asked in amazement. "We're missing a wall!"

"We'll put in a window the length of the room. It will be an architectural knockout."

"There's no furniture," she said.

"So? We'll rough it a little until our furniture comes."

"It's coming by boat," she protested. "They said it

would take two to six months."

"What's two to six months? The Jewish people have been dreaming of coming to Israel for two thousand years."

"Maybe you have – not me. This is a nightmare. I'm not living here. There's Arab graffiti all over the walls!"

"The place needs a painting, that's all. With all the American Jews here, there must be a top interior decorator from New York. Please, Sandra," Elliot appealed. "You promised to give Israel a chance. If we had made the move sooner, we could have gotten a beautiful apartment in Jerusalem or Tel Aviv. Thank G-d we got here at all. Do you know what Moses would have given to live here in the Holy Land in an apartment like this?"

"I'm not Moses. I'm a spoiled rich girl from America, and I want to go back."

"Please, Sandra, I don't want to fight."

"This place doesn't even have a working kitchen," she exclaimed, walking through the debris on the floor.

"Master of the Universe," he thought to himself. "Why didn't I marry Miriam?"

The bathroom was even worse. A mortar shell that hadn't exploded was sticking out of the toilet.

"There are portable toilets on the street," he told her. "We passed them on the way."

"That's just wonderful," she answered. "The dream of a lifetime. Elliot, I'm sorry, but this is not going to work."

Her husband let out a sigh. He knew the change wouldn't be easy, but it was a time of miracles. He thought a miracle could occur with his wife.

"Let's open the *Aliyah* Kit," he said, trying to change the subject.

There were four *mezuzahs*, a *kippah*, two women's kerchiefs, a pair of *tzitzit*, a *tallit*, a *siddur*, a *Chumash*, a *Kitzur Shulchan Oruch*, two gas masks, a complimentary Selcom cell phone, a Guide to Israeli Expressions, two blankets, two pillows, a can opener, a can of pickles, and two containers of army *Luf* that smelled like expensive dog food.

With a look of disdain, Sandra held up the kerchief. "If you expect me to wear this, you're crazy."

"Sandra, this is a religious country. As Israeli citizens, we have to obey the laws."

"I want to go back to the airport right now," she insisted.

"I'll buy you a wig that looks just like real hair," he promised, raising his hands in a gesture of prayer.

"Listen, Elliot, you may get your kicks from religion, but I don't. I get high when a television camera is pointed at my face, and I know that millions of eyes are focused on me. I feel those looks like the sun at high noon. It makes me feel loved."

"I love you. Why can't my two eyes be enough?" he asked softly.

"They just can't," she replied, walking away toward the missing wall that looked out over the ocean and beach.

"I'm certain you can get a job with Israeli TV," he assured her.

"Without knowing one word of Hebrew."

"They have broadcasts in English."

"Oh, Elliot, don't you see? It isn't enough."

"The eyes of the world are focused on Israel. You can be more famous here than anywhere else. Just give it a chance, sweetheart. You'll see."

Sandra didn't answer. Elliot didn't know what more to say. He asked her if she wanted to go out with him and see about buying a bed, but she was too tired.

"We've had a long trip. After a nap, you'll feel better," he said, spreading the two Jewish Agency blankets onto the floor. Then he left to do some shopping.

"Don't forget to call someone to get that mortar shell out of the toilet," she shouted after him as he walked down the stairs.

He returned two hours later with a wagon loaded with furniture – beds, a dining room table, a sofa, two mirrors, a bookcase, a carpet, a portable fan and some chairs.

"Enough to get started," he said.

Two giant black men hauled the furniture up the stairs. They, and thousands of others like them, had converted to Judaism with the incredible discovery of the Ark. Since then, the Chief Rabbinate had banned all conversions, turning literally millions of people away.

Even with the new furniture in place, Sandra still looked depressed.

"OK," he admitted, trying to cheer her up. "It's not the Upper East Side look, but it's something to get by with until our stuff arrives from the States."

While he was directing the movers, a bomb squad showed up and went to work in the bathroom. Before leaving for the barbecue, Elliot put up the *mezuzahs* and said the blessing that was written out in their *Guide to the Oleh*. It was a beautiful evening with a big yellow moon glowing out over the ocean. Hundreds of people were on hand for the party. Festive fireworks lit up the sky. The men *davened maariv* around a bright bonfire while hot dogs and chicken legs were grilled over coals. A representative of the Jewish Agency gave a short speech. Men and women danced in separate circles to the tune of old-fashion, religious Zionist songs. Elliot had a great time, but Sandra sat alone in the sand down the beach, staring across the sea toward America. Later, after some more speeches and dancing, Elliot felt relieved to see his wife socializing with a group of TV and movie celebrities.

"She'll find her niche," he assured himself. As every new immigrant to Israel was told, "*savlanut*" was the key.

Three beers later, Dr. Elliot Miller was in the greatest of moods. Back in their new apartment, he collapsed down on the couch and gazed happily out at the glistening sea. In the distance, he could make out the roar of the ocean.

Sandra sat meditatively down on the floor by the missing partition, as if she were relaxing outside on a terrace. Crossing her legs in a yoga position, she too set her gaze out to sea.

"You wouldn't believe it," he bantered. "At the party tonight, I ran into my dentist, my accountant, Larry's old shrink, and a friend from high school whom I haven't seen for over twenty-five years."

His wife made no comment, as if she were deaf.

"Didn't I see you with some people you know?"

"I suppose that you did," she answered.

"Didn't I tell you that things would work out? It isn't the end of the world."

With a practiced fluidity, his wife stood up from her meditative pose. "To me it is," she replied. With that, she walked down the hall to the bathroom. Moments later, she returned.

"It still doesn't work," she announced.

"I'll call a plumber in the morning."

"And tonight, what do we do?"

"I guess that it is our turn to suffer a little," he answered.

"Who wants to suffer?" she said.

"It comes with being a Jew."

"Who wants to be Jewish?" she asked.

Elliot didn't know how to respond. Though she was clearly exhausted after their long, drawn-out journey, the look in her eyes said she meant every word.

"I can't get into the role, Elliot. It just isn't me."

"It has to be you. You're a Jew."

Her silence unnerved him. She didn't say anything. She looked at him with a cold, haunting expression and gazed back out at the sea.

"My father was Jewish," she said. "Not Mom. I lied to make you happy. So your parents wouldn't try to stand in the way."

Elliot couldn't speak. He felt as if he had been shot at close range in the stomach.

"All of these years...," was the only thing he could think of to say.

Suddenly, he understood why his son, Larry, had always been indifferent about living in Israel. He wasn't a Jew.

"You wanted to marry me that much?" he asked her.

"I guess I did then," was her icy reply. "You were going to be a doctor, and my family was poor."

The next day, he accompanied her on the bus drive back to the airport. She had made up her mind. She didn't want to convert, even if she could have. And she didn't want to live in Israel, acting out a part. She wanted to go back to America where she grew up and where she belonged.

Elliot was anguished and broken. At the entrance to the airport, a huge billboard of *Mashiach* with the slogan, "DON'T WORRY," towered over the highway, but Elliot didn't take heed. His wife was walking out of his life. And there was nothing he could do to stop her.

Elliot stood by her at the ticket counter. He walked with her past the security guards. In the duty-free section, he waited outside a bookstore as she chose a paperback novel to read on the plane. At the departure gate, they stood facing each other, sensing that they might never see one another again. There wasn't a need. Their lawyers would draw up the papers.

Dr. Elliot Miller remained by the boarding gate several long minutes after Sandra had gone. A short distance away, a woman wearing a kerchief waved goodbye to a man carrying a laptop computer and briefcase. Elliot didn't think twice about her until she appeared once again outside the terminal as he waited for a group taxi to Aza. Strangely, as if throwing away an unpleasant memory, she reached up and pulled off her kerchief. Though years had passed, she had the same gentle expression, the same soft-spoken eyes.

"Miriam? Is it you?" he asked in amazement.

"Elliot?" she replied in a voice just as startled.

"What are you doing here?" he asked.

"Like everyone else, I came too," she answered.

"The man… at the boarding gate?" he stammered.

"My husband," she replied, lowering her gaze in embarrassment. "At least he was my husband. I thought he would get used to Israel, but it wasn't for him."

A passenger jet roared overhead. So that was her non-Jewish lawyer, Elliot thought. Maybe he and Sarah would hit it off on the plane.

"What are you doing here?" Miriam asked him.

"My wife left me too."

For a moment, the two old sweethearts stood speechless.

"You're going to Aza?" she asked.

"To Aza? Why yes," he replied as if waking up from a dream. "I'm going back home to Aza."

"So am I," she said softly with the same tender smile he remembered.

Just then, the driver of the next *sherut* in line walked over clutching a falafel and Coke.

"That's all? Just you two?" he asked.

"Seems that way," Elliot answered.

"You'll have to wait until the car is full," the Israeli said gruffly.

"I'll pay for the whole cab myself," Elliot offered.

Stepping gallantly forward, he opened the rear door for Miriam.

"It's your money," the driver said, biting into the *pita*.

With a schoolgirl blush, Miriam got into the car.

At the terminal exit, as the taxi pulled out onto the highway, Elliot caught another glimpse of the giant "DON'T WORRY!" and the smiling, confident face of *Mashiach*.

Other books by the author:

Tevye In The Promised Land
Dad
Secret of the Brit
Jewish Sexuality
The Discman and the Guru
Fallen Angel
Heaven's Door
Best Blogs

Co-authored with Rabbi David Samson:

Torat Eretz Yisrael
Lights On Orot
War And Peace
The Art Of T'shuva

TEVYE
In The
Promised Land

"I thought I knew everything there was to know about Tevye, but reading *Tevye In The Promised Land*, I kept turning page after page after page...."

Chaim Topol

If you enjoyed "Fiddler On The Roof," you are sure to love *Tevye In The Promised Land*. Now in this sweeping historical adventure, Sholom Aleichem's beloved milkman from Anatevka is back. In *Tevye In The Promised Land*, Tevye's trials and tribulations continue as he journeys with his daughters to the Holy Land to become a pioneer settler in Israel – a novel your whole family will never forget.

Made in the USA
Lexington, KY
20 January 2013